Further reviews of Volume I

"Lovett Jones's timely rewrite of a classic novel provides a shocking reminder of how much and how fast our environment is being despoiled and degraded – often with the assistance of those who should be acting for the public interest. Read it – then join an environmental pressure group."

Tony Juniper – Executive Director, *Friends Of The Earth*

"I screamed with laughter."

Sir Roy Strong – writer and historian

"Gareth Lovett Jones has captured the essence of Grahame's writing style and acute observation, turning the original story upside down in a way that is uncomfortably close to home. As I pass through the streets of our cities, the business parks and commuter villages that now invade so much of our countryside, I am constantly reminded of scenes and characters in this book. Read it and look around."

Brian Johnson – *Eng*

This is a hugely entertaining as well as a deliberately disturbing and provocative read. I enjoyed it enormously whilst appreciating Mr Jones' deadly serious message about fighting social injustice and building a sustainable future. At the end we leave Mr Mole on a borrowed bicycle setting off "in search of England", to be chronicled in a second, must-have, volume. I for one will be looking out for its publication.

John Grimshaw – *Sustrans*

I felt compelled to let you know how much I enjoyed *The Wind in the Pylons*. It presents a perfect blend of poignancy, humour and righteous anger and is a wonderful exposé of our corporate-controlled political system with all its negative consequences. The innocent presence and incredulous reactions of Mole are a delightful reminder of the simpler view that we have forsaken in exchange for the ever-elusive dream of happiness through consumerism and growth. I shall certainly be recommending this book to friends as I can sincerely say it is one of the most enjoyable, heartening books on topics close to my heart that I have read. I can't wait for Volume 2!

Unsolicited e-mail to the publisher from **Pamela Forsyth,** a reader in Scotland.

The Wind In The Pylons

Gareth Lovett Jones is a photographer and author whose past work includes a novel, *Valley With A Bright Cloud*; *English Country Lanes*, a cyclist's eye-view of the countryside; and *The Wildwood*, an exploration of British ancient woodlands. His photographs also appear in Richard Mabey's *Flora Britannica*. He is currently working on an exhibition on the subject of veteran yew trees. He lives on the Oxfordshire/Berkshire border by the reach of the Thames where Kenneth Grahame made his final home.

The Wind In The Pylons

Adventures of the Mole in Weaselworld

Gareth Lovett Jones

Volume II

Hilltop Publishing Limited

First published in the United Kingdom in 2004
by Hilltop Publishing Limited
PO Box 429
Aylesbury
Buckinghamshire HP18 9XY
UK
www.hilltoppublishing.co.uk

All characters in this novel are fictitious and any resemblance to weasels,
living or dead, is purely coincidental.

IBSN 0 9536850 4 7

Cover Illustration by Judy Hammond
Book Design by Judy Stocker
Typeset in 11½pt Centaur by Avocet Typeset, Chilton, Aylesbury, Bucks.
Printed and bound by Biddles Ltd, King's Lynn, Norfolk.

Cover illustration

He kicked the golden globe as if it were a football, to send it rumbling directly towards his rival.
(page 201)

THE STORY UNTIL NOW

Following a mysterious tunnel he finds behind his kitchen cupboard, the Mole emerges into an unrecognisable landscape where horizon-hugging factory farms have erased much of the old familiar countryside, and hulking shed-like shopping zones rear beyond derelict valley pastures. This is Weaselworld, a place in which Nature herself has been all but forgotten, and every big decision is made in reference to a quasi-mystic principle known as "The Mystery Of The Market". It is also a world of the future, for the tunnel has carried the Mole forward into the England of the 1990s.

Attempting to cross the slip road of a gigantic Clearway, the Mole is knocked down by an irascible driver, one Mr Gordon R. Rette, a water rat and overworked Head of Degirthing at the City HQ of global petrochemicals giant Toad Transoceanic: it is Mr Rette's job to oversee the firing of his colleagues. Through him, the Mole comes into the company of the transnational's Chief Executive, Mr Humfrey Wyvern-Toad. The wily Toad is not slow to note the curious effect the Mole's presence has on anyone who stands near him: in a world in which *the lie* is an indispensable tool of the professions, animals begin to speak the truth to him, and are quite unable to stop.

Having successfully tested out the Mole's truth-drawing gift on Gibbert Phangachs, a rising star of the Grand Old Toad And Weasel Alliance, the Toad offers him a post as Special Directorial Consultant at Toad Transoceanic—a fact the Mole himself never quite grasps. The Toad takes him and Mr Rette to an interview with Mr Probity Stote, leader of the chief opposition party, the New Animalists, and from there to the Party Conference of the GOTWA (also known as the To-We Party), where the Mole's powers have a devastating effect on the Prime Minister's keynote speech.

On one of his days off, the Mole walks into the path of a fox hunt, ending up inside a subterranean outpost of a group of idealistic burrowers who call themselves the Animale Liberation Front. Led by the powerful and serious-minded Badger, this group has sworn itself to oppose the force the Badger describes as "Weaselmind", and the Mole agrees to go with them at night to a barbaric chicken battery where the birds are set free and the Press makes an attendance.

On another such day, the Mole walks down-river from the Rette family home, where he has been staying, to rediscover the tiny midstream island on which—in his earlier life—he and his dear friend Ratty encountered Pan, god and protector of all animals. There is no sign of Pan there now, and the Mole sees that since he is unable to go back down the time tunnel—a Retco ThriftaCenta having been built over the entrance—he must leave the Rettes, and this damaged future version of his Valley, and try to find somewhere else in England where there may be a suitable spot to make a home. In Mr and Mrs Rette's absence, and borrowing a bicycle from their teenage son, Justin, the Mole packs up some camping gear and sets off, in a generally easterly direction.

CONTENTS

PART TWO
Mole The Wanderer

PART THREE
In Farawaysia

PART TWO:

Mole The Wanderer

Fortunatus et animal deos qui novit agrestis ...
(And happy the animal, who has knowledge of the woodland gods ...)
Rattus Rattus

CHAPTER ELEVEN

THE MOPIN' ROAD

During his last evening at "Kennylands" the Mole had spent almost two hours poring and squinnying over the finer details, such as they were, of his *Hollowmew's Motorist's Map Of The South East Of England*. Bit by bit, and very reluctantly, he came to the conclusion that to get anywhere from here that was properly *east*, he would first have to get all the way round London; and London, he saw, was huge—huge—HUGE! Even on this many-decades-old map, the western side of London seemed to begin somewhere in the vicinity of Slough: the capital beyond it sat like a forty-five-mile wide octopus, sending out black-shaded tentacles in every direction.

Some earlier owner of the map had made a number of additions that might now be of use to the Mole, marking in what he thought must be later developments. So, for example, there up to the north was a large pencil-circle, heavily scored in, with the words *Milton Keynes* scribbled next to it. Luton had also been greatly enlarged by the same hand, absorbing Dunstable into it like a graphite amoeba. Due east of this, another scored-in circle spread across what the map itself showed simply as open countryside: it bore the odd name *Stevenage*. Also roughed in were the lines of various roads, marked as either *C* or *Clearway*. These radiated out from the capital like the spokes of a bicycle-wheel the size of four counties. The Mole had grasped, not unmoaningly, that each must be waiting there now for him to cross it, one fresh nightmare at a time.

But by sticking to the arc of hills that faced on to Mr Rette's front porch and then spread away north-eastwards at least as far as Luton, the Mole thought he might still find a way through to that distant eastern country where, encouragingly, all the towns appeared to be much smaller and fewer and further-between. A way through, this meant, that avoided both the black tentacle-tips of the enfolding metropolis and the uninviting-looking blodges dotted around and beyond them. Big towns—towns of any size at all, in fact—were not on the Mole's list of must-sees.

It may well be that the most courageous thing an animal can ever do is to act for the best against his instincts. If that is so, then the Mole's first two hours' travelling that April morning were his finest to date. Over and over as he turned the pedals or walked and pushed his bike, or stopped in his tracks like a quick-set blancmange, he found himself muttering, "But *Mole*. You don't want to *do* this!—You don't! You *don't!* You're a home-loving mole! You're a *hole*-loving mole; you like to know there's a hook there for your tea-cosy, and an armchair, and an old soft cushion by a grate you call your own.—No, Mole. An Englishmole's *hole* is his castle!"

Yet each time such objections slowed his progress the dogged little animal would somehow rally, and argue himself onward. After all, he thought, even if the sun was lost behind cloud today—and even if that sun *was* the sun of so many years too late—nothing could stop it being spring. Here and there, the last of the blackthorn blooms still foamed creamy-white or a toasted whitish-brown to the points of their long spurred branches, and the lane verges had begun to stretch their soft new coats of shining green. All about him, trees and hedgerows were in that first stage of explosive release when the buds stand out as if thrilled to be opening, prolifically speckling the networks of branches they will soon obscure. One or two of the old plants the Mole knew and loved so well could be found along the hedge banks, too: in one place he saw the tiny crocket spires of dead-nettles cresting the grass; in another, cuckoo-pint's gloss-varnished spear heads, still tender as the first cut lettuce.

"Who knows, Mole?" he reasoned with himself as he tramped on. "Who knows? Mayn't everything be for the best after all? Don't you have the best start out an animal could ever have on such a journey? Aren't you—truly—awfully lucky? A wonderful, brand-new bicycle. A wonderful, brand-new, soup-coloured tent to live in. A stove to cook on, a set of new cycling—um—ah—clothes, and even—O my!—a two-day supply of sandwiches! The way is open, Mole! *Your* way is open! Yes. Out of the old life, into the new. And ... O dear, O dear ... you have all that money too! O dear—all that *money!*" He drew in a deep breath, padding harder as he did so. "Well ..." he said. "All must be for the best—it must—in the best of all *possible* ..."

For whatever unplumbed reasons, the Mole left that thought-end ragged, tramping on in silence with the gradient still not on his side. "... And in any case, Mole," he said, some twenty paddings later, "you'll *never* put up a hook for a tea-cosy now if you don't go on!"

Once, long ago, the hills the Mole was penetrating had formed one of the borders of the world as he knew it: their bold chalk outlines—here, steep-sided and dark with yew woodland; there, rounded and green under pasture—ranged along the whole curving length of the Valley on its northern side. Even during his most adventurous forays, he had not gone very far into them: the truth was, he had never felt quite at ease there. He could not have imagined a place more distinct from that of his Valley with its flat meadows and rich, dark, *tunnelable* soils. This was a deeply-indented hill country: its friable white rock was, at best, thinly covered with flint-speckled clays, where beech grew well enough when it was planted, and where ash and yew, white-beam and spindle-tree grew when the land was left alone.

The Mole reached the first of the big beech woods on high plateau-land within three quarters of an hour of setting off. They were open to the road, and he could see into them as if into a vastly extended cave whose airy roof rested on uncountable thousands of sinuously bending pale grey pillars. In their far recesses, the slightest of spring hazes had changed the trunks into forms resembling the limbs of prehistoric beasts. The Mole knew that he could never have lived in this country of stony bottoms, without a hint of flowing water. And what were all these miles of woods being *used* for now? He could remember animals here, felling and carrying with great boat-like waggons drawn by steaming, sheen-coated cart horses, while others turned legs for kitchen chairs on knocked-up lathes ingeniously hitched to the trees' lower branches. Why, there had been a whole tribe of workers camped out in these woods from spring through to autumn—a tribe of flat-capped, leather-aproned chair builders without whom everyone else would have had no choice but to sit direct upon their kitchen floors! Yet for all these silent woods showed of them now, they might never have existed.

The Mole emerged from the trees into a stretch of narrow lane framed by thick hazel hedges, along which even quite gentle bends were enough to hide any sight of what might lie ahead. So it was on one such bend—confused, perhaps, by the wind waffling about in his ladybird-helmet—that it seemed to him that he heard some of the familiar old sounds ahead: the clinking cloppety-rattlings, crunchings, creaks and squeaks of a horse-drawn cart. Beaming in anticipation of the sight, and of a possible stop for a chat with the driver, the Mole gazed hard up ahead of him. Within moments, though, the sounds had separated out and rearranged themselves.

What the Mole heard ahead now was an all too familiar noise—both roar and scream, both whine and wail. In the next split second, the road was filled by a blob on wheels, electric-blue as a mandrill's bottom and bearing directly down on him without a sign of slowing down. At the very last moment, the driver made what the Mole already suspected might be a norm of compensation when passing something so lowly as a cyclist: a deviation of some six and one eighth inches—six and three sixteenths at the outside—into the verge, the mud, the stones and the sticks, several samples of which were thrown high in the air as this *largesse* was granted.

"*Don't slow down!*" sputtered the Mole to the departing missile. (It took a lot to make him angry enough for irony.) "It's only another animal, isn't it? Of no possible importance!" He could not help reflecting, when he had cooled down, that this might well be an accurate description of his own status now in this world of weasel aspirations: *Of No Possible Importance*. Yet, as he continued now, an image of horses in harness lingered on in his imagination, and behind them a load of golden hay, overspilling the cart's top raves like an ice-cream perched atop a cornet. He heard the farmer's cheery greeting, imagined the talk they would have had at rest in the road about the state of the weather and the crops in season. The scene clung on; then slipped aside, finding no replacement.

Nor was this the last experience of the kind the Mole was to have on his journey east. As he moved on that morning, he began to realise that over the first few miles he had probably been unusually lucky so far as other road users were concerned. After this, there seemed to be little escape, even on the smallest back roads. It was not that he faced an un-interrupted flow of traffic, but the *threat* of the next act of gross, life-endangering incivility was now a permanent feature of the way. The Mole could never quite tell—until the last, appalled moments—which of the machines con-tained the worst of Mr Rette's *bobbing-gnats or birdlice*.

One such—it was a *Razzle*, for what that may be worth, and accident-red—came on him helmed by a ferret with suede-cut so close its wearer resembled a freshly-born rat baby. He chewed as he drove, still somehow managing to wear a lip-twisted sneer of disdain for all aspects of the irrelevance beyond his windscreen. This vehicle did not simply roar and wail but drubbed as well—inconceivably loudly—with an embracing, relentless beat-out-of-nowhere, as if under the vengeful hammer of some unseen god of thunder. It sailed straight at the Mole at twenty times the speed of any cart in antiquity, infecting the flow-ers, the grasses, the air, the very idea of spring itself with its thudding, insensate industrial racket, dragging the row on behind it into the distance (having granted him his ninety-nine sixteenths) like cannon-shot, like a miniature war.

Not a quarter of an hour later, the Mole found the lane ahead completely blocked—to *motors*, if not cycles—by two white vans which lay crunched together into a large metal "L" across the tar. One of these bore the bold *impri-matur* BURGERBURGADOOR TO-YOUR-DOOR PERSONALIZED DELIVERIES, next to which was a picture of a grinning trans-speciesial holding out a box with a round-thing in it. The other read PIZZAWIZZA— THE ORIGINAL PIZZA-DELI. Two young stoats stood adjacent, prodding one another's chests in the moments when they were not snapping at the air near the other's snout. When they did this simultaneously, their duckbilled logo-peaks clacked together like some kind of medieval head-weaponry.

"You wouldn't *slow down*, would you?" screamed Burger-burgadoor.

"No ... No! *You* wouldn't slow down!"

"No, *you* wouldn't slow down! Why? 'Cos YOU'RE a bleeding MORON!"

"*WHAT* DID YOU CALL ME?" shrieked PizzaWizza, who must, the Mole thought, be very hard of hearing indeed not to have recognised words delivered so close to one of his ears. "*WHAT* DID YOU JUST ... *WHAT* DID YOU C ... Yu ... Yes ..." he went on, in a far quieter, and slightly stunned, tone of voice. (Coincidentally or otherwise, the Mole was now gingerly wheeling his bike along the verge, close past both animals, attempting without much success to stop at least one of his ears against further expletives.) "Yes," he said, matter-of-factly. "I'm a moron. Aren't I? I'm a total, brain-dead sludge-maggot, obviously I am. I couldn't hardly do one circuit at Brand's Hatch on me tod in a milk float without it going over on its roof ... er ... could I? Even only nudgin' twenty miles an hour."

"No ..." suggested his opponent calmly, "No, *I'm* a moron. *I'm* a sludge-maggot. Oh, I'm a total, total terebellid worm, to be honest. I couldn't drive me way through a large, wet paper bag, if one were to be placed there for the purpose, without a very large amount of assistance from the Police, several traffic wardens and a Official Diversion. Not even if someone had wrote "HIT THIS BAG" on it in large red letters."

After a few moments of panicked stalling in a hidden and weed-filled depression, the Mole had just about got himself past both animals and the remnants of their vans.

"Yeah, well," he heard PizzaWizza say behind him, in

what was still a tone of some confusion. "There you are then. Aren't you? We can agree on that, then. You're a moron."

"No … No. *You're* a moron! That's what we agree on. You just said so!"

"YOU just said so! You just said it, you said it, I heard you do it! And you're right! That's what you are! A bleeding MORON!"

"*WHAT* DID YOU CALL ME?"

For his part, the Mole had had enough of such exchanges even before he set out. "O dear," he breathed, as he remounted and rode on alongside a queue of *motors* that was rapidly extending itself beyond the scene of the crash. "O dear! I just *have* to get away from this!"

He stopped at a crossroads to pore over his map, in the hope it might yield some fresh clue as to how to go about it. He was standing next to a tall thorn hedge bordering on woodland: it had not been layered for a generation, at least. Underneath and beyond this, amongst many other things, he saw an old ice-cupboard, stranded and weeping with rust, a decayed, blackened mattress twisted into the shape of a discarded snake-skin, a pile of violent-yellow cardboard boxes (marked "IntraStott"), and a clutch of black shiny-stuff bags, two of which had burst and were spewing forth a rankness of carpets. Sweet woodruff was just going into flower around all this, where it had not been crushed, and there was a *smell* in the air that was not floral.

So this was what the woods here were used for now, thought the Mole sadly, turning back to his map. But, without looking further, he already knew that he would find no respite from the *motor* here. These country roads too, no less than the Clearway, were runnels of rage and despair along which the poor half-mad animals of Weasel-world roamed in their wheel-traps, cut off forever, it seemed, from the very source of life itself. And when they

did stop—he glanced again at the back-of-van evacua-
tions—*this* was what they stopped for.

Though it was well disguised by all that had happened to
it since, the Mole was following the general line of an
ancient ridge-road, and not half an hour later he had come
close enough to the hills' steep scarp to be able to look
down as he travelled into a series of wide, grassy combe-
mouths lying between projecting spurs of upland. It was
close to one such combe—and still with the idea of alternative routes in his mind—that he spotted a gated track
with a small sign next to it. This read:

ASTON HARTSWICK

This Nature Reserve is of national importance for its
orchid population, and in particular for the rare Chim-
panzee Orchid, of which only five specimens are known to
survive in the wild. It comprises a series of former hill
grazing pastures now under renewed management. Some
regeneration of prostrate Juniper is also being encouraged
here, whilst ...

But at this point in his reading, the Mole's attention was
distracted by a high, thin, needling scream. It fell on his
hearing like a thread of iced water and was completely
unfamiliar to him—what *could* have made it? His curiosity
aroused—and wanting now to see what lay beyond the
gate—he entered the "reserve". The track led steeply down
into the combe-mouth, while on his right a much less def-
initely surfaced way, if taken, looked as if it might carry
him on into woodland on one of the spurs. The first didn't
seem a sensible choice—if he went down, he would surely
have to come up again—so he marched on into the trees,

turning off once more (it was a mistake) on to a sub-track whose surface had recently been badly churned. Here he squished and squashed and, as it got worse, splooped and splurpled, along the edge of ever more impassable white-paste sloughs until, with an "O *blow!*" of feeling, he abandoned the way altogether for the much more solid ground of the woodland floor.

Now the Mole was wheeling his bike over the pale and dimly gleaming undersides of whitebeam leaves fallen in circles under the trees that had produced them, and over complex weavings of well rotted top-branches, thickly upholstered with the soft stuffs of mosses both smooth and feathery. The dog's mercury here had reached its poisonous bloom-time, while in places a tangling of ancient stems of traveller's-joy littered the ground like detritus from a rope factory. Out of this—massive as any hawser ever to groan against rigging—the occasional cable reared up to spread a broken snowy penumbra of spent seed-heads across the canopy.

Drawn ever deeper in—against his instincts and yet, in some way, with them too—the Mole could see the darker-than-dark outlines of a group of big yews: they resembled tree-shaped holes in the pattern of intervening branches. Yet the Mole sensed that the place was not unfriendly. No matter how dark the foliage nor gothically angular the shapes around him, he did not feel threatened here as he did on the roads. No gamekeeper had uncrooked his gun in this place for half a century or more—he could tell—and as to the wood's less civilised, hole-dwelling inhabitants—those of the pattering and pointed-toothed kinds—they were all, to an animal, long since gone. He looked up at the light in the sky. "Why, it must be not far off five o'clock already," he thought. "I suppose ... I suppose I could stop *here* tonight."—Why not, after all? His legs and knees were keen.

The ladybird tent snapped back and ate the Mole no more than three times before he succeeded in getting it to stay up and open. He had chosen the middle of a small clearing—or, more exactly, a sausage-shaped strip of sky between branches. From any distance, the tent's camouflage colour made it almost invisible, so much so that the Mole left the bike standing in order to be able to find his way back to it, for he had not quite finished his exploring for the day. Immediately he was organised, he walked on beyond the densest area of yews, emerging into the direct light of a sun just dropped from below the cloud-edge. He had heard the iced-water cry once more, and it had come from this direction.

But before he could get nearer to its source, the Mole was distracted by another magnetizing sound: a bold, staccato, rapidly accelerating whistle, emerging in bursts from a cluster of hazels. Noisy and insistent, this sound seemed to have in it some idea or feeling of interest to the Mole, though at first he was unable to decipher more than fragments. Very quietly, he walked closer to the hazels to find perched high in one of them, and still well hidden, a buff-and-dun little bird with a stumpy bill and streaked dark patternings down its head and breast.

"Hello, Bunting," said the Mole. "And what may *you* be doing here in this old wood?"

The little bird fired its whistle at him in a slightly different fashion. Concentrating now, the Mole heard it to mean, "And why s-s-s-shooooouldn't I be here? Why s-s-s-shooooouldn't I be here? See a b-b-b-branch to be pe-e-e-erched on? P-p-p-*perch* on it! That's my philo-o-o-osophy! That's *my* f-f-f-f-f-f-philoooosophy!"

There was a pause (the Mole was slightly at a loss), and then the Corn Bunting whistled again. "Not so m-m-m-maaaany of us about, these days!" it told him. "Not so m-m-m-maaaany of us about! It's a fact! Not seen any f-f-f-f-eeeemale b-b-b-b-uuuuntings in these parts, I sup-p-p-poooose?"

"'Fraid not," said the Mole, only just suppressing the urge to ask the Bunting if he had seen any female moles. "But don't you—um—I mean, far be it from a mere bur-rower-of-the-earth to suggest it, but—mightn't you be bet-ter off in a place where there's a bit more seed about?—Open fields, and so forth?"

"No g-g-g-g-ooood! No g-g-g-g-ooood! No g-g-g-g-ooood! No g-g-g-g-ooood!" answered the bird in a gatling-gun whistle of feeling. "Can't go far, in the fi-i-i-elds! Can't go far, in the fi-i-i-elds! All stops! World finishes! Comes-to-an-end! Can't-get-across-it! No f-f-f-f-ooood! No f-f-f-f-ooood! D-d-d-d-eeeeadworld! Can' t-get-across-it!"

"O ... dear ..."

"Stay in the r-r-r-rooough! Stay in the r-r-r-roooough, Mole! Stay in the hills! No-no-noooooo! No-no-noooooo! Don't go out, don't go out, don't go out in to d-d-d-d-eeeeadworld!" The Bunting fluttered its wings as if throw-ing off water droplets after a bath, then flashed up into the sky only to circle back, high above, its frenzied *pizzicato* whistlings seeming now to convey another variation on its theme: "Stay away—stay away—stay away—stay away! Stay away from the p-p-p-p-ooooisonous vooooids!"

"The poisonous voids? ..." echoed the Mole dismally. This did sound some way less than inviting. Could there, he wondered—*could* there be *worse* ahead of him than he had seen already?

But he was not able to dwell on this, for once again the other cry—that disturbing, trickled, ice-water mewing—was finding its way down to him. His spine thrilled to the sense of ancient threat in it even though he knew, of course, that it could not possibly have any relevance to *him*. Then—through the top branches of a group of massive overhanging beeches—he spotted an outline, circling effortlessly, and as near black against the low grey cloud as were the yews beyond the ashes. Two broad wings, the tip-feathers spread out like open fingers, a long rudder-tail split in two like the tail of some fish—what could it be? And was the bird closer to him than it seemed through the complex, confusing filigree of branches, or was it ... well ... rather bigger than even a quite-unmistakably-civilized mole might have hoped?

But even as the Mole was craning his neck, another large outline drifted into view to glide and circle exactly as if suspended from wires above him. And now—O, no—there was *another*—and one more! As the Mole watched, instinctively drawing back into the cover (the nonexistent cover) of the hazels, the sky beyond the beech canopy was colonized, monopolized, by big black silhouettes. When next he counted there were thirteen of them. Occasionally, languorously, one would make its trickling, freezing cry: a long remote *me-e-e-ew* ending each time in a kind of decorative, tailed-off trill.

The Mole reached to his neck to clutch at his tie-knot and tighten it, only to remember that he was both knotless and jacketless today. This disturbed him. It was complete nonsense, of course, to fear that these birds might attack an animal such as himself: he was not large, he knew, but he was not *that* not-large. Even so he would have been much happier if he had been standing there decently dressed rather than shapeless in a shift with words on it. These birds might not believe that *Mollusk Cares*.

One of them called again, and the great dark forms circled, and circled, each describing its imperceptibly, delicately yawing wing-ring, as if urgency of any kind was alien to the species. Another bird dropped just a little closer, and the Mole—in an instant jellified beyond recall—clung to the nearest hazel as if it had been a friend.—No, but he *would* be their dinner! He would. How had he not seen it?

Mole à la——, Mole à la——, Mole à la *nothing*! Mole à la
T-shirt! Raw, unseasoned Mole! Not even part-braised, no
gravy, not even with mustard! Not on a *plate*!

Another bird cried, and then another. But as they did so,
the Mole released his grip on the hazel stem just very
slightly. For in that moment he had begun to be able to
understand the cries.

"Other hills! Other hills!" one was mewing. (Could that
be it—what it meant?) "Searching! Searching!" (Yes,
thought the Mole, that was clear enough.)

"Searching!—Searching!—Searching!—Searching!"
called others now in a chill overlapping of fine-spun, faintly
echoing sounds.

"Not our country! Not our country!" one bird seemed
to be crying, at the edge of the group. "Other hills! Other
hills! Other hills!"

"Searching!—Searching!—Searching!—Searching!"
came the response from the centre whilst others were
shrilling something else, a call with which the Mole had
difficulty. He thought it meant something like, "Not
east!—Not east!—Not east! Better here than *there*! Better
here than *there*!"

Then, without any interruption in circling or crying,
and carrying the same messages off along the spur, the
birds began to clear the sky above the big beeches and drift
away *en masse* to the west, dark forms growing gradually
smaller, until all the Mole could hear was one last faint
and barely audible iteration from a single, singing razor-
beak: "Searching!—Searching!—Searching!—Searching!"
And as he heard this so the Mole shuddered, neither in
fear nor relief, but in *empathy*—or something as close to
empathy as possible when an animal has only moments
before believed he might make such creatures' supper,
without mustard.

The Mole was wakened unreasonably early the next morning by an unseasonably early cuckoo. But against all the odds he had slept well in the night, pleased to be so independent, and capable of coping too. (He had heated up some powdery dry-stuff with water on the stove, and it had warmed him: through the disturbing strangeness, it had tasted almost like food).

So it was with some vigour that he unzipped and flipped his rip-stop zip-flap and stumbled out from his tent with a sense of freshness, and latent energy that might perhaps be harnessed (though not, of course, until well after breakfast): a sense of new horizons that could ... that could perhaps be crossed.

"You're before your season!" he told the cuckoo. "Aren't you? You're at least a fortnight early!"

"Phupp-poo!" responded the cuckoo, one hundred per cent invisible in the depths of a shrubbery, as cuckoos always are.

The Mole decided he should begin his first morning as he meant to go on, and try to make some use over breakfast of the magical voice-box which Justin had lent to him: it did seem to be a valuable source of information about the world. The Mole persisted in calling this device a "voice-box" despite the fact that Justin had told him, four or five times, that it was a "ray-jo". In his heart of hearts, the Mole felt the word "ray-jo" was just a little silly: his own word was not only more dignified, it was also a rather better description of what the thing *was*.

But how to work it? That was the problem. He stared at the small black object and its arcane layout of buttons and numbers. "Just move the POWER switch to ON!" Justin had explained to him despairingly. "'POWER'?—See? ...

'ON' ... there? That's it—yes! N ... N ... *Yessss..!*" Nervously the Mole slid the little black-thing to the right with the tip of a claw, and nearly dropped the box as a voice jumped out of it, so loud it seemed the object might vibrate itself apart. He jammed it off again. "Too loud! ... MUCH too loud!" said the Mole. Then, recalling other instructions, he fumbled apprehensively with another little black-thing marked as "VOLUME" and tried again.

"... reports coming in," said a by now not unfamiliar, ebullient voice—very clear, not too loud, not too soft—"of what is feared may be a major chemicals-spill from the huge Toad Transoceanic complex in northern Teesside. Our north-east correspondent Mike Moledredge is already at the scene—at the other end of a Deracitel, unfortunately ... Mike, can you hear me?"

"Yes, John," shouted another much less distinct voice, fading in and fading out through crackles, "... there has been a leakage here ... we know it is from an acid storage unit at the edge of the complex, though we don't have any other details yet ... ver several miles of coastal marshland ... ly this appears to be a very serious incident, and local naturalists fear ... ny years, if ever, before ... could return to a healthy state ... huge area of marine life could be threat ..."

"—Mike ... sorry to interrupt you there. You're breaking up on us, I'm afraid. We'll try to get back to you later on. NOW—the time *is*: six forty-seven precisely. And appropriately enough, perhaps, after that last report, we have here now one of the rising young stars of the influential Mart-wing think tank the Feral Studies Institute, Mr Farris Ferris, who is to give a talk later on today at the London Temple Of Economics in which he will be putting forward the challenging idea that even the future existence of plant and animal species could eventually be decided through the actions of the Market.——Can this be right, Mr Ferris?"

"I believe that's now pretty clear," drawled a much lighter, boyish voice. "Yaahh. What we have to recognise, I think, is that it's in the power of the Market-Mystery to be able to determine every last detail of our impacts on the world we live in——"

"——But not, *surely*," interrupted the first voice, "whether there are still tigers in the jungle, say? Or butterflies flapping about in the fields? Some would argue, wouldn't they, that that kind of thing is a matter for Nature alone? Just so long as we don't mess it all up in the first place, of course?"

"The real issue, John——one I think we should start to grasp——" breathed Mr Ferris in tones of airiest detachment, "is this: the world *is becoming* increasingly global. You mentioned fields. Every field is a workplace, isn't it? And your other example, the jungle? Every sector of jungle on the planet may and indeed can be regarded——with reference to vastatabulatagram produced for us by the BCF at Cambridge University——"

"——Sorry, the BCF——the Barter Conducement Facility——?"

"——that's right——may and indeed can be regarded as, at least, a potential workplace. What we need to do now is conduct a comprehensive analysis of every square millimetre of the planet surface in terms of its potential usefulness to the Market. So, if there are butterflies——here——or tigers——here——we can begin to think in terms of their presence as *profits foregone* by businesses which might otherwise, if unconstrained by their presence, make rather more intensive use of the fields or, of course——"

"Cut down the jungle?"

"Yaahhh, modify ... improve ... harness ... and no doubt, in the process, cut down some jungle. We should begin to see things like butterflies and tigers for what they are in reality—as the Mystery sees them. Those little—rather exotic, in some cases—luxuries of life which we may in some cases be able to afford, and which, I think, in others we may find that we can't. Of course," went on Mr Ferris with the same blithe casualness, "if this was done across the board as I'm suggesting, then certain species and so forth might end up going to the wall—"

"Indeed! Quite a lot of them, no doubt?"

"—but of course, they are already doing that anyway. What we need to do now, quite simply, is put a price on them. In the future Global Mercantocracy, what we keep with us as—er—fellow-travellers, very much depends on what animalkind as a whole is prepared to pay, in compensation to Business, to secure it."

"So, Mr Ferris, are you saying that Nature, and the worth of Nature, can be measured entirely in terms of profit and loss sheets?"

"It's indisputable," said the fledgling ideologue. "Yaahhh. Indeed, in his most recent book, *Commoditizing Mother-Love: Are There Limits To The Market-Mystery Principle?* (from which I shall be quoting at some length today), the visionary U.S. Martist Milton Trappratt shows clearly and for the first time how Merchandise-Price Analysis can be applied to a theoretically limitless range of abstracts, on the principle that there is no action that is not, if you follow, in some measure also a transaction. In another BCF Study it has been conclusively demonstrated, I think, that even a model such as the standard mother-child relationship can be—"

"Costed?"

"In a word, yes."

"Well, Mr Ferris, I'm afraid that on that *stimulating* note we shall have to leave it, as it is now time to go over to Michael Fish at the London Weather Centre ... Michael!"

When, more than two hours later, the Mole approached

the nature reserve gate, he paused again by the board there. At the bottom of this, next to an outline-drawing marked *Red Kites*, in which he recognised the shape of the birds he had seen, he read: "... in a pioneering experiment, twenty breeding pairs have been reintroduced to this stretch of the Chilterns from Northern Spain ..."

"Were *they* put here by the 'market'?" he wondered, in deepest perplexity, looking about him in vain for someone to ask. All he saw as he left were the green criss-cross wires of the nature reserve fence. This kept him company for a quarter mile or so of his second day of pedalling, then stopped abruptly.

<hr>

The Mole crossed the first spoke of the Clearway bike-wheel, having paid no higher price than thirty seconds of low-grade moaning: the road he was following passed straight over it on a bridge. The Clearway ran deep below it—no less choked with traffic than any other—along a vast trench through the hill that looked like the result of some geological disaster. From this the Mole urgently averted his gaze while his pedalling feet accelerated to a blur. Three miles or so later, he found himself in the centre of a "village"—settlement, in any case—arranged around a series of greens and *motor* repair establishments on a busy main road. Here he spotted what he suspected must be a shop: it had a name—LORIS—above a caged-in window you could not see through. But people were entering through an open door and emerging again with groceries, and there did seem to be shelves inside.

For all that he still had half his sandwiches, the Mole thought it might be sensible to do a little reprovisioning, if only because this was the first shop he had seen. Thus he came to that difficult moment—put well out of his mind until now—when he would have to take out one of those many, many fifty-pound notes, and break into it. The only other choice would have been to sing for his victuals, and he was noted for his singing voice only in so far as animals mostly begged him not to … And Justin had *said* the money was "his", he reasoned uncertainly. Whatever that could possibly mean …

Some forty minutes after he stepped through the open shop door, the Mole emerged again, reeling slightly, and severely in need of a firm park bench. For he had at last come to grasp something of the limitations in buying-power of this sadly depleted currency-of-the-future, with the assistance (not entirely patient) of the assistant and, later, her boss. Grasping it was one thing, though—believing it quite another matter. Why, in his own time a pound, if he had had it, would have bought him a long-lasting winter overcoat, or a new pouffé with leather where the feet go! But the "pound" of today would buy nothing more than a loaf made of mysteriously sloppy sliced white bread, and a small, shiny, near-weightless packet of *Whoopzits*, whatever they might be!

"… and if 'fifty peas' really is ten shillings," he muttered, still worrying at the detail of what he had been told, "… TEN SHILLINGS!—O my, O my!—Why, that means this little bit of sausage (or whatever it is) cost … ummm … ahhh … No! *Six shillings?*! And *thruppence?*! *And* they divide it all up into these wretched 'peas' now. Why should a 'pea' have replaced the penny? And whatever happened to half-crowns and florins? And shillings and six-pences?—And are there really no thruppenny bits any more? No …" (he barely suppressed a sob) "… no *farthings?*" The Mole's whole life had been measured out in farthings.

But there it was. It really did seem as though these "fifty-pound" notes ("I don't *bullieve* it!—That isn't all you've *got*, is it?") were worth nothing like as much as the Mole had first thought. At the same time, he realised, each one of them could be made to go a fair long way, not least if an animal shopped as he did, parsimoliously. And he did have an awful, awful lot of them. (He really ought to count them, somewhere, he thought. Though on reflection he'd rather not.)

Once he had taken in what he had been told, he had scrupulously ranged the bright-lit shelves of the shop for foods that cost as small a ransom as possible. Things in cans, he saw—some of them—were "cheap", if also heavy. But his kit contained a can-opener, so he had finally opted for "Economy Beans" (fifteen peas per tin), "Economy Marrowfat Peas" (oddly, twenty-three peas per smaller tin, which, he hoped, had more than twenty-three peas in it ... "A pea for a pea, a pea for a bean?—O! It doesn't make sense!"), and a mysteriously-sloppy-sliced loaf. He had, sensibly, rejected the atmospheric *Whoopzits*, but added a banana—rather too brown—and something that might perhaps have been liver sausage. This was called *Livvery-Baconny*, and was wrapped in alien shiny crinkly-stuff: with it, he noted now in reading the packet, he had also purchased some "sodiose molyphisphate", a touch of "sodiose flitrite" and more than a dab of "dio-dioxxinophites" as well as unnamed "flavourings" and some "smartracine" in the marrowfat peas.

When eventually the Mole departed the settlement of LORIS, dropping down a sloping lane from the main road with relief, he did find himself thinking on about the ticklish problem of *enoughness*: a subject which, in his own quiet way, he had pondered more than once in the past. For the nuts-and-bolts of his journeying—thanks to Justin—he already had more than enough, and after the relative success of the previous night's camp he knew he would be able to carry on like this, if necessary, more or less indefinitely. But nylon walls do not a burrow make, nor ripstop-flaps a hole.

He might be able to *survive* like this, as a rootless wanderer—yes, and slake some of his curiosity into the bargain. But to be *happy*, if that was possible at all in this world, even so underreaching an animal as the Mole had need of something more.

He thought of Mr Wyvern-Toad and his twenty-seven "residences", and his stable of bit-champing killer-machines, but simply could not take it in. It wasn't just that no sane animal needed anything remotely like that much: in the Mole's way of seeing, no sane animal could *cope* with that much. The Rettes, too, seemed to have loaded themselves down with complicated objects for which they mostly had very little use. He thought again of the several long conversations he had been unable not to overhear between Mrs Rette and *Zipp-O-Swhitt*, on the subject of magical self-closing curtains that refused to magically self-close; and the no less several heated and tedious debates between herself and her spouse on the case for exchanging her present *Range Crusher*—already old-hat, apparently—for a Yakuzaito *Bludgeoner*. (The latter could be rolled to the bottom of a desert gorge with little more than scratches to the paint-work.) The Mole wasn't about to do it, but if you were to multiply such exchanges across a lifetime, he thought, you *might* find they occupied an unreasonably large part of it.

And there was a deeper problem here, at least for one of the Mole's predisposition. For exactly how little must an animal want, or "need", he wondered, in order to avoid capitulating to Weaselworld and joining it as a fully paid-up member? To pay for anything in this world you must earn money; and to earn money, it seemed, you had no choice but find a job, which in turn meant working for a company such as Toad Transoceanic; which, in the turn that followed, meant giving up everything in life that was worthwhile.

Was there no alternative? To revert, perhaps, to the life

of the *old* old days, cast aside one's smoking jacket for good, and dine on earthworms? What could his hole amount to, in its first stages, anyway, except a return to such a life— assuming, of course, he ever found a place to dig it? Yet, he thought—as a hedgerow of fully-fattened hazel catkins drifted past him—he might still dare to imagine something better. If he couldn't find a fit bit of turf for a hole, why, then, mightn't he be able to build himself a tiny cabin somewhere—out of second hand floor timbers, say—next to some humble little freshwater pond, by an old oak wood? Maybe he could find the space to turn over the soil, and plant it out with potatoes, and beans, and peas, and turnips? Over time, who knows, perhaps he could even earn enough from his surplus crops to purchase himself a teapot and cosy. To the astonishing luxuries of his old life—his brewing flagons, his framed pictures, his armchair, his skittle-alley—he could not aspire. And he could not help wondering, now, whether in that past life he had not been just a little greedy.

But his thoughts would not stop there. For, he chafed, even if such a place existed and he could find it, it would still have to be located far, far away from all the threatening monstrosities of Weaselworld; and especially far away from any Toad Transoceanic "komplecks" or the like, if only to be certain the pond's clear blue waters were never overrun by a flash-flood of acid. ... And then, you see, wasn't that the worst problem of all? For where might such a place *be* now, on the face of this compromised earth?

The irony of all this, of course, had the Mole only known it, was that he was already carrying with him in the bottom of his left-rear pannier enough hard currency to have purchased an entire hamlet of tiny timber huts, and filled each of them to the roof with teapots and cosies. For even at the Tip-Top-Scale of tax (provisional, and to be amended radically *down* though the skilled manipulations of his yet-to-be-appointed firm of City accountants), the Mole's salary as Special Directorial Consultant at Toad Transoceanic for one (nominal) Calendar Month came to £33,333.33—or, to put it another way, the price of 107,525 packets of *Livvery-Baconny* with just enough left over for a tin of Marrowfat peas.

If, on the other hand, we were to quantify this figure in terms of the Mole's potential for roaming the British Isles by bicycle, and, for the sake of the argument, build into the calculation the occasional grossly self-indulgent luxury-stop in, say, a low-end-of-the-range farmhouse bed and breakfast (one per month?) or Offspring Hostel (one a fortnight?) then—once he had confronted the truth of his purchasing power—he would find that he had earned enough in a nominal month at Toad Transoceanic to spend the next nineteen years, eight months and fifteen days of his life in transit. (This calculation allows for one full renewal of major equipment over the period concerned, but assumes the Mole's fortune would not be subjected to gross inflationary pressures. It is, nevertheless, one that any of his fellow high-flyers who secretly craved the open road, and the simple life, might well have borne in mind.)

At the end of a row of houses, the Mole came to a building of a type he recognised: it was an old brick Infant School. Through the tall, white-painted windows he could see children forming a queue for lunch. (The Mole had already used up the morning, what with his little problems with the shopping, and packing, and gears.) There were diminutive rats, and mice, and voles, and rabbits, all but a few of whom looked so amply rotund that if you had done nothing more than flick one of them lightly, it would have rolled helplessly away. (It would be unkind to do this on a hill.) In the seconds they were in his passing gaze, the Mole saw the first in the queue stacking their trays with plates of chips and curious, seeded, bun-like things framing thick circular wedges of something brown. The drinks they carried, in glasses, were of much the same colour.

In the classroom next door, already empty, the Mole saw the teacher packing up her books. Beyond her, on a wall next to a notice board, there hung a large poster showing a picture of a ... was it a panda? The Mole very much suspected it was. Bold, unmissable print at the bottom gave out the simple legend, MOLLUSK *CARES*. The Mole glanced down at his own apparel in embarrassment, clutching it together in a vain attempt to fold up the letters. One could have just too many caring declarations in a single spot, he thought.

Yet even as he was doing this, another cyclist, weaseline of mien, was approaching from the opposite direction. This individual too was decked out in the *dernier cri absolu* of the age, his clothes and machine barely visible under a hectic snow of logos, of which—the Mole clutched harder—the largest by far was inscribed across his thin, hard chest. It read:

McMINC

The MultiCorp

McMINC

The Way

None of this dented the Mole's commitment to civility.

"Good m—" he said.

The 'orning' element, as normally used, got no airing here, since before the Mole could get it out the cyclist had flashed on by in the fixed-dead-ahead silence of the very serious sportsmal, head dropped almost to handlebar level as if in preparation for a stag fight. For one brief flash of extreme high-techno-nastiness the animal's lanky pumping form was blobosely imprinted across the Mole's egg-shaped Shaydes, exactly as the Mole himself was being stretched and striped round the centres of the other's face-wrappers.

It was enough to decide him. Directly he reached the next small wood, the Mole lifted his bike off the road into the dark green seclusion of some hollies to open the bag containing his comfortingly antiquated weeds. Five minutes later he re-emerged, his old identity restored, and if Mollusk Still Cared it did so now only within the privacy of a waterproof pannier-lining.

<hr>

By a series of arduous ziggings and zaggings away from his chosen compass-point, the Mole eventually found his way back up to another spot on the top of the scarp. Here, with no other sensible choices open to him, he made a bold decision and carried on along the ridge on a rough track signed as *Byway*: it did at least point in the right general direction. But now, a couple of hundred yards along it, a pothole bumped one of his panniers into the "dragging-along-the-road" position, so he stopped to restore it and tighten up its stays. In the drama of the moment he had barely noticed that he was in a rough-surfaced car park, where a dozen or more animals were just at that moment getting out of their *motors*. All but one—a hare—were weasels, stoats, ferrets, or ... but let us call them weasels for the say-so. As they gathered in a tight huddle not far from the Mole, more than one of them glanced about apprehensively at the vista of oaks and beeches bizarrely misshapen through long-distant pollarding, at the long view down the hill through the wood, and at the pastures running away on the flat hilltop land.

"Over here, please, yes, thank you!" boomed one full-bearded weasel, taller and much stockier than the rest. "OKAY! Over here, please! Great! *Great!* Well, here we are!" (..Did one of the ferrets to the rear emit a low whimper, then? ...) "This is *the start* of *the* introductory, three-and-one-*quarter*-mile walk from my book—which I think you all have now?—let me know if not—*Les Wezelpleze's On-The-Ground Actuality-Walks For Beginners*. And, of course, many of you will also be getting to know my new and, though we say it ourselves, quite revolutionary product, the TQ-MOP *Pathways Through Kasements* ..."

"I've been over every one of them five times so far," said a small, pale-grey female stoat proudly.

"Good! Good!—Fiangona, isn't it?—Just for any of you who haven't got it yet, let me say, this syllagram contains everything any serious Indoor Walker will *ever* want to know about the very best routes in England and Wales—over 200 miles of really superb high and low level paths, selected personally by myself and my team. You can *zedd*-straight-in on to any area you choose, *slick* on to a path, *follow* it step by step over the ground on-*tect*, and of course, *exprint* copies of the routes if you ever did think of walking one out here in the, ha, ha, Actual." (At this, a little ripple of subdued, nervous laughter dampened the whiskers of the group.)

The Mole was having quite serious trouble with his pannier-stays and the exasperating, ungrippable press-clip-things that for some reason would not close up as Justin had showed him. So he had little choice but to remain where he was and fiddle.

"—Also!" reverbed Mr Wezelpleze through the russet-orange of his beard, "—We'll get the commercial over soon, don't worry!—But may I just mention, for the benefit of those of you who don't yet know them, my two earlier and also *hugely* successful volumes, *Forty-Five Two-Mile Walks Beginning And Ending At A ThriftaCenta Car Park*, which probably speaks for itself, and my unbeatably comprehensive volume, *THE Definitive Guide To Footpath Guides*—as there are now over twenty-three thousand, five hundred such guides in print or on tect.—Quite an achievement, when we only have one hundred and twenty thousand miles of paths, and half of *them* are still hard going!" (Another little drizzle of laughter.) "Or completely nonexistent!" (Now, that *was* a whimper.) "And in any case, almost no one ever walks them if they're not in the Lake District!" (Whimpering laughter, or vice versa.)

The Mole could not fail to notice—though politely, of course, and only out of the corner of his eye—that this gaggle of strangely timid weselians were each and every one of them kitted out to the jawbones in complicated and aggressively-coloured waterproofs and magnificent boots such as might have seen an animal across the breadth of the Arctic Circle on a six-month unsupported tow-your-own-sledge race. Had there ever before been so many hoods, flaps, zips, pockets, logo-clutches, fleece-linings, strappings, mappings, sockings or glovings gathered together into a single English bridleway?

"—ALL RIGHT, then!" gonged Mr Wezelpleze. "This is it, team! The moment you have all signed up for! We have precisely *three and one quarter miles* of footpath to consume. IN-the-Actuality!"

No doubt about it this time: two thin ferrets near the Mole clasped one another and whimpered shamelessly, as did a less-thin stoat. "Courage, mals!" shouted Mr Wezelpleze. "With my expert assistance—and remember, please, I will remain in the lead *and in full sight* for the length of the walk—I won't allow any one of you to fall behind— we *will* and *can* do it! ... Now. This rather quaint object, here" (he pointed) "is what we call a *stile*. Some of you will already be familiar with the design, yes? Right. And what do we *do* with a stile?—Anyone?"

"We get over it?" suggested the Hare, jogging demonstratively on the spot in his logo-loaded *Shrikes*.

"We get *over* it!" agreed Mr Wezelpleze.

"... But not ..." said one of the small ferrets in a proportionately sized voice, "... not ... We don't have to go across *that field*, do we? Not with all those ... big, woolly *sheep* in there?"

"The 'big woolly sheep'," responded Mr Wezelpleze beamingly, every last shining denture on view in a grin of magisterial reassurance, "are the basis of lamb chops—no more, no less. There is no reason whatsoever to be afraid of them."

"Sir, I ... I can't go!" flatly stated one individual dressed in desert-attack gear, his species obscured by what he was wearing around his head. "My geosputni-collocationer is down."

"You won't need it, Edmund! Trust me," responded his leader, emanating warmth and reassurance. "Trust me! This is a *very* well-used path. The Pond-to-Pond Walk, the Councillor Alfred P. Twigletail Memorial Ramble, the Grand National Ridge-Path Trail (in one of its rare ascents from the hill-bottom), *and* the South Bucks Figure-of-Eight Revivifier all pass over and along the very route we shall be following. Or most of it. See how worn-in that path is, Edmund. That path has been *used!*"

"But ..." responded the obscure one brokenly, staggering a little under his load as he did so. "I just feel ... I'm very sorry, Mr Wezelpleze, but the truth is, I just *haven't spent enough!* I ... *can't go*, sir, unless I part with some more money!"

"We'll organise a second fee for you, Edmund," replied Mr Wezelpleze in a practised voice. "Directly we're back at base, you have my word on that. All right?"

"Thank you sir," replied the other, standing just a little more erect. "... Thank you. I'll be fine now."

While this was going on, one pale young ferret had been staring into the depths of the twisted old pollards and the woods beyond them with a pained but also—to the Mole—mystifying expression on his face. There was something very close to sadness in this youngster's eyes, he thought, almost as if he had been recalling ... what? Things he had almost certainly never known in person, but which he *knew*—in some other, less tangible way—to have been the day-to-day experiences of his ancestors, in quite another age than this?

"Yup!" said a plump stoat near to the Mole, squatting and putting a paw over one ear as he did so: he was using a Deracitel. "We're going in now. Coupla minutes, I guess. Yup. We're at the car park. Getting the briefing? ... Yup ... Yep—*outside.*—Outside the cars, right? ... Oh, you know ... woods ... grass ... sky ... bitta mud ... Ye—*Don't worry*, Honey!—no ... No! It's *nearly dry*. Call you later, Possum! Check ... We'll make it! ... Bye ... Bye! ..."

"—Now remember, mals!" thrummed Mr Wezelpleze. "You have freely chosen this challenge! It is *your* choice to make this Lifestyle Statement, not just there on your chests and backs but in the great *out-here*. Nobody said this was going to be easy—"

Just when he was least expecting it, the Mole's idiot-clip-things clicked firmly into place, as a result of which he had no further reason to tarry. But as he pedalled on, he could not fail to hear Mr Wezelpleze's voice—perhaps just a tri-

fle strained now—as it boomed out, "ALL right then!
Emergency measures! All link hands! ... That's it! Now—
all right? You mals at the back there, you all linked up there
OK? Right ... *Good!* Now—nobody let go, and let's get out
there, team, and *take on nature!*"

When the Mole looked back, he saw the iron-willed
author of *Pathways Through Kasements*, amongst countless
other publications, as he stepped boldly over the stile followed by a wavering, hand-holding daisy-chain of animals,
then drew his charges on into the shining sunlit pastures of
what was now a glorious April afternoon. Voices drifted
back to the Mole as he bumped on: "... Are we nearly
theeerre yet? ..." "*Miiind* the *sheeepp!* ..." "... I want my
screeenn! ..."

The Mole did find it difficult to believe that a once-
proud country—cradle and origin of explorers as doughty
and varied as Whiskielia Fynnes, Burr'ton, Livingbone and
Scottie of Antarctica—could have sunk *quite* so low as this.
Shaking his head, he pressed forward through the tree-
branches' criss-cross and waving shadows, on his own,
rather more open-ended expedition.

Of the Mole's efforts to get around map-blodges Luton
and Stevenage there is, unfortunately, little good to set on
record. After his second overnight stop in one of Berkham-
sted Common's larger thickets—a successful camp, if the
persistent yapping of dishmop dogs on walkies is over-
looked—the Mole used every bit of ingenuity at his dis-
posal to plot a route along the pale double-lines of minor
roads that would take him in the right general direction.
What he could not avoid, though, for all his efforts, were
the regularly spaced examples of bolder double-lines,
infilled with red, that ran at right angles across his direction

of travel. Several times that day he had no choice except to turn on to one of these in order to get himself a few hundred yards along it, and so reach the next back road east.

And on these blood-and-guts-red routes, the Mole found himself in wheeled company aplenty. As his undergeared stub-legs span crazily around, pumping him along each strip of gutter edge just as fast as animally possible, he was forced to share the road with near unbroken caravans of great screaming white monsters. One by one, their sinister dark-windowed cabs flew down upon him as if with the sole purpose of adding him, as mole-Wiener-Schnitzel, as mole-in-the-hole, to the mulched jaffa-cake boxes and crumped-flat beer cans he was rattling over.

"But WHY is all this carriage on the roads?!" he muttered, when he could, in a ferment of incomprehension. "WHY isn't it on the railways and canals?" Yet, he realized, railways and canals were notable largely by their absence, just about everywhere he had been in this world. Why, the *river itself* had no freight on it! The old conduits seemed to have disappeared as surely as the elm trees: perhaps there had been a Dutch Railway Disease, or a Dutch Canal Disease, to carry them off as well?

A shower of rain had stopped falling just as he reached one such road, and each remorseless thunderer was trailing beside and behind it a fluted cloak of spray-filth. One after the next, these grey clouds wrapped themselves around the small traveller in an embrace that dirtied as it blinded as it drenched. Even where the roads were dry, he still had to contend with the warm-wind-punch of each new phantasmagore, belting down upon him from the opposite direction: *their* cloak-tails, invisible, were generously stocked with eyeball-filming grits.

Indeed, the Mole did not find air along these roads at any time. What he gasped at instead was a spicy-sweetish-peppery *miasm*, liberally recharged by each vehicle that slammed past him. This sugar- and pepper-flavoured gas percolated its way inside him like the finest—the most exquisite—of fine dusts, coating first his tongue, then the roof of his mouth, then his nose and his lungs. As special seasoning came the occasional less well maintained grand-slammer, flatulating past in a blue oil haze: what he tasted or smelled then were, presumably, bits of its engine. Every so often he would sneeze splutteringly—it was almost a relief. But this is a dangerous thing to do when you are balancing along your allotted five inches in the company of monsters.

Most memorably awful-in-awfulness of these experiences was the section he rode of the trunk route between Stevenage and Hertford. Here, the Mole was locked into a stream of thirty to forty thud-passings at once, and just for variety at one point there was a fine long artillery fly-by of big, shiny, deep-voiced motorcycles. All along his left side, the thick stems of a hacked-down thorn hedge protruded from a verge where nothing else grew: an eternity of wheel-spray had reduced it to a beach of exposed grey dust. Yet here in this waste as he passed, the Mole saw young rabbits (of the non-waistcoat-wearing kind): five, ten, twenty, forty, more. Each sat beneath the hedge-skeleton staring into the pestilence of noise as if hypnotised by it. They looked to the Mole almost as he had heard rabbits sometimes look when trapped by a hunting animal, in the last moments before it their *quietus* makes.

"What are you *doing?!*" he shouted to one after another of them. "Get away!—Get back! Don't you know how dangerous this place is?!" But not one of them responded, not even when he shouted to them from right close by. They remained there, quite unmoving, little dust-hued statues ranged along a tiddlersland of dust.

Strangely, even in the spaces between the main roads there were few moments that day when the Mole felt himself to be away from the influence of the town. For the countryside had been invaded here whichever way he turned. There hardly seemed to be a strip of woodland left, even in the middle of seeming-nowhere, where there did not now sit rows of poky white or cream slumgullion-bungalows in every variant of the New-Abysmal style. In one quite typical spot, mockingly named *Oak Leys*, these had been stuck up very close together in long, thin gardens as if, absurdly, each might claim the woods behind it as its own. In all such places the Mole found himself riding along a jangling deranged motley of this, that, and anything other: low walls made of perforated greystuff lumps, crazy-paving tilted to the vertical, strands of chicken-wire on greystuff posts, slumped and bulging woven-pinewood fences that looked as if they could be punctured with a prod.

The commonest barrier of all was the one made from those same tall and suffocating conifers so inexplicably favoured by the Rettes and their neighbours: ghastly, sixty-foot walls of the things—ranging in hue between crypt-green at the one extreme and grave-green at the other—shut out all sight of house from road, and road from house wherever there were settlements, and loomed over the Mole as he passed. In places, too, they had been jaggedly lopped half way up as if by the bungling hand of panic, to reveal dust-dry, lifeless, bird-repelling centres. To the Mole, these decapitations looked like nothing so much as rows of huge, deformed feather-dusters.

And, indeed—to an animal from an earlier, harmonious age of well-made brick walls, white picket fences and the neatly trimmed, rounded shapes of thorn and box hedges—all this was chaos pure and simple. Here there was no order, no centre, no common taste, no hint of community; and the wall simply as a thing to lean on to have a chat with a neighbour was rare enough to deserve something in the order of the Mole Prize For Keeping Neighbourliness Going In Adverse Circumstances.

Worse still, if possible, was that more than once that day the Mole emerged from such places not into farmland or anything resembling it, but into strange, synthetic-looking landscapes—countryside struck down with some disease. He passed through rolling expanses of unnaturally close, carpet-like grass afflicted simultaneously with polio and mumps: the land broke into low bulges and swellings—some of them marked with posts bearing flags—interspersed with ugly circular pock-marks. Across these holed carpets—they recalled to the Mole the inescapable floor-coverings of the Rette house—small groups of animals walked very slowly, carrying sticks, or rode in odd little self-driven invalid carriages, or stooped to place a ball on the ground and hit it, or try to. When, eventually, along one busy back road, the Mole found himself passing gigantic brick gates with balls and eagles in the Botched-Overweening manner, and saw one generously gilded sign proclaiming *The Hertfordshire*, another announcing *Extranational Golf*, he understood even where he did not comprehend.

Throughout this same blighted region, the explorer came up against more than one variety of what he thought must be later stages in the colonization of the country by the town. None impressed him. There were jam-packed, boxy little terraces of miser-minded weeness, made of gloom-brown bricks and murk-brown tiles, hemmed in around kerb-lined little car-parks. Most of these had been done as if in some groping, idiot imitation of the plain and honest styles of the Mole's own day, rather as if those who had thrown them up had been going on rumour even when examples of such old buildings stood only a hundred yards away. They looked as if they had been crushed together to shoehorn a fit, and the song sung by all of them was clear enough: "Life is a grim, relentless battle, and don't mention it, but we're probably not the ones who are going to make it".

More privileged colonists, meantime, had been able to erect individual structures—the Mole could not honestly have called them houses—some of them the width of entire tiny-terraces and made in every kind of luridly-coloured brick but never—never—in brick pure and simple. Along one ex-lane, the Mole passed a row of such things squatting in a sublimity of vileness atop a low, steep bank, beneath which open garage mouths gaped blackly at him over barren ramps of mauve-grey briquettes. At one such low-slung fort, *The Ponderosa*, every available sloping surface—entrance, drive-sides, even the high ground beyond the house—had also been revetted with lumping greystuff blocks as if in terror of a single blade of grass appearing. The anthem here ran, no less clearly: "Life is a grim, relentless battle, and by the way, *we're* the ones who won, in our opinion. Got that?"

"Not a place to settle," thought the Mole, his spirit gripped as if in a vice. Nor did he linger.

<hr/>

Towards the end of this third day of his journey, the Mole emerged from the urban-outbreak lands. He found himself in a new kind of topography, too, so that along with uncharted brick acreages and symptoms of golf, he had left behind hillsides of any steepness, and woods of any size. Now, the land rolled on before him in a vague and gentle way, neither hill nor vale, and everywhere he looked there was ploughland. At first the fields were merely very big, but then they were bigger still, and the Mole began to wonder whether he might have come to the beginnings of the region known—to one small corn bunting, at least—as the poisonous voids.

It was not long before he found out. At five o'clock he
confused a junction, turning north where he should have
turned east. After this, as he rode on, the land became more
and more sweeping. Hill-swells reappeared as once again he
drew close to the extension of the long chalk scarp he had
been following from the outset. Here he found himself
cycling alongside what looked like fields metalled with
stones: pavements of loose grey flints and broken white
chalk lumps in which crops were set almost as if there had
been soil there to support them. Guessing he must have
come the wrong way, the Mole still climbed on up the last
long rise only to stop and stare, open-mouthed, across—
what else might it be called in his pantheon of titles?—the
greater nothingness?

None of the country he had seen or traversed since his
emergence into Weaselworld could quite have prepared the
Mole for the vista that lay before him now. He looked back
the way he had come, to see that an impression of the old
countryside had been maintained, up to here, by the reten-
tion of thin hedges and the occasional hedgerow tree
around the far-too-big fields. Such hedges ran on up to the
top of the last land-swell, riding across it like a net on a
wave. But beyond this—where the land dropped away to a
great flat vale spreading northwards to the horizon—it was
just as if, at a certain point on the hill, the lines had been
rubbed out wholesale by some giant eraser. There was no
further pretence of any kind here: the countryside itself
had been rubbed out, and anything left standing—isolated
houses, a set of huge white sheds, lumping greystuff water-
towers, wire-carrying posts, concertina-skeletons and the
incessant earthbound glide of *motors* themselves—stuck up
into the sky out of a nakedness of young wheat like outlines sketched on a sheet of green and blue paper.

Way down to his left, the Mole could see the outer edge
of a small town. It was two miles away, at least, yet noth-

ing—*nothing*—stood between him and it but rows of young crops and a couple of melancholy thorn bushes, far off and tiny, by an angle of road and ditch. The town's edge projected like a row of broken teeth, boxy houses framed by another ramshackle line of short-life fencing, with here and there a white motor-home parked leaning on the verge of nothingness. Had the place been a Saharan stronghold standing mud-walled in an infinity of sand, it could not have been more starkly isolated.

"The poisonous voids ..." whispered the Mole to himself, summoning all his strength as he did so. "The poisonous voids!" And as he stood there, he began to be gripped by an irrational, but also irresistible, fear: that if he stayed much longer he might be sucked out into this emptiness before him, to ricochet and blow about there forever like some small black ping-pong ball. Shivering, he turned and remounted, swiftly retracing his route south as far as the crossroads of his error.

This junction was shaped like a pair of half-open scissors, and to one side of it was an odd little brake that he had barely noticed earlier, but came back to now with gratitude and relief. It was nothing more than an oblong stand of tiny crinkle-oaks and tendon-barked, immature hornbeams growing amidst thorns and bramble clumps—a bit of rough that had somehow, even here, escaped the plough.

Testingly, tentatively, the Mole wheeled his bike off the road to stand amongst the hornbeams' strange ridged boles. Almost amused at himself now, he remembered how uneasy he would have been, in the *old* old days, standing amongst trees like these. These were Wild Wood trees, no doubt about it. But the Wild Wood here was shrunk to a scrap, a toddler's handkerchief, far less threatening than threatened, with the big bare fields pressing in on every side.

At the brake's bottom end, the Mole found a stream:

there must be some clays here, he thought. It moved in a flickering pulse round a series of left elbows and right elbows over little drifts of gravel. Somewhere close by, a blackbird began to sing. The sounds floated out from one or other tree, filling and echoing in the narrow bough-space, a set of variations on a beautiful, unstable theme that was at one moment like a lullaby, at another, a valediction. Just as this happened, late afternoon sunlight flooded into the copse when a cloud carried its shadow eastwards on the breeze. A single young hornbeam twenty yards from the Mole was picked out by the light, as prominent now as a suddenly spot-lit stage player. Its leaves were already open-ing—delicate, skin-soft pointed ovals in miniature constel-lations of palest green: the lowest of these seemed to hang in space against the woodland floor as if unconnected to the branches, rising and falling in some primordial sema-phore for which there never was a handbook of interpreta-tion.

Such beauty! thought the Mole. Even in this world, it is still possible! He walked his bike towards the tree, resting a paw hard against its bark. "O Pan, O Pan!" he said out loud, and a vigorous chill shudder of emotion shook his small body as the words came out. "How I have loved your realm, and all that you protected in it!"

The Mole stopped that night in the crossroads-brake, perfectly hidden from the road—except perhaps for the few minutes when his stove was lit—by a three-quarters-circle of impenetrable old thorns. He awoke just once, and when he did so he found his eyes and nose and blow-up pil-low slightly damp. The dream he had been dreaming had been of shimmerings, and summer sunlight, dancing from wavelet to wavelet across the breeze-ruffled surface of a River. And it had been of quietly creaking rowlocks, and the gentle rocking of a boat, and the sound of Ratty's voice (he had been beside himself, in raptures). They had been searching, and searching, confident of what they would find, and drawing very slowly—O, so very slowly—closer to a flower-rimmed and, in some quite inexplicable way, awe-inspiring island.

CHAPTER TWELVE

ANCHORAGE

"Ja, ja, you *schoot zem down*, ja?—You schoot zem—you schoot zem! Ze idea iss *vewwy, vewwy szimple*—zat ve szet up bick, bick laser-guns—ve'd need, accortink to pwesent calculashions, fife huntret tousant uff dem, maybe eight huntret tousant—schtationed schtratechically aroundt ze vurldt—und zen ve szimply *blaszt apart* ze carbomortuofluorons, ja?—"

"—the CMFs—"

"—Ja, ja, *before* zey haff ze chance to destroy ze nözöne—"

"But surely, if—"

The Mole was listening to his voice-box. The morning sun had cast its rays across his brake, as it had over the rest of eastern England, and on ABC Radio Paw the day was, as ever, marked out in pulses of warmly adversarial debate.

"—ja, you szee? No 'ifs'! Ve *blaszt zem apart*. It's szimple!"

"—Well, thank you very much, Dr Gottlieb Strangevole, of the Leveritt Research Institute, for that."

"—ve blaszt zem!—"

"Dr Strangevole . thank you! 'Fraid we have to move on now."

"—ja, ve *bl*—!"

"—Now *meantime*," said the ebullient voice—one which was, by now, almost as familiar to the Mole as any in this world, "down at the University of Deadmal's Gulch in Alabama, another eminent scientist and his team have been working on their own possible solutions to the nozone-hole issue. Professor Wally Brockheimer, hello? Can you hear me?"

"Loud and clear."

"You ... I believe you had some kind of plan to fill huge fleets of Dumbo jets with nozone and then *fly* it up there? Can this be right?"

"Yup, we did, but that's shelved now, for a number of technical reasons. Our present thinking embraces two broadly defined practical strategizations. The first is to get the nozone up in balloons, rather like upscale helium balloons, and then set them off one by one—"

"With laser-guns?"

"No, no. Ha, ha. No, that's not quite our style down here at Deadmal's Gulch. No, er, they'd self-detonate. We'll be equipping them with remote-detonators, right? The other line of attack, most likely at present for tandem-syllagractivization, is simply to cover the surfaces of the world's oceans with a layer of sputofoam chips."

"But—surely—that would involve billions of tons of the things, wouldn't it?"

"Oh, maybe not much over a couple of billions. Sputofoam is very light stuff."

"But wouldn't it make rather a mess of the place? I mean, the oceans wouldn't look quite the same covered in a layer of little white bits, would they? And what's the point, anyway?"

"Oh, the *point* is to greatly increase the reflectivity of the planet, overall, thus reducing the temperature-incrementualization process."

"I see ... A bit like, what, wearing a white shirt on a hot sunny day?"

"Exactly. Exactly."

"Except that in this case the shirt is big enough to cover the Atlantic, the Pacific, the Indian Ocean, the Solent, The Wash, and any other stretch of salt water you care to name?"

"Exactly."

"Some shirt! Well, Professor Brockheimer, if it saves us all from frying then I suppose we must wish you luck with it. Just so long as you can clear it all up afterwards! Thank you very much.—And now, back to that big chemicals-spill at Teesside, which it has now been confirmed has spread across at least six square miles of—"

The Mole clicked off the "OFF" switch. He was in no less of a mood to learn things than he had been the day before, but, he thought, he might just have to start narrowing down his choice of subject-matter. Nose-own (whatever that might be) was one thing. But there was so much else to think about right in front of him.

He got up, mug in paw, and walked a few paces to reach the wood-edge. There was that smell again—that sickly, briny, chemically smell. The ploughlines ahead of him reached out across an expanse of soil in which he could see nothing growing except the crop—not unless you counted a few stalks of fat hen dotted here and there amongst it. And what could lie beyond it for him except more nothingness, more absence?

"... No, Mole," he thought, unable to resist the idea now. "Perhaps, after all, you shouldn't have done this. You could go back.—You could. All you have to do is point the bicycle that way." He turned in the direction of his previous day's journeying, and all such theorising was stopped dead in its tracks. Wherever he went now, it would not be there.

Once he was packed up again, with his tyres on the tar, the Mole followed an impulse. Instead of immediately setting off on the lane that would lead him east, he went back up to the high point on the scarp where the land dropped away, and all the world had been shaved to its skin. Here he stopped, gazing out once more across the great space, less scared by it this morning than challenged—and wishing to challenge it back in return. With the informed eye of one who had, after all, lived through a part of ancient history, he read closely each line of the place's nakedness, seeking out ditches and changes in the colour of the cropping, distant isolated lines of trees and low, vestigial, grass-covered banks. He stood like this in the westerly breeze for ten to fifteen minutes, piecing together a picture of what might have been there in the past—B.V.—before the void.

By the end of this time he was, if not convinced, then at least very deeply suspicious. This, too, had been countryside—hadn't it? This, too, had allowed room of *some* kind for Nature. There had been fields here, too—surely, surely!—just like anywhere else in England. Why else could he see isolated thorns standing in rows here and there in one distant sector, like small dark ships afloat on an ocean of green? What had grown along those banks? Why were those trees standing there, in a line, if they had not once been part of a hedgerow? Hadn't all this too been just another part of the familiar English scene, mixing arable with pasture, and woods, and copses, and wet ground, and bits of old rough?

"A terrible—" breathed the Mole. Then his voice faltered. But he tried again, if only to make clear to himself what he suspected. "A terrible crime has been committed here," he said. "... I think so. O, I do think so."

For the second and last time, the Mole returned to his brake: it felt like "his" brake now. At least here, he thought, he was back in something that might pass for countryside, if you looked at it from just the right angle. The blackbird sang to see him off, its melodies overlapping the slick whirr of his immaculately oiled freewheel like one stream flowing into another. The bike rolled on effortlessly over the smooth black road surface, and the Mole attempted—and made—a single non-clattery gear change. The bumptious little breeze was with him, too, gusting his exposed bits of fur into velvety channels, and in the first sheltered dip— amazingly early—he found cow-parsley just coming into bloom.

There did also seem to be one other, almost unimagin- ably good development: *motor*-infestation on these roads had dropped to far lesser densities of incivility-per-hour, at least along the wiggliest back roads the Mole was trying to favour. "Look on the bright side," he said to himself, as the tiny white points of the cow-parsley danced past him on swaying heads. "Remember, Mole. Look on the bright side! Even when there isn't one!"

What the Mole discovered about this rolling country as he angulated slowly east-north-east across it, was that though the open road was often far too open, and though the void absolute constantly threatened, it became absolute only across isolated expanses. And these, he deduced, must be the estates of single vast "farms", for want of a better way of describing them. Their work-places—his chief sin- gle clue—were always much the same: brutally looming, hangar-like sheds that reared out of runway-seas of pale cracked greystuff. Rows of boldly coloured machines— outdoing even the titans of the tar in bulk—stood in or near these sheds. (The Mole in person would barely have come up to the middle of one of their crunching great wheels, not that he was about to make the comparison). Many such monsters had already died—of their very unwieldiness, perhaps—and stood in great ranges suggestive of abandoned battlefields, rusting down among the docks and sow-thistles.

Inside some hangars lay the produce, old or new, in roof-high stacks: great cylinders of wheat, occasionally sprouting grasses, or similarly-proportioned blackstuff-bags, or simply hills of grain. Half dry, tyre-moulded mud lay in broad pale channels wherever the dessicated greystuff ended, and hardly an enclave had not also been struck down with an outbreak of crypt-conifers. These stood in rows like flags of mourning—who knows, thought the Mole, perhaps that was what they were, planted in memory of the world that was gone—drilled along side-walls, on guard along end-walls, their vegetable gloom isolate and blackly visible over distances of miles.

As he stared more and more obsessively into the spaces around him (it was not good for his eyes), the Mole began to work out the patterns of clearance, seeing how field-systems had been swept away for the convenience of the giganti-plough and the giganti-reaper, leaving only the "difficult" bits—this small angle of very steep ground, that horseshoe-bend in a stream—to themselves. The terrain had been scraped, and combed, and scraped again over every variation in its gently rolling surface, to within inches of that broken, dead-elm-bleached covert, this low wood-land edge. Nowhere here was any longer its own place: to have used the word "local" of any part of it would have been a nonsense. All was subsumed into the wider—the utterly anonymous—flowing of the tilth.

But beyond this madness was another yet deeper. For although across most voids and part-voids every last quarter-inch had been cultivated, there were places where the Mole found the land left as if permanently abandoned, a grubby mess of last year's (or the year before's?) rotted stubble, invaded now by mosses. Worse still, he found himself pedalling past wastelands where nothing grew at all.

Because of their colour—as starkly unnatural as anything he had seen—he called this condition of the land the orange death.

It was nearing noon, and the Mole had just pushed his way as bright-sidingly as he could manage across one green desert, only to find himself approaching another of the engorged spokes of the Clearway-wheel. But he saw with relief that this, too, would be easy to get past—easier still, in fact, since the road he was on went directly under it through a tunnel. Here the formerly narrow road verge suddenly bulged outward, spreading into a space of litter-strewn grass big enough to have supported a market garden. Next to this, the Mole saw ahead that extreme rarity, another animal, standing as exposed as he was himself to the sky and the wind.

This individual was a hare of venerable seniority, somewhat stooped, somewhat scantily furred, and dressed in an old suit-jacket over worn canvas trousers. He was wielding a hoe whose blade had been reduced to a stump by many decades of use, and doing so with skill and speed. But he was not working the soil of the fields, nor even the expanse of verge. What he hoed at instead was the road surface, along the edge of which there lay a thin coating of mossy humus—the target of his attentions.

"Mornin'!" said the Hare as the Mole got closer.

"Mornin'!" replied the Mole, delighted to have been addressed first for once.

"Off on yer 'ollydays, then?" asked the Hare with sweet simplicity, eyeing the Mole's load both rheumily and rejectingly as he spoke.

"Well, um—yes.—In a manner of speaking."

"Which way yer 'eaded?"

"O. East. Generally, you know.—East?"

"Oh, yeh. Goin' in ter Suffolk, then."

"Will I? O—yes. S'pose I will. Sooner or later!"

"Got ter get acrost the rest of Essex first, though."

"Yes!—yes ..."

"Not too many 'ills ter trouble yer there. You'd not want 'em either, would yer, loaded down with that lot?" (It was only then that the Mole registered the horizontal presence of the old fellow's bicycle—one of a design he recognised instantly, though thoroughly blurred from its historic sharpness of line by what might have been half a dozen coats of thick black paint.)

"Do you—um—?" The Mole paused, as so often, wondering just how best to phrase the question he wanted to ask. "I mean—is there a lot of call for this kind of work, hereabouts? Hoeing the, er—the road?—Gutter?"

"Can't say 'bout that exac'ly," replied the Hare with all the caginess of the country animal who does not have an answer handy. "Sure thing is, though, thur ain't too much other work about."

"Not in the—not in the—um—fields, for example?" asked the Mole, his gaze roaming to the horizon-embracing union of void and road beyond, against which the old Hare was framed like the first astronaut (in old suit, and canvas, and sporting a hoe) against the moon surface.

This was a "B" road here, and zippers were therefore zipping noisily and in numbers, breaking into such rhythms of conversation as the two animals established. But the Hare did cut through a roar, with an effort, to reply "... In the *fields*? What, round *'ere*?"

The Mole's gaze transferred to the rollaway-runaway surface of the ploughland beyond. A mile or so distant, a monster-with-spraybar was snailing its impersonal way, towing its curtain of chemicals. There was, of course, an animal inside it—as anonymous behind his opaque glass screen as a surgeon behind his mask—one animal, to how-ever many square miles of land?

"No—S'pose not," said the Mole. "Bit of a stupid ques-tion."

"You're not *furrum* these parts, I 'magine," said the Hare, leaning heavier on his hoe. "Where you come frum?"

"O ... Oxfordshire-Berkshire? Berkshire-Oxfordshire? That sort of direction. Upstream of Toad H ... Toad Tow-ers? If you've heard of it?"

"Oh yas, oh yas! Toad Towers. I 'eard o' that all right.— Bit pricey there, though, entit? So I 'yur. *I* wouldn't go there," said the Hare decisively. "No, I would *not*."

The Mole thought he might steer the conversation towards a subject that had been troubling him. "Um—not too many birds about at the moment, it looks like?"

The old Hare dropped his gaze to the ground and shook his head. "Can't live 'ere," he said flatly. "Jus' can't live 'ere any more. Used to be blackbirds and song thrushes all over round 'ere, *and* yellow'ammers, buntings. Couldn't 'ear yerself think for 'em sometimes. We 'ad corncrakes, all acrost them leas" (he nodded, as if to land he could see, beyond the Clearway) "when I wuz a lad. *Bwerrp-bwerrp*, 'e used ter go. *Bwerrp-bwerrp*. Keep you awake, 'e wud. Oh, we 'ad 'im all over, when we 'ad medders, noisy ol' devil! All gone now."

The Mole nodded, sighing.

"—You ain't seen no larks, comin' over 'ere?" asked the old fellow, brightening just very slightly.

"One or two. Back in the hills, on the top. But they ought to be—O!—*everywhere*. Oughtn't they?"

"They shud. They shud. Don't see 'em round 'ere. Don't 'ear 'em. Not like you used to. You'd 'a seen six, eight maybe, far out as the sprayer, hoverin' over this back by now." (He swept an arm to the void.) "Not so long ago, either. All gone now." He cast an eye briefly, rheumily, and

rejectingly, towards the empty sky above. Then he straight-
ened up. "—Wal, s'pose I better be getting' on."

The Mole had many, many other questions already
alight now, that this seasoned animal might have been able
to answer. But he had already turned back to his work, and
so the time-traveller had little choice than to travel on.

"Pleasure meetin' you," he said.

"Oh, an' I shud say the same," replied the Hare. "Always
good ter talk a bit! You 'ave a nice 'ollyday, now. An' keep
the wind be'ind yer!"

***

The Mole crossed a bend-crimped little centipede of a river
(it appeared from the map to lend Cambridge a part of its
name) at a point a few miles north of Saffron Walden. Its
valley was the first of any size he had encountered in the
region, which is not to say much: the Mole had not quite
noticed he was in it until he reached a bridge over water, the
distinction between "valley-bottom" and "valley-sides"
being, apparently, a fine one in those parts. He entered a village whose bending street of attractive old flint, brick and
timber houses had been invaded—infested—by a number
of slablike grey structures which made even the briquette-
forts of Hertfordshire seem charming by comparison.
These looked to the Mole like nothing so much as fifty-
foot-long double sandwiches made of petrified grey bread,
with fillings of glass, and could only be standing there, he
decided, as part of some *Put Up The Ugliest New House In An
English Village* competition. The place's only thatched cottage,
too, had been struck down by the blight, trailing at its rear
a clutch of hideous box-shapes that seemed to have sprung
out of one another, the smaller out of the larger, like a set
of tumours in living timber. No watercolourist of the Mole
School would ever again be setting up his easel here.

An embossed metal sign to a tree-shaded side-road bore the words *Mill Lane*, and the sight of it sent the searcher swerving where it pointed. After fifty yards or so he found a footpath, running off to the mill itself athwart an elder corner. But here—once he had rounded this—he found himself back in contradiction-land. A solid old clap-boarded mill building faced him—just such a one as might have sat on the River itself, and done its work at no more than the cost of an occasional repair so long as water flowed there. It was marvellously well maintained, too: the roof tiles all looked new, the paintwork was impeccable, the big sash windows positively shone.

In a split upper door, looking out, stood a figure in beige overalls, sporting a flat check cap. He was a character, it seemed, his long rat-face just a little hard, guarded, with a hint of penny-pinching about it. It was the miller, of course, and that was fine, except that here the miller was nothing but a dummy. At a distance the Mole had been completely fooled. But as he moved closer, waiting for the animal to spot him or move on back inside, he saw his mistake and laughed, and groaned.

There was a great quiet settled on this place—the quiet of absolute redundancy. A small round plaque set into the bricks by the unturning water wheel read:

EUROPA ASPICA
Preservation Award
1988

And the little river flowed, its flow that old, familiar thing, the waters dropping into the mill pool through a culvert as all waters did and should. Two very early swallows circled over a calm surface reflecting reeds between duckweed patches. From beyond the mill came the single clap of a fish's tail; a wood-pigeon landed to drink; and beneath the Mole's arm the rounded coping-bricks of the wall he leaned on felt warm, lulling him, making him think of sleep.

"I must go on," he thought. "O! I must go on."

He returned heavy-footed to his bike, and was just about to turn to regain his eastering trajectory when he felt again some whisker-tickling, light-as-air touch of curiosity. He peered along the lane running northwards in parallel to the river, then paused, and peered again. "It is a *valley*, after all," he thought, "—a kind of valley, anyway! Are you going to leave it straight away, Mole, without even pedalling a *little* bit downstream?"

So the Mole did pedal a short distance downstream, and across and away from the water, and within four minutes and forty three seconds of so doing he was hearing a throbbing and a soughing from beyond a strip of elders on his left. Then he saw a high wire gate, topped enticingly in the modern way with three strands of heavy-duty barbed wire. On it a sign said:

Another such gate to the elders and buddleia bore another sign. This suggested:

EXTREME DANGER

OF UNPLEASANT DEATH

!!! KEEP OUT !!!

Deep Sludge Pits

It was then that he recognised a new, zingy-strange smell in the air, and in moments his nostrils felt tightened, his lungs taut. He saw a long pillow of cream-white smoke, then the black top and shiny lower parts of a pair of chrome-silver chimneys, embossed in a kind of lattice work. The buildings they were attached to lurked beyond a high wire fence that wrapped itself into a quarter-mile-long row of mourning conifers. Through gaps in these the Mole glimpsed stacks of huge drums, bilious flashes of bronze-mirror windows that reflected the light as do puddles with spilt petrol in them, and a sign that read (he thought) *RESEARCH BLOCK A.* Then, finally, there was a recessed entrance-proper, complete with multi-staffed gatehouse (*No smoking, No parking*) and another sign at the road that told him little he could not perhaps have guessed:

AGROCHEM LTD

An ImpAgrocon Associate Company

AGRIMASH
INSECTOSLAUGHTS

Research, Development, Manufacture
APPLICATION

This sign and what lay behind it stood not three quarters
of a mile to the north of the somnolent old watermill with
its static race and wheel, marking the way in to a place of
work that was, whatever else, alive. At it, the Mole did a
neat, sweeping U-turn and found his way swiftly back to
his next road east. For two hours afterwards, strange tastes
were to cling to his tongue and throat. This was not the valley.

⬤▰▰▰⬤

Whether by some inner magnetisation or just because it
was the best way to keep the wind behind him, the Mole
meandered on for the rest of that day in a north-easterly
direction across the low undulations of the Essex-Cam-
bridge chalk lands. Most of the back roads he used here
proved uncomfortably straight, or broad, or both; and as
ever the land was very, very open, with such woodlands as
existed low and dark and always to be seen at great distances over ploughland, remote and inaccessible as offshore
islands. Once again, too, the Mole found himself pedalling
alongside what looked like fields of broken stone. He
could hardly have chosen a less fitting country in which to
search out the qualities he most cherished: intimacy, enclosure, rich alluvial soils, water-flows more generous than
those that make their homes in ditches.

Yet for all that—perhaps, in one sense, because of it—
the troubled wanderer would stare intently across each new,
saucer-shallow depression as if *there* or *there* along the valley—beyond the next five or six hundred acre expanse of
barley, or the one beyond that—the place he was searching
for might be keeping a low profile.

The contrast between what the Mole saw and what he
felt he ought to see was like a shard of glass lodged in his
heart. For the truth was that, in all simplicity, the Mole's

Valley had been England to him. Just as it must be for all those who do not travel far, his idea of a wider England had been assembled out of the neighbourly constellation of known things he saw about him daily: the River and the framing hills beyond, the networks of valley fields and orchards, the old brick and timber-frame farms and cottages with their boundary walls of "imported" flints, the village downstream (to the Mole it was *the* village), the compact, rarely-visited little market town in the other direction; and, of course, the gravel-surfaced lanes, the green ways, the footpaths, the ponds, the ever-changing bits of rough, the Wild Wood. He had no more questioned the continuance of these things than he had questioned the worth of his friendships: they had been timeless. How long would the gloss-winged rook be seen to rise to the distant elms? How long would the honeysuckle-draped hedges enfold his walks? How long would the river-leas dance to a haze in spring with the speckled, plummy caps of the fritillaries? Forever. *Forever.*

And if the Mole's Valley had been England to him, so the England beyond it, as he pictured it, had been nothing so much as a joyous, endless garden: a place of just the same richness and intricacy, in which crops were sown and livestock reared across the years and centuries alongside and amongst Pan's flower-carpets and old wild ground, his stream-courses, reed-beds and pools, in harmony. But in these emptinesses he found around him now—where Pan's domain had been boned and gutted and driven back and back into tiny, vulnerably dried-out pockets, and the rest drenched, as he strongly suspected, in "Agrismash Insectoslaughts"—*harmony* was less an ideal than a conceit.

Yet even though this present landscape bore not the faintest resemblance either to his memories or his hopes, the Mole still could not let go of the idea that once it had. Somewhere deep inside him, too, he continued to nurse the belief that if he pedalled on for long enough he might eventually find his way into a region of the country where things were still done in the old, familiar, comfortable fashion. Empty as all the land ahead of him might be, the Mole still scanned the distances for any sight of fellow-animals, out at work in incomparably smaller fields than these with their horse-drawn waggons (O, *where* were the horses?) using hand tools and the efforts of their own backs. Still, too, he would listen out with abject hopefulness for the sounds of animals singing as they worked or walked home; as once they had done. Yet who would ever sing here now in these silent expanses, from which it seemed history itself had been erased?

The Mole looked and looked as he travelled for the old wood gate with its use-shined catch and chain that would admit him once more to such a world, but instead he saw only bare grass banks and shaved-open ditches of geometric straightness, in which lay huge empty turquoise bags bearing names like *Lasso* and *Thrash* and *Scorch*. And any number of chucked *Gnome* oilcans. The only wooden gate he saw in that day's travelling lay on its back in the coarse grass, rotted down to no more than a crumbling outline of its upright shape.

During the middle of the day, as he was crossing this country, the Mole had stopped in a village south of the county border to purchase provisions. This village was interesting in several ways, not least since it still possessed a Post Office and Stores, in which the Mole bought a tin of tuna shavings, a packet of something called *Gerbils' Original Crunchy*, some floppy yellow celery and a pulpy juice-bag of a tomato, the only one in the shop. After long and weighty consideration he also invested in another map—a shiny

modern publication in the *PathRoamer* series, produced to
the extraordinary scale of 1:25,000, and giving a picture of
the country round about in what seemed to the Mole a
quite fantastic amount of detail. He just could not resist it,
for all that it was the price of an oakwood chest-of-draw-
ers decorated with smart ceramic knobs.

The Mole had looked hard for shops in each of the settlements he had come through so far. Surely, he thought,
the *shops* will have survived, especially as there seem to be at
least ten thousand more animals on the roads now, at least
in some parts. What did he find? He found buildings—all
of them just houses now, and prominently pocked with
burglar alarms—sporting names such as *The Old Butcher's
Shop*, *Old Bakery*, *Old Laundry*, and, commonest of all, *The Former Post Office or Stores*. *Old Smithies* were also common, and he
saw one low cottage named as *Wheelwrights*, another as *Brew-
ery Cottage*, another as *Farriers*, as well as any number of
Quondam Schools.—But where do animals *go* now, he wondered, to get the things they need? What happens if they
need a tailor urgently (he checked himself—most of them
obviously wouldn't), or a blacksmith, or a shoe- or paper-
maker, never mind the fact that they had to buy their food
from *somewhere*?

In this particular village, one rival store had closed
within living memory. Above its protruding square Victorian shop-space and big glazed window a supported board
still read *BREADRET AND WHOLEMOLL: PROVIDERS*. A
smaller sign next to this, its heavily flaked paint now barely
legible, gave up: *Essex Cured Bacon, Ham and Chaps*. In the
window, in front of sun-rotted lace curtains, a handwritten,
yellowing piece of paper announced: "Clearance Sale Auc-
tion, June 21st", whilst next to it another, perhaps more
recent, warned "This shop is now PERMANENTLY
CLOSED. No further enquiries please". There was wall-
barley growing bright and brisk across the step of the pad-

locked entrance doors. These showed up both olive-green and peacock-green beneath the last two coats of cream, whilst the plaster had fallen in broad patches from the cottage beyond. It was—had been—exactly the kind of shop the Mole would most happily have frequented.

And the village as a whole was—what? ... No, but—*what*? As so often, the Mole struggled for any kind of words. Alive, but only in a dead kind of way? The old street here, with its oversailing decorated-plaster houses bending away along the stream did feel *nearly* familiar to him, as did the later brick cottages and the sight of a pair of low thatched roofs visible on a bend in the distance.—Alive, but *what*?

For one long, painful moment standing there he remembered the lovely feeling he had sometimes had as he stood on the kerb-free gravels in the middle of The Village, with its slow-moving carts smelling sweetly of hay as they went by, or a herd of cows turning into one of the many farm entrances. He remembered the jingle of harnesses, the sheen on a carthorse's flank, the polished gloss of brass and leather. ... O, but what *was* that feeling? It had been beyond all that, yet a part of it too. There had been mosses on the roofs, and yellow lichens patterning the old brick walls, and a long perspective of rounded green hedges dreaming away to the fields beyond. It was—wasn't it?—a feeling of *joined-upness*—of the place being linked inseparably, as if by the very air itself, with the land it stood in. *This* was localness, what made a place a place: its self-reliance, or something very like it, with its life solidly, confidently based in the land that framed it. And wasn't this just the very feeling he had had himself sometimes, sitting by his fireplace in his own small home, writ—if not large, then at least not so very much bigger?

The Mole stood staring down this village street now like a seer in the grip of a vision, and clutching his paper-bagged tomato hard enough to explode it, striving and striving to connect what he remembered—what he knew—with what he felt all around him here. A wood pigeon in a sycamore above him made its idiot-rhythmic "*Woo ... hooo ... poop! Wooo ... hwooo ... pwoop!*" A child shouted, once, from a hidden garden. Two houses down, a well-dressed elderly otter stepped out to get the milk in, glanced at the Mole, did not speak, and went back inside. One motor breathed past, slowly for once: the entire village street on the far side was parked-up with the things for as far as he could see in either direction. Then another too-early swallow swerved and banked over the ditch-stream's grassy "V", in a place that would once have attracted children.

The Mole walked on a little, admiring bits of ancient carving on the lowest parts of some of the houses' projecting upper storeys. Through the low window of one of these, he caught sight of a furred hand, jabbing away urgently at a little grey keyboard.

One thing was certain, he thought: the place was connected now to what Justin Rette had called the "There-and-here". (Or was it "Here-and-there"?) But to the fields round about? (*What* fields?)—To *itself*? It was "in" the countryside still, this place. But there was no hint nor breath of the rural left about it.

"... O! ..." thought the Mole, finally letting go of the thought that so troubled him. "Whatever that feeling was, I just don't feel it here. It isn't—it just isn't here." Slowly, he got on to his bike and pedalled, and freewheel-trickled, and pedalled on.

That night he camped, compromisingly, in a long, thin tree-belt in country seven miles or so to the south of a place called Newmarket. During supper, he pored over his brand-new map in deepening fascination at all the things it showed him (he spent a long time studying the details of the key). It was very strange how so many of the place-names he found on it suggested oldness, past-ness. How could *Lambfair Green* or *Hobbles Green* or *Cock And End* or *Meeting Street* or *Chimney End* or *Duck Street* be anything but old? And seeing such names on the map helped to decide him on the next, painstakingly intricate stages of his expedition.

⚜

It was around eleven thirty the next morning when the Mole confirmed finally, and with no more room for doubt, what had been done to this country he was traversing. After he had crossed the Suffolk border, he stopped at a crossroads of the nakedest variety to check the direction of his route. Various objects stood stark against the void here: a *Give Way* sign, a direction signpost, a phone-box erect and isolate as a rocket prepared for launching, a printed sign on a wooden post that read simply and with manifest untruth, *You are being WATCHED!* All around him were the great parallelized swellings of the alien corn, with a single oak lost in it at a distance, and just a suggestion of a wood-presence beyond the next rise east.

Yet on the map..! On the map, the land was divided up by black lines, which the key unambiguously interpreted for the prentice detective as "field boundaries". And what was a "field boundary" if not a hedge or wall? These thin drawn lines enclosed small, odd-shaped spaces and large, long, thin ones: they had inlets, crooked zigzag bends, little twists and quiddities. The Mole needed only to look at them for an instant to begin projecting himself imaginatively into the spaces they represented—almost exactly the kinds he knew and loved best, such as had been enclosed painstakingly, century upon century, from the Wild Wood that had once been everywhere. And what was here now in their place? A void. *The* void.

He looked back to the map again to double-check.

Could he possibly be at the wrong crossroads? He read the sign once, then again, but every name confirmed it. He was exactly where he thought he was; and it was not as it had been. This map, then, he thought—shiny and modern as ever it may be—this map too was out of date.

He rode on another half mile in the pursuance of his enquiry, towards the vague wood-presence. The map showed this spot as a landscape of real promise: a complex of woodlands, clearly marked as deciduous (he had worked that symbol out as well). *Waterleas Wood, Black Wood, Long Wood* were all named, in an area of about a mile and a half north-to-south by a mile wide, with four small fields clustered between them. And when the Mole reached the place, what did he find there? What did he not find there! There are only so many ways of saying "absence". Black Wood was completely gone; Waterleas and Long Woods had both been reduced to little more than tree-belts, rind-parings of their former selves. The entire centre of the woodlands had been scooped out and with it had gone the birds, the animals, the shrubs, the flowers, the mosses, the lichens that had lived and reproduced themselves on this spot since woodland's first days.

For just one blazing moment the Mole was able to picture the process of destruction as it might have taken place here, and he knew that if he had been present then he would have become, for his size, an animal to be reckoned with. No, he would have given no quarter to those who controlled the uprootings and drainings and bonfires. What they had destroyed here and across all the territory-of-nothingness beyond was the very stuff of his heart, his inner being. This was destruction that touched him personally.

As the days passed, the Mole moved slowly on across the centre of the broad county of Suffolk, following the bends and turns of lanes whose shapes could only have been formed in prehistory. And he did not give up hope—how could he? Now and then, too, as he approached some reach of valley meadows still willowy and sallowy, where undrained or undrainable wet ground had escaped the plough, his heart would—if not quite leap—then at least do a tentative skip-and-a-jump as once again he seemed to see something resembling, however faintly, the place he hoped to find.

One such damp spot he had approached when the sun's strong late afternoon light was picking out the detail of every blade of grass, every shining bluebottle perched on a bright new hazel leaf, every shadow of a twig against a stem. The bridleway he was following had led him down in the direction of water, and hedges, no less, were drawing in around him. Instinctively he gazed ahead, though any palpitating sense of arrival was firmly held in check; he could risk no more disappointment—not now, not at any time.

Sensible Mole; for within another two hundred yards the hedges had disappeared, the willows were passed, and he was looking at just one more long naked vista down a valley greenly cultivated to the very edge of the stream. In this space, about half a mile away, stood another black isle of mourning-conifers, beyond which something—some old place that had once stood friendly and open to its meads—lay hidden.

As he drew closer to this, the Mole saw the first, not entirely unexpected, signs: *Private: Keep Out; Danger: Keep Out; Beware: Guard Dogs—DO NOT Enter.* From beyond barb-tipped fencing around the tree-wall he heard the hoarse, thundering barks of two unseen creatures he very much hoped stayed hidden. And when he turned to cross what here, he knew, could only be a mill-front bridge, he found barbed wire in rolls, blocking his way completely, with more of the same defending the bridge on its far side.

The Mole had hardly begun to consult his map before there came a manic woodpecker-rapping at one of the small panes of the handsome brick-built mill he could now see straddling the river. Beyond these panes he could just make out the form of a female hedgehog, gesticulating with abrupt short movements of her hands and arms that even the world's most determined optimist could only have taken to mean, "Would you very much mind becoming absent?" The Mole did his level best to smile back—an effort little less than heroic through rolled barbed wire and the hollow snarls of salivating hellhounds—and pointed to his map with a gesture of confusion.

A few seconds later he heard the slam of a door. A few seconds after that, he found himself staring through the wire into the face of a small animal barely able to suppress some powerful and incomprehensible fury. (The Mole noted that the soft furs framing her teeth-rich mouth were flecked with foam.)

"Can't you READ?" she snapped. "This is private property! Now turn around, and go right back the way you have come!"

"... But ..." The Mole stumbled slightly under this attack, which he seemed to have brought on merely by the fact of his presence. "... The map says ..."

"I don't care two hoots what the map says!" returned the Hedgehogess, who was impeccably dressed in dun tartan co-ordinates of timeless tastefulness. "There is a bridleway to *there*," (she indicated the approach to the mill bridge, on which the Mole was standing), "and there may or may not be another bridleway to *there*," (she turned and waved vaguely in the direction of the far side of the bridge) ... We're in dispute with the Council over that ... but *this*," (she indicated the paradigm of privacy lying between the two sets of barbed wire strandings) "is PRIVATE! Now go your way, sonny, before I let the dogs out—"

The Mole drew himself up to his full height. "Madam," he said, "I am not accustomed to being addressed as 'sonny'. And what you are saying does seem to me—if you don't mind me saying so—like stuff and nonsense. A bridleway is a bridleway. It *goes* somewhere." The mourning-conifers were positively shaking now with Cerberian yells and snarls.

"These bridleways are BOTH *culs-de-sacs*," responded the champion of seclusion, "and that is that! Now push off!" The Mole could not fail to see that this was a face that had completely lost its amiable, ground-snuffling hedgehogularity. Here again was that same disturbing, minatory quality: the bright, hard eye of the acquisitive predator that would grip what it held in its jaws and never let go.

But the Mole was determined, too, when he believed himself on the side of right. "Why should you want to stop animals going over this bridge?" he asked sadly. "They must always do it—um—have done it in the, um, the past?"

The glitter in the Hedgehog's eyes was positively crazed now, perfectly complementing the lights that were dancing off her jewellery. She drew just a little closer to the Mole across her trench-front barbed wire. "That's just *rubbish!*" she hissed. "No one has *ever* come acro ... No one has *ever* come ac ..." Here she hesitated, for not more than two seconds, a gauze of puzzlement crossing her sharp, long-snouted little features. "No one—Nu ... Damn it! ... You don't think we paid *three and a half million* for this place just to share it with travellers like you, do you? Ho, no! I'm very sorry! We have our *security* to consider. How do I know you're not a burglar? We have paid for Seclusion, and believe me, animal: we've got it and we're going to keep it! I couldn't care two hoots what happened here in the past!

Two hoots! I own this place now, and what I do here is my own business! And ragamuffin … *cyclists,*" (she mouthed this word with particular disgust) "*and* walkers, I do not intend to allow anywhere near here. Now, get your bicycle *away* from my property—" Here she grabbed the Mole's handlebars, difficult as this was over a roll of wire, as if to push the bike away.

"Madam," said the Mole warningly. "Kindly unpaw my pawhlebars."

The Hedgehog's eyes blazed back at him with a crippling hatred, which seemed to pass directly through him to greet an entire tribe that he—quite unperceived for what he was—was taken to represent. "*Just get out of here, will you?!*"

The Mole could perhaps have fought his way on, wire and dogs and all: his tool-kit did boast a pair of good strong pliers. He could perhaps have gone and found a policemal (though—where, exactly?) and applied the force of law to the problem. Instead he did neither, saying simply, "I am very sorry for you."

"*Sorry* for me?!—How dare you! How *dare* you …" For the briefest of moments, the harpie-Hedgehog's expression softened sufficiently to allow something resembling doubt to creep upon it. It was as if she had just then recognised before her—if not a ghost, exactly, then at least some part-affiliated representative of the Ghosts' Trade Union. "… Who are you, anyway?—What kind of clothes are *those* for pedalling around in?"

"I am very sorry for you," repeated the Mole in an unsteady voice. Again the Hedgehog stared through him, shivering now both with rage and with another, less easily defined, emotion. And her visitor wheeled his bike away to the ongoing accompaniment of the hellhounds' raspings. He was far too upset to ride.

The Mole may have been searching for a place he could call both "home" and "England", but in some part of his mind, deep beneath the surface channels of conscious thought, he was involved in another quest as well; and he did know what drove him on. But he would no more have dared admit it to himself in so many words than he would have acknowledged just how far out on a limb he now found himself. For any country the Mole could call both "home" and "England" must also be Pan's country—nothing less: some region, or county, or part of a county where the god of Nature's influence still flowed unabated.

Here, though, across each new expanse the Mole traversed, Pan's presence was open to question at best, and at worst ... Back in the long-lost time-before-now, the Mole had had no more need to be reassured Pan was there than he had to agonize that the River might stop flowing. More than that, it would have seemed odd to discuss the subject at all except, perhaps, in moments of unusually heightened springtime-rhapsody; and then, in any case, he had left that kind of thing up to Ratty.—No, no. Pan had been simply *there*. Not in person, of course: not as he had been on that one occasion. But he had been there even so, as a force informing all the Mole saw about him, in the living interconnectedness of growing things—everything from the leaves on the opening lime trees along the Toad Hall drive to the fine little root hairs on his own transplanting-carrots.

So he pedalled on through the days that followed, in search of more than he would say. He took encouragement where he could: in the wind-gusted foamings and churnings of the cow-parsley that now lined the roadsides, waving him eastwards on his journey; in the clotted droopings of some too-early May tree, shining bold and isolated in a scrub of green; or—during rare periods of bad weather, as some blue-purple bank of rumbling anvil-heads was rolling on ahead—in the multitude of tiny oscillating prisms that clung to leaves and blades of grass, throwing back to him the light of the freshly-uncovered sun.

His nose for the worthwhile campsite in this country also improved by the day, and he got better and better at lifting his bicycle over fences, or squeezing it through holes in tree-screens meant to bar his way to the middles of bits of woodland. When such spots were not available, he might find himself a low-profile recess, snugged into a bank on a bend in a small stream or—just as likely—waterless ditch. Here he would put up his tent amongst a miniature forest of butterbur, still round in the leaf, or sit overhung and hidden by a clump of knobbled hollies. And whenever he lay on the ground again each night, he would make renewed contact with the firmness and bigness of the earth, and take strength from it.

On and on he was drawn by the uninterpretable distant foldings of the land—a land he saw along, when on its higher ground, but never down from, as he would have done in hilly country. Again and again, compressed by distance, some surviving, not entirely voided area with woods or hedgerows would suggest change ahead, tugging the Mole towards it as if by a rope attached to the centre of his chest, only to open out, and disappoint, and not be as he had expected. And there were some moments—just a very few, and always towards evening—when the Mole did think he might have heard ...

No, but he would not so much as think, let alone say, the words. But did he—*did* he—in that low gilding light, out of some dark block of distant woodland all but lost behind a neck-high sea of acid-yellow flower-stuff—*might* he have heard something, O, so very faintly, that resembled ...? No. It was too much.

Alas, poor Mole! Sturdily as he resisted this thought too, there did come times when he grew lonely. Why, he was on an adventure—an adventure no animal he knew had more than dreamed of. Yet who would he ever tell about it? Who would he turn to, even to complain about his decorating, if ever again he possessed a wall that he could paint? It was at such moments that the duvet of despair would sink down most softly, most insidiously, over him. For after all, he thought, *wasn't* he like a ghost searching only for other ghosts? He sought a spot to dig his hole but found only its very opposite, and slid endlessly on across the slippery surfaces of this world, following his ever-lengthening shadow along lanes that ribboned away from him as if they were making themselves up as he went on.

One evening, when he had yet to find a camp, he spotted three small white clouds ahead against a sky of delphinium blue, moving above a close horizon. They resembled pieces of a jigsaw puzzle, scattered away from the rest. "You are like them, Mole," he thought. "And you will blow on with them like this, won't you?—Just like this, forever." He kept his eye on the three white shapes as he climbed the slope, and for a few disorientating moments the crops and roadside banks seemed to be rolling back towards his motionless form while the earth turned itself independently beneath his tyres. For nearly a minute he pedalled harder—as if by so doing he might catch up with these clouds and join them as a rearward—and the creamy-white foam of the fisherman's lace tossed into a boiling on either side of him while the great irridescent, dry-haired pelts of barley fields collected the wind in snaking patterns beyond.

But then—tut-tutting to himself at the unmolelike, the very unmolelike, madness of it—he relaxed, and free-wheeled, and allowed the strong wind to give him little pushes onward. That night, he stopped in another low streamside brake next to a long but very narrow meadow; and in the morning, as ever, he broke camp and moved on, almost as if he felt it wrong to rest.

CHAPTER THIRTEEN

PRINCES OF THE FIELDS

The Mole turned more and more frequently to his voice-box as the days went by. His thirst for insight did not leave him—quite the opposite—and each time he switched on, he experienced the same nebulous pulse of hope that this bizarre little object might reveal to him something fundamental—give him some yardstick by which he could measure what he saw, and understand.

It is difficult to say whether it did so or not. One day, for example—he often switched on now at lunchtimes, and *Gerbils'*-nibbling inbetweentimes, too—he might hear the latest report on the attempts of that caring company, Mollusk, to dump its most recently redundant oil-rig full of thick, black, clinging killer-sludge into some conveniently forgettable stretch of deep ocean. Then he would hear the spokesmal—the Mole noticed that these animals always spoke with an affable, salt-of-the-earth, neighbourly reasonableness—defending the company's actions as if they made the most perfect sense and were in the best possible interests of the sea-bed concerned.

Later in the same day he might hear the familiar foot-dragging drone of the Prime Minister himself, defending

Mollusk's proposed action as *perfectly legitimate and well within the Government Guidlines*. Gradually the Mole came to realise that Mr Nuttmutch was prepared to drone on ABC Radio Paw with quite astonishing frequency, and his job always seemed to be the same in principle: to defend what to the Mole, in his simplicity, seemed indefensible, as though it was nothing more nor less than the right thing.

The Mole's peregrinations continued to take him eastwards toward the coast, but not quickly. Any cyclist of the whippet-esque, Flykrasofted variety could have covered Suffolk west to east in a single day's ride along main roads, head down and stag-style, getting passing impressions of filling-stations and trunk-route furnishings as he did so. The Mole, in the most striking contrast, ruminated over every place and junction he came to, nor did the tyres of his bicycle ever touch main road tar except to get straight across it to the far side. In diagram form—if anyone had attempted to chart it—his trajectory would have borne far less resemblance to a Navoleonic route-march than to a series of caterpillar-on-cabbage-leaf meanderings taking in wide, looping deviations north and south. Once or twice as he went on, he even succeeded in recrossing the line of a previous day's journey at a right angle: such moments were always a trifle strange.

Subtly, and sometimes less so, the entire late-spring landscape smelled to him of things non-natural. More than once he passed animals out walking their dogs in the lanes, and was amazed how casually they were behaving. Was it possible, he wondered, that they didn't *notice* the things in the air all around them? And might it be that they were all now slightly ill, without so much as knowing it? The Mole himself had developed an annoying, wheezy little cough (he had never had a cough!), one that simply would not go away.

Even along the lane-sides themselves, not everything was

well. The Mole would find stretches where the heads of the ever-present cow-parsley hung bunched and bulbous, as if in a permanently aborted effort to form, fixed to distended stems above tanglings of foliage that looked as if they had been burned to brown or black. For the rest, though road-side plants grew well, he saw the same few unappealing species ruling the roost—docks, thistles, stinging nettles, hogweed—all of them neck-and-neck in a race to overblown rankness. As in the fields, it seemed, so along the verges too. The old balance had gone, and these few plants were thriving here almost as if someone was nurturing them at the expense of others. Only the strongest com-peters—burdock, oxeyes, white campion, mallow—seemed to make much headway against them, and even these were far from common.

One morning, the Mole was progressing across a flattish upland of heavy clays in the north east of the county, utter-ing the occasional muted "Moo!" or "Baaa!" (He did so miss the sight and sound of livestock.) The lane he was fol-lowing was lined on the left by a surviving quarter mile of blackthorn hedge whose thickest branches had somehow been ripped or slashed into a long line of frayed, heart-wood-yellow stumps and points. Beyond it a machine was working, and it took the Mole no more than a few seconds to realise it must be spraying only a few yards from him. But because of the thorn barrier, the operator could not see him; and because the Mole was a cyclist he could not roll up his window, shut off his air intake, and put his foot to the floor to escape. So the smell drifted at him through the savaged branches like some stultifying perfume from a fop-giant's ruffled kerchief, and in seconds it had filmed the insides of his mouth and throat.

The Mole passed directly downwind of this sprayer, doubling his pedal-speed to try to put himself ahead of it. He might have succeeded, too, had not the machine itself

suddenly accelerated from a point of rest behind him—
not, as it proved, to continue spraying but to leave the field
altogether. Twenty seconds later it was there on the road in
front of him, the driver seated high in his steel palanquin
behind a sloping dark window, and adjusting to the fact of
the Mole's own presence. The thing was finished all in gar-
ish gut-jolt orange, and with its wing-like bars now folded
up at the rear it resembled a great misshapen, squared off,
gut-jolt-orange fly. The engine whined and roared as the
driver—incapable of waiting the few seconds it would have
taken for the Mole to pedal on by—accelerated towards
him, the great insect lurching and springing on its vast fat
tyres, first along the tar and then, at that very last moment
of Weaselworld convention, along the beaten-down verge
to his right.

The Mole was able to clear the intense taste from his
palate only by eating an orange, and even then he was not
completely successful: something still lingered, metallically.
He longed for a stream of clear spring water to scrub out
his mouth, and wash down his fur, but did not expect to
find one. When he stopped for lunch, some two hours later,
he found himself looking with freshly sceptical eyes at the
drawing on the packet of his Gilded Harvest Homegrown
Wholesome 100% Wholemeal Loaf. As if in the style of
an old line drawing, this showed a scene from his own
memory—his experience: a row of animals, bent forward
and scything wheat, with stocks and a loaded cart beyond,
and tree-shadows falling across the stubble. Fray-stumped,
isolated hedges and great misshapen, orange sprayer-insects
were, oddly, nowhere to be found in the picture.

By the fifteenth (or was it the sixteenth?—no, *seventeenth*)
day of his journey, the Mole had at last found his way into

the beginnings of a marginally different kind of country. Here, the stream-indentations of the claylands behind him had broadened out into something much more like valleys as he understood them —valleys, that is, possessed of wide, flat bottoms, readily distinguishable from the slopes at their sides, some parts of which had survived until now as grazing marshes.

At much the same time as he made this discovery, the Mole also noticed a change in the soil. There was sand in it here, and as he continued eastwards it grew sandier and sandier, to the point where he began to find little scraps and corners of old heathland, some of them crossed by tracks so full of sand from edge to edge they might have served as bathing beaches. He saw isolated oaks along the lanesides, one or two of them old and round in the belly, hinting at some ancient tree-presence. But he was by no means out of the prairies yet. There were other kinds of enormous farm here, specialising in potatoes, carrots, sugar beet, wherever they could to the furthest horizon. Some framed their cultivations with regimented strips of Scots pines, but the final effect was no less of Nature in thrall or retreat. Had the Mole gone first into one of the larger areas of heath he might have been more greatly cheered than he was, but he was put off by the near-impossibility of cycling there: the bike slewed about in the powder-fine sand with each turn of the pedals.

At last, though, he was tempted enough by a track to think of using it. It fanned out at a gentle angle from an adjacent Private Road and was signed clearly as a bridleway; and its surface consisted largely of soft dry grasses. Thus enticed, the Mole turned down it, ignoring both the admonition on the Private Road sign (*Legal action may be taken against unauthorized persons found on the property*) and another, newer-looking sign that stood next to it. This read:

WEASELHAM HALL

LAND AMALGAMATIONS GROUP PLC

POTATOES GROWN EXCLUSIVELY FOR THE

retco thriftacenta chain

Five minutes later, the Mole found himself passing a group of great grey sheds that came well within the national guidelines for lumping-hideousness, beyond which a couple of Clearway-miles of smashed up road surface was ranged sculpturally in piles. Here the track broke into two parallel strands, and since the Mole had spotted what he thought might be viper's bugloss just breaking into intense blue flowers along the left-hand way, he followed that one.

It was a matter of no more than a minute before he heard the sound of an engine behind him. Turning, he saw a silver-metallic shoebox-with-snout bumping slowly along the parallel track, and when it caught up with him it slowed to his pace. A window rolled down. A furrily ferretacious face leaned across and looked out, its eyes narrowed to slits by the sun or by mistrust, or both at once. "Are you following the bridleway?" it demanded coolly.

"Um—yes," replied the Mole, stopping. His heart had already sunk to his knee-linings: was this to be *another* confrontation about bridleways that for some reason could not be followed?

"You should be up here," said the Ferret, no less remotely. "That's a private ride you're on there."

"O—" said the Mole. The distinction was quite lost on

him, but even so, as a law-abiding citizen, he did not hesitate to transfer himself over the nine or ten feet of grass that separated the one track from its neighbour. "There were more flowers on this one," he said.

"... Flowers?" echoed the Ferret, in a voice so flat he might not have recognised the word as English. This was another animal in his later years, the Mole saw, his greybrown face-fur whitened slightly about the mouth. His very pale check Tweed jacket and cap were in much the same colours, so that animal, clothing and vehicle presented themselves as a rather monotonous tableau in grey and silver.

The Ferret withdrew stiffly to his steering wheel, and had put the *motor* into reverse before the Mole realised there might be an opportunity here for him to learn something—and a good one, too. "Um—excuse me!" he shouted.

Sighing slightly, the Ferret paused. "Yes?" He regarded the Mole with the chill gaze of one who sees nothing beyond, perhaps, the breed called *Trespasser*.

"O, well, I was just wondering," said the Mole, going around the front of the *motor* to the driver's side. "—Don't want to waste your time, of course, but I was just wondering: might you be able to tell me what happened to all the—um, countryside—in these parts? I mean—you know—where it all went to?"

"'Where it went to'?" chimed the Ferret, again in a voice of dry incomprehension, his grey-circled eyes narrowing to gun-slots in the pillbox of his face. "It didn't go anywhere, my mal. It's all right here, just where it's always been."

"The soil may be," said the Mole. "Not much besides, though, is there? I mean—apart from anything else—where did all the hedges go? If you happened to know?"

"—Oh well that's just a myth, of course, all that rubbish about hedges!" retorted the Ferret, rather more forcefully.

"All these stories we hear about farmers ploughing everything up. We ploughed up the land just where we were told to, by the Government, for the War Effort, *if* you remember that, and that's all there is to it. Just show me where the hedges were before, in the East of England. There weren't any."

"I *could* show you!" said the Mole warmly. "That's easy. They're all marked there on the map—where they used to be." He gestured westwards. "—Further over, anyway."

The Ferret leaned a little closer to him through his high-up *motor* window, curiosity or its cousin qualifying his earlier unseeing gaze. "... Well, of course," he said. "That's quite right." He looked away from the Mole, turning his head with difficulty in one direction, then the other, much as if scenting the air for danger. "... What? ... No. ... What?!" he said. "Yes. That is quite right. What I said before is just the lie we settled on at the National Agribusinessmals' Union. You understand: the NAU puts it about where it can—to the media, and so forth. Has done for years, now—years!"

The Mole looked at the ground in embarrassment. It was always embarrassing, after all, to catch a fellow-animal in the midst of a lie, not least a lie to which a matter of seconds later, for whatever reasons, he had openly admitted. This was no less the case even in a world in which *the lie* was a tool possessed of many and versatile professional uses, and confessions to its use quite common. "So it is true, then," he said, sighing deeply. "It was all like England here too. Once."

The Ferret hesitated, not replying, and looking at anything but the Mole himself. Then, rallying a little, he turned back to him and said, "But this is England too, my mal! There's no need to get sentimental! This is the New, Modern, and Greatly Improved England. And an animal must always be free to do as he wishes on his own land."

He glanced at the Mole dubiously. "Im sure you'd agree?"

"… Well—" replied the Mole, haltingly, "if you're going to plough everything up—all the old hay meadows and pastures — and grub up the woods—and get rid of all the wild bits—then no, I don't. You drove out all the hedgerow animals, didn't you? And the birds. I don't understand how you can say any of that is 'improved'. I don't understand how you can use the word at all. It's the opposite of improved. The opposite!"

"Well now, my little mal," replied the Ferret weightily, "the trouble with all you animals who come out here from the towns is, you-just-don't-understand-modern-farming."

"I don't *come* from the town," said the Mole, with emphasis enough to make the Ferret turn a half-turn towards him, adjusting his view of him as so many seemed to do at a certain stage in such conversations. "And I do beg your pardon, but I don't really see why I should *have* to 'understand' it, if what it does is against—" (The Mole almost used the word "Pan" here, but kept his counsel) "—against Nature," he said gravely.

"'Nature'?" spat out the Ferret derisively. "'*Nature*'? It's 'nature' that is the problem! It's 'nature' that's got to be kept out of the picture! Eliminated from the calculation!"

"But it's all—it's all being *killed!*" said the Mole hotly, recognising that he was, right here and now, confronting the enemy—Pan's enemy—and, doubtless, one of the many. He looked about him at the void of the moment: a square mile or so of potato-land to the south, with more of the same beyond, sugar-beet in the other direction, framed by a narrow belt of pines. "This soil is full of—I don't *know* what. Strange, strange scents—scents that shouldn't be there!"

"Scents?" echoed the Ferret with derision. "—Damned funny way to put it. You mean the insectoslaughts, I suppose?"

"—Yes, yes, the 'insectoslaughts'!" said the Mole, upon whose vision the word was still vividly sign-written.

"Well, my mal, it goes without saying, they are all perfectly harmless," intoned the Ferret, much as if revealing a secret from on high. He clearly meant to lay the subject to rest there and then, but within range of the Mole's candour-inducing force field it simply would not lie still in its coffin. "... That, eh—that's what the researchers always prove, in any case ... *What* am I damned well telling him *this* for? ... The researchers the Min of Agg always use, you understand, to prove things to everyone's satisfaction—?" The *motor*-bound farmer's voice died away, and he gripped and regripped his steering wheel after the accepted fashion. "Whu ...? Wha ...?"

"—Um," said the Mole. "Could you tell me—pardon my ig'runce—but you couldn't possibly tell me what this 'Minn of Agh' *is*?"

"That's a—It's just a little joke of ours," said the Ferret in a low voice. He stared at the Mole, then, relaxing just a very little, reached forward to turn off his engine. "On the Weaselham estates. Not intended for public consumption, needless to say, nor, obviously, for the ears of animals like yourself. Whoever you may be. It's the Ministry Of Agrichemical Growing, of course, but amongst ourselves we call it the Ministry Of Aggrogrow? Ha, ha.—Aggrogrow? The Min of *Ag-g*?" The Ferret laughed again drily—so drily, in fact, that had the sound been a landscape it could not have supported life.

"And the 'Minn of Ag-gh' is the—um—the Guvvn'ment again, then—is it?"

"Well, yes, of course it is!"

"But it does this 'proving' thing for—um—"

"The industry!—Yes! Well done! The manufacturers, and the users! And 'users' means, of course, us big, big firms. The only ones that matter."

"Even if it isn't—well—true? Completely?"

The Ferret stared ahead through his windscreen and clawed at his steerer anew. His brow fur was deeply lined, as if under pressure of inner conflict. "The whole point here, my mal," he said, "and I know you won't understand this—the whole point is how these things are *seen*. All the basic proving is done by the chemical companies themselves, and they are very, very thorough in making out the case for their products. The dossiers they put together on each new thing that comes out! You'd be amazed! Why, even if you'd just died from getting too close to a canister of *Aphisplat*—oh, if you read the company's notes on it you'd go up to heaven *knowing* it wasn't that that killed you!"

Dry as dry, the Ferret laughed again: the Mole did not join him. "And if anything does set alarm bells ringing where it shouldn't, there are perfectly effective ways of dealing with it. The Insectoslaughts Inspectorate can take years—decades, in some cases—getting around to checking up on a product! And we get some use out of it in the meantime, I can tell you! Government research committees are always under the most *enormous* pressure to agree things are fine. Any 'experts' on possible ill effects are simply kept off them in the first place. —Standard, absolutely standard, practice, as long as I can remember!"

Shaking his head in shame, and sniffing warily, the Mole looked at the ground beneath him. "... But if animals get ill ..." he said.

The Ferret snorted. "Survival of the fittest, my mal! That's the name of the game today! The animals of this country will just have to learn to adapt to meet the needs of Modern Agrigrowing. Any who can't may have to go by the wayside. That's how I see it. It's only a matter of time before new breeds evolve that can survive—thrive!—on the crops we grow for 'em. What could be more natural than that, eh?"

"But if your farms have all turned into—I don't want to be rude, but—" (The Mole gestured to the land all around them) "—a kind of dead place, then that's the *opposite* of Nature …"

The silver Ferret flinched at this, though so briefly the Mole hardly saw it. "I mean you know, for example," he persisted, "do you ever hear the lark singing over this country nowadays?"

This time the Ferret's reaction was unambiguous. He tensed visibly and squinted hard toward the horizon. "You hear them sometimes on the heath," he said hoarsely. "—But let me tell you, my mal, it isn't my job to go around breeding larks! We don't get any subsidies for *larks* on our farms. The larks may go elsewhere."

"—But what if there *is* no 'elsewhere'?"

"That's just a shame, then, isn't it?" barked the Ferret, his face twisted into an unamused grin. "There's no profit in larksong, my mal!—No, no. Larksong won't pay the dividends for Weaselham Hall Land Amalgamations Group investors!"

The Mole looked down at the blue flowers by his feet dejectedly. "Profit". It was a word he had heard more than once these past few weeks. But the enquiring animal in the modern world cannot afford to be dejected long. "Why, um—why do you call yourself by that long name? No offence intended, but you are a farmer, still, aren't you?"

"A 'farmer'!" The silver Ferret laughed his remote and enervated laugh. "You should catch up! We don't have too many plain-Jane 'farmers' left round these parts now, you know!"

"What do you have, then?" demanded the Mole, who was not entirely surprised to hear this.

"We have Contract Farming Companies! As any *country* animal with half a brain would know already! We have Land Intensifier and Gilt Gilt-edging Groups, of which the

WeHLAG happens to be one of the biggest in the county. Oh yes. Yes, yes! WeHLAG controls tens of thousands of hectares across this county alone, *and* we're growing by the day now as the last of the quaintways one-mal-and-his-tractors give up and sell out to us! We are, as it happens, right now in the midst of a very major Reconglomeration, of the *most* Top Secret nature, and certainly not for the ears of traveller-holediggers on bicycles. During this very next quarter, the WeHLAG (of which I, O. Messhof Pottidge-Pherytte, am Managing Director) will be selling itself on to a vastly better financed Gilt-regilder, set up in collaboration with certain City institutions—Insurance Groups, Pension Funds—the names of which I think I may manage not to mention (though the Monarchical Life Group Of Companies is, as it happens, *the* key player.) This new giga-Company—*Farming Improvement-Systems And Amalgamations Group And Partners PLC*, as it will be known—is fair set to become one of the very largest and most Efficient businesses of its kind in the country. *Everything* on our far-flung estates will be done under remote-management: by *sub*-sub-contractors, sub-*sub*-sub-contractors, and quite possibly sub-sub-sub-*sub*-contractors. The one thing you will not find on them, of course, is farmers. In the old, fustian, quaintways sense of the word.—Animals living on the sad little bits of land they work, that kind of nonsense."

"And so, what will you be—um—'farming' on all this land?" asked the Mole, stalling slightly until he could think of a better question.

"—*Subsidies!*" spat out the Ferret, as if this fact also was far too obvious to mention. "For as long as we can make them last. Hell's *giblets*, I did not mean to say that!"

The Mole was stuck once more. "Er ... Er ... Sub-ziddeys?"

"Damn it, animal! You know what *subsidies* are! Where were you born, Talpa Miniscula?"

"Just down the road from there, most likely. It's not—um—it's not a type of mangel-wurzel, by any chance?"

Silver-shooned as any moon, the Ferret fumed on quietly inside his silver shoebox. He grasped out toward the ignition key with palpitating paw, but did not touch it. "Well, now," he growled, clawing lightly at his scalp-fur as he did so. "—You have heard of the SAP, I hope?"

"... the—um—S-A-P," repeated the Mole, very carefully. "As in—O—not as in 'trees', by any chance?—It mightn't be?"

"*Not* as in 'trees'! *Not* as in 'trees'! The SAP! The S-A-P! The Selective Agricultural Policy! Damn my *gumboots* it's no wonder the-public-doesn't-understand-modern-farming, now is it?! The *Selective Agricultural Policy,* devised in Brussels," ("... brussels? ..." thought the Mole) "and intended, originally, to help support tiny inefficient olive-farmers and the like on their crumbling Mediterranean terraces; but now, thanks to the marvellously skilful sleight-of-paw of our mals in the Ministry, used in *this* country almost entirely to support The Efficient Agri-Grower! Out of, needless to say, the public purse!—And by Efficient, of course, I mean—?" The Ferret waved at his corporate void like a hard working second-form chemistry teacher at a symbol-cluster on a blackboard.

The Mole hesitated. "... Big?" he said, with eggshell caution.

"BIG!—Big, very-*very*-big, and very-very-*very*-BIG! Big *is* Efficient. Everything you see here in front of you—everything you might ever see, on any FISAGAP farm of the future—if you ever visited one, and I very much hope you don't—is Efficient Farming Of The Very Highest Order!"

"—But if it's 'efficient'," said the Mole, who did not have to ponder long to ask this, "—well, then, why should it need any, um, you know, sub-zidees? Out of the public's purses, wasn't it, you said?"

"Because Efficient Farming," responded the Ferret through distinctly clenched teeth, and leaning towards the Mole to drive the point home, "—Efficient Farming, under present conditions, could not possibly go on without them! We couldn't *begin* to afford all the chemicals we use! And the upkeep on the machines—the new-equipment costs—the roads—the buildings—impossible. Impossible!"

The Mole was thrown just long enough by this to allow the Ferret a "Well. If you will *excuse* me—", before he could speak again. "But—but 'efficient' means a thing works well on its own, doesn't it?" he protested. "It did in my day. If a thing has to be—I don't know—*propped* up all the time, then that's the *opposite* of efficient. It's a great big—"

"Of course it is!" exploded Mr O. Messhof Pottidge-Pherytte, fuming through his windscreen at a nearby sugar beet. "Of *course* it is! As I told you, we have a system here! Look ... say, for example, some new subsidy for flax comes in, as it did not so long ago. All well and good. We find the land to grow the flax on. If we have to cut down some wood, or plough up another stretch of useless old turf to do it, then that is what we do. (Don't you worry, my little mal, we'd plough up cousin Daphne and her Argentinian boyfriend's garage-forecourt if there was a subsidy to do it.) Then—if the flax doesn't happen to be needed at the end of the day—because so many other Efficient farmers have also been growing it—fine. We store it awhile, and then we junk it."

"... You..? ... You..?"

"We junk it.—We destroy it."

"... You *destroy* it?" wailed the Mole. After all, it seemed, he was still capable of being astounded.

"In the fullness of time. Obviously. This, my little mole, is what lies at the heart of Modern Agrigrowing. The Efficient farm isn't here to grow crops. Not first and foremost, Pan bless my credit ratings, no! Nothing so banal! The *Efficient* farm is here to crop the subsidies on whichever products happen to bring in the fattest varieties in a given fiscal year. That is what Efficiency is. But beyond that, we have the very gilding of the gilt-edged lily—the noblest, the most cunningly ingenious masterstroke our mals at the Ministry have devised for us so far. By which I mean, of course, StickaBy."

"… sticker-buy …?" said the Mole, in a not unhollow voice.

"StickaBy!—StickaBy! Everyone has heard of StickaBy! It does get into the papers, no matter what is done to keep it out. StickaBy—the No-Crop Crop!"

At once the Mole thought of all the orange-coloured fields he had pedalled past, where something deadly to all plant life had been applied. "… you can't mean you are paid to …"

"Not-grow-things! Of course! That's StickaBy!—In which—just in case we have missed the point here—the land is *Stuck By*. For a year. Two years. Ten, if necessary! The longer the better, the longer the better! Oh, there are millions to be brought in, if you know what you're about, in the not-growing-things stakes! One of the key growth areas for FISAGAP PLC, no doubt about that! Our colleagues in the City will certainly expect it."

"Doesn't anyone ever ask all the other animals what they think?" asked the Mole hopelessly.

"'All the other animals'," parroted the ferret, a sneer hovering at the very corners of his lips. "You do put things quaintly, my little mole. I suppose that is only to be expected of a mal of your sort.—You mean the *public*?"

The Mole nodded.

"—No, no, *no*. No, no, no, no, *no*! Luckily the SAP is so intricate in design that an animal would need a PhD in

Quantum-Economics even to begin to understand it. It may be that there isn't anyone who does! We certainly don't, though of course we know just which ropes to pull. Mrs Hoghidge of Herne Hill won't ever get past 'Go', I'm afraid, and a lot of work goes into keeping her in her bliss of ignorance."

"—But if Mrs Hoghidge did know," returned the Mole stoutly, "I don't think she would like it. I don't, and there it is.—That is, you see, she may not want the money out of her purse being spent on—" (he nodded at the greater absence) "this. I certainly wouldn't."

By now, Mr Messhof Pottidge-Pherytte's face wore the fixedly frustrated look of the highly intelligent animal who finds himself talking to a rabbit. But he made no move to leave. "... It has taken *over fifty years*," he breathed, "to refine the modern agricultural system to this, its present state of near perfection.—Now, who—out of your great and in-depth grasp of the way of the world—who, do you imagine, might *sit* on all the many committees that advise our good friends at the Min of Agg on policy? Make a guess, make a guess!"

The Mole paused. "—More of your friends, then, I suppose," he muttered. "Is it?"

"Eighty per cent—four fifths, to you—I think it is, are now either top-top-agribusinessmals" (the Ferret cleared his throat) "such as myself, or company mals, who are by definition right-thinkers. The wider view is represented by members of respected scientific institutions—ones which often owe a certain debt of gratitude for support to?" The Ferret waved a paw irritably, as if to draw forth an answer.

"—O," said the Mole, and nodded. He was indeed beginning to get the picture. "The chemical companies, then, is it? But not—not, for example ... Toad Transoceanic?"

"Toad *Transoceanic!*" said Mr Pottidge-Pherytte with a

trace of surprise. "Mollusk! ImpAgrocon! McMinc! At the heart—the very heart of the game! Oh, you get a point for that! And so, then—just take it as it comes, now—what would you say the general thrust of those committees might be, so far as keeping our Mrs Highodge in the frame on how her sixty-pounds-a-year is getting spent?"

The Mole ruminated once again. "Whatever it is," he replied, "it didn't ought to be!—It *didn't*. That's what I think."

"Well, my little mal! Luckily for us, what you think counts for no more than—no more than—"

"... larksong," said the Mole sadly, gazing up at the empty skies. "But what you do here, what you've done—all of it, you know—it's wrong," he said firmly. "It's *wrong*."

"Damn you, you little burrowing vagabond-nobody! Don't you come out here on to one of my estates and start preaching to me!" Beside himself as he now was, the Ferret remained, waiting, like a witness in the dock who knows he must go on giving evidence.

"I don't understand why the Guvvn'ment can't give purse-money to *little* farms—ones where they use the muck to fertilise the crops, like they always did, and nothing goes to waste. And there are lots of flowers in the fields. And the birds are singing. And they don't use all these horrible—poisons."

"Well that just shows how ignorant you are, then, doesn't it? Because the hill farmers do get their nominal pittance, every year that comes around. And I suppose they're worth it, in their way. They have their annual crisis—one thing or another—and all the journalists flash off to Wales to talk to them about their heroic efforts to survive. It does help keep the spotlight off the real action."

"But there aren't any little farmers in these parts," objected the Mole. "Not that I've seen.—What about round here?"

"This is prime agricultural land!" yelled Mr Pottidge-Pherytte. "This isn't some valley-head in the Lake District where a lot of sad old blighters are still being paid to keep the stone walls standing for the tourists to climb over! This is the very heartland of Efficient Agrigrowing! There is only one rule for these parts, my mal: Big is Beautiful. And small—small is completely out of the picture. Let me tell you, my little mole: standing here, as you are, in the midst of this flawless place—you are looking straight at the future of cultivation-systems in this country. Take it from me: it's all going to look like this—every piece of land we get our ploughs onto. Oh, when the FISAGAP gets into its stride, by *Pan* we'll see changes! Half of Dorset could go over. (Most of Wilts already has, of course.) Huge tracts of lowland Staffs—yes, and Shropshire—and Northants—like this. *This*. It will all be The Same. The same crops, the same inputs, the same equipment, the same storage, the same view. And as the FISAGAP grows as it must, oh, we'll be buying them out—the ones that give up, on the land that's worth the ploughing—one by one, one by one. Any parcels of land we can't put under subsidies will go for golf courses.—We are, as it happens, already in top-secret discussions with one of the biggest of the Japanese banks (the Ho Seismo, no less), with plans to set up our own Extra-national Golf Course Subsidiary. Don't you worry—it's a real possibility. There's big money to be made in golf courses. *Big* money!"

Disgust was rising through the Mole as surely as if he had been standing over a pile of rotten eggs. So *this* was how the golf disease was spread! The thought of the things being imposed right in the heart of all he had once known as countryside might in itself have bound him to a pitch-fork revolt, had there only been one to join there.

"Yes, yes—'all the world's a golf-course!'" blithed Mr Messhof Pottidge-Pherytte, his little pink eyes bulbing slightly under pressure of greed. "And in ten years time—fifteen, at the outside—it will be four-fifths of *everything* amalgamated-down and in the hands of the few—the very few! And the FISAGAP is set pretty damn fair for being the biggest of the lot, because by then of course they will all be companies. Oh, I have dreams some nights where I see myself sitting high, high up—like I was in the cab of the biggest combine they ever had on Jupiter—I mean, so big, high as one of those tower blocks they have down in the City. And I sit there, watching its great long shadow fall away in front of me—half way across Suffolk, as it mostly is. And I know we've done it, and I'm the one in charge of everything. The Great Farmer Of The East—"

"The *Wicked* Farmer Of The East," thought the Mole, though even now manners restrained him from saying it.

"—And if there is any competition left then, well, it's pretty simple.—The Great Farmer Of The North? He doesn't count for very much, with all those mountains. Just a big sheep and deer rancher.—The Great Farmer Of The South? That will be us, too, by rights.—The Great Farmer Of The West? He'll be a golf course consortium, of course.—Us, yes, us, with luck! And there I am, riding high in my cab with the clouds blowing towards me and wrapping themselves around my dustscreen, and I look down on some last small unacquired farm (there are one or two of them around here, that get my goat) and it offends me so much I *combine* it with my vast machine, and all that's left when I've gone over is a pattern of pink brick dust in the soil! And I look down on some village or small town and I think, 'They're for it next!' Oh yes—marvellous, marvellous! Always did have good dreams, ever since I was a pup. Though in the real world, of course, by then it will all be done by robots."

("... now ...?")

"—Satellite-controlled, naturally!"

The Mole had been experiencing pulses of powerless, despairing anger as he listened to this last soliloquy. But now he was calm again. When he spoke, he did so with the conviction of an animal who may have no proof-positive for what he says, but who knows, nonetheless, that it must be true. "It will all go wrong," he said. "Nature will stop you."

The silver Ferret lost his smile at this, and no mistake, meeting the Mole's steady gaze with something that might almost have been a look of fear.

"Pan will stop you," said the Mole simply, and meant it. Pan, the god of diversity, *would find* some way to break this tyranny of sameness. He would; he must.

The Ferret stared on at him, the faintest lines of doubt inscribed across congenitally doubt-free features. "... Pan?" he repeated hoarsely. He said the word again and then once more, much louder, in a deeply scathing tone. Then he laughed until he wept.

"I must be going now," said the Mole. "Thank you for sparing the time."

"We're not going to fail," snapped Mr Pottidge-Pherytte as he reversed his vehicle, crunching viper's bugloss in the process. "You just remember that, my little mole. *We're* not going to fail!"

The Mole watched the *motor* as it bounced off, a silver-sheened box dwindling against the open sky, then turned grievingly back to his own way.

❧

Within twenty minutes of this parting, the Mole had come back again to bump-free asphalt, though it was unlikely he had yet left the purlieus of the Weaselham Hall estate. In any case, the farming style was unaltered, with a single exception upon which the Mole's gaze fell now almost greedily. A quarter of a mile ahead of him along the tar there stood another small island of the familiar-antique. To the right of the road there, a high hedge with oaks in it enclosed what must be fields. To the left and facing this were a stand of thin young elms, a clump of thorns in bloom and, sticking above these, but only just, a brick chimney with a thread of smoke in it and what might have been part of a low thatched roof.

There was another complication too, now: during the time he had been talking to the Ferret, all the sky to the south west had been blackly repainted with the folding velvet inks of a towering storm-bank. A single broken row of balsam poplars, that might once have sheltered an orchard, blazed blowing against this darkness, every bright green leaf wind-shaken. The storm looked to be coming in a north-easterly direction and, as the Mole immediately saw it, was now in dread pursuit of one small animal in particular. (Who else? The very horizons were deserted.)

The Mole knew enough by now to put his waterproofs on well in advance of any downpour, clinging to the super-stitious belief that if he did this thoroughly enough, with every zip and flap done up, and all his cycle-pannier-toggles tightly tugged, the storm might decide to go elsewhere. But that tall, tree-lined hedge ahead was three minutes' ped-alling at the outside, so he decided to take the risk and make for it unencumbered.

He had estimated the distance correctly, and was able to change near one of the oaks with the darkness-impending no closer, so it seemed, than it had been before. After that, of course, there was not much for him to do but wait, yel-low from head to knee in cape and sou'wester. Even stand-ing as close as this he could see little more than details of the old house opposite, lost as it was behind its thicket of thorns and sickly young elms. Such walling as was visible was lumped over in dun, ancient pebbledash, while the centre of the thatch seemed to be under tarpaulin. A rough grass track with two neat tyre-ruts in it curved away beneath a May tree heavy under pink-scarlet blossoms. Beyond this, the Mole could see the end of some kind of half collapsed timber structure jutting into the air, with next to it the slatted elevator of a crumbling bale-lifter that had been modern, not to say new-fangled, in his own day.

In the long grasses at the roadside opposite him lay a stone horse-trough, cracked and flaked by decades of frost, in which wiry, skeletal wallflowers had taken root. Against it, all but hidden by grass, lay a piece of timber on which the words *Little Ekings* were just discernible, daubed in pale blue paint. As to the fields behind him, the Mole could see nothing through the tall hedge except that they were under grass. But it was the cottage that kept drawing his eye. Should he—might he?—go in and knock on the door? This was *his world* here; he recognised it instantly, even in this state—this final stage—of overgrown decline.

"Pardon for knocking," he muttered, in rehearsal for something he was not yet ready to do. "But you see, I happen to be a mole from the past. I am—in fact—*the* mole from the past. The famous Mr Mole from the *completely forgotten* past.—The famous-for-being-forgotten Mr M—"

"Waitin' for the weather?" came a voice from up the road. It was a voice both light and badly-oiled on its hinges, and the accent could not have been stranger to the Mole had he tunnelled-up in Newfoundland.

He turned to see an old harvest mouse, supporting himself on a pair of crutches that resembled walking sticks made from knobbled wood. He came slowly up the road in the company of his dogs, a pair of Welsh collies who approached the wandering cyclist with silk-soft rubbings and ice-nosed demonstrations of affection.

"You're gooen ter hev a long wait! That's set for the

north, you ma' depend." The Mouse nodded in the storm's direction. "*Down*, dawg! He's a rare good dawg, that one, ... *Down*, now! ... Bit-too much on th' friendly side.— Where you be from, then?"

As the Mole was explaining, in much his usual fashion, he could not fail to take note of this old fellow's dress. In its way it was just as antiquated as the observer's, and spoke as if in as many words of a life of enforced frugality. On his head, the animal wore a round green woollen hat, stained and holed, and pulled down well around the ears. His shirt was collarless, worn onion-like beneath more than one layer of holed cardigan and a waistcoat to which were attached three pieces of twine. His trousers were brown and misshapen as potato-sacks, and his overcoat looked as old as the century: its arms were no longer at one with the rest of it, hanging by a few threads of drawn red cotton. If straw had stuck out of the holes it would not have looked entirely out of place. The Mouse himself had a frank and direct gaze, with humour somewhere beneath the surface, and for all his lameness there remained about him a quality of soldierly toughness: he walked on his nut-tree sticks with a straight back. His eyes, the Mole saw, were both a little milky.

"You coome alawng thet green way?" asked the Harvest Mouse, jerking his head in the appropriate direction. The Mole nodded. "Meet anywoone alawng et?"

"I met a Mr Pottage-Ferret.—In his *motor*."

The old animal nodded grimly. "The dawg-in-chief himself, eh?—An' wor thet a pleasure?"

"Not awfully, no. To be frank. Though I did ... hear some things I didn't know. Talking to him."

The Harvest Mouse wheezed as he laughed, or vice versa. "I bet you ded!" he said, still laughing. "I *bet* you ded!—Down dawg! Git *back* here now."

The Mole glanced about him. "... Nice to see somebody still doing a bit of—well—proper farming," he said, as much out of hope as conviction.

The old mouse dropped his eyes beneath brows like small grey thorn bushes, and looked for a moment at the road. He nodded. "Not too much of et hereabouts noo lawnger," he said. "Safe there ain't."

"But it's not going to last, is it?—All of that, out there?" said the Mole, nodding himself—and hoping perhaps for some knowledgeable confirmation of what his instincts told him.

"Et will not."

As if following a joint impulse the two small animals walked silently to the point, a few yards distant, where the hedge ended and the enclosed green space of the Harvest Mouse's island of fields beached up against the ocean surrounding it. They looked out at the wash of barley to the right of the road, like an incoming tide, and at the vanishing perspective of young potatoes on the other side, their still-bunched leaves poking up from ridges as straight ruled and beige as a depressive's cords.

For all the passing isolated storms of the last few days, where rain had not fallen—and even perhaps, for the most part, where it had—the soil stayed dry. The Mole stooped to the earth, grasped a handful, and crushed it. It collapsed in his palm as softly as crystal salts, leaving a residual stain of orange-brown powder on his fur, and as it streamed back to the ground a miniature dust-cloud rose up to knee height. "I have *never* seen soil so dry," he said. "If anyone had ever said it could get like this, *my* how I'd have laughed!"

The old mouse looked at him intently. "That's what happens when you plough it year on year, ten-year on ten-year. They niver rest et. They *niver* rest et! They think, when it's woorn out they cin throw it away and git a new woone. Well, they're a-goen' t'larn different, you ma' depend on

thet. Woon't be able to grow *nuthen* on thet, at the end o' th'
day. Then we'll see.—Put et back under grass, then! Or
furze, if grass woon't grow noo more. Thet river down
there?" (He indicated it with a nod.) "It's got the fields in
et, now. All silted up. Used to be full of trout, thet river.
Full of 'em!" The old animal leaned towards the Mole and
touched him on the arm, country-style, to underscore his
point. "They'd jump straight up to your fryin'-pan, not far
off. An' the crayfish, they'd coome up when you wor
standin' there—you could tickle 'em. You could *tickle* 'em!
None there noo more. Nawthen there now save the silt. Et
all leaches down into thet water. Thet river is full of the
fields now."

The Mole breathed deeply, struggling with his feelings.
It was not that he still expected to find his place of rest in
these eastern coast-lands: by now, he had given up expecting anything very much. But he had still—so *very* faintly—
hoped.

"Thet there," said the Harvest Mouse, raising one of his
sticks to the potatoes. "When I wor a 'squeak' thet big ol'
aerodrome of nawthen, atween here an' thet plantation
there, thet was thirty farms. Thirty, now! They had eighty,
ninety animals woorken' on 'em back then. More at harvest,
Et was *alive*. I woorked 'em! I woorked on three of 'em, all
through my young years, an' et was damned hard woork
too. You try pitchen' sheaves from dawn to dusk, six days a
week! We still did et like thet then, on the little farms. I
knew every last tiddy li'l piece of 'em, I did."

The old fellow paused, staring out across the corduroy
sea with his damaged eyes as if dwelling on beauties he had
known there. "I wor a prince amongst these fields," he said.
"Et's the truth now. I wor a prince amongst these fields,
bor, in my day. Ploughen'. Sheperden'. Ditchen'. Plashen'. I
did 'em! I did et all. Show me woone animal round here
now who cin use a billhook like I! Et was a hard life, you

ma' depend. But et was companionable."

The Mole nodded, but could not speak.

"An' you could walk all the paths there, 'long th' hedgerows, woone field to another, woone farm to th' next." Again the old mouse touched the Mole's arm, and pointed as if to details of the non-existent fieldscape. "Always met some woone out there, had a joke or two—we wor all over. All over! An' now look at et. 'Nivver a ploughman, nivver a woone ...' Who said thet, now?—Ah, but it's true though, ain't et? Et's all bin killed orf, jus' like the plague took 'em."

"—By the Guvvn'ment?" asked the Mole, who was beginning to show some promise by now as a political analyst.

"By the *Guvvn'ment*. They killed orf the little farms, woone by woone, woone by woone! You worn't prepared to grow? They put you out of business. An' the woones who got the money wor the like of Pottidge-Pherytte. The destroyers. They might as well hev put up a big sign sayen' 'Destroy An' Be Rewarded', naw thet's the truth of et. Safe *I* don't git noo grants for what I do! An' they're still after ivery last farthen' now." (The Mole nearly jumped when he heard the word "farthing").

"Any little farm thet coomes up for sale—they're all after et. Down on et like a falcon on a—whatever et ma' be. You want to git a field, they outbid you. But they'll not be gittin' *my* bit o' land! Coome on now, bor, an' I'll show you somethen'."

The old animal turned on his sticks and went ahead of the Mole to a gate in the tall hedge—a gate of wood, no less, and bleached by age. They entered a field of no great depth, but perhaps two hundred yards in width. Isolated thorns had colonized its turf and there was a skeletal pear tree, very old but still in bloom, two balls of mistletoe clinging to its top branches. At the far end, beyond a wire, six pigs were lazing on the exposed earth in front of a short section of hedge that had been most beautifully laid into a living basketwork. "A-keepen' ma hogs in her for now," said the Mouse as he walked on towards a second gate. A few seconds before they reached this, the easternmost tip of the storm cloud—which had been holding back the sunlight for the past two minutes—moved on, and the surface of the field beyond was progressively picked out by the light, as if by the swift removal of a veil. And it was all colour there beyond the gate now: an old hay meadow, so jam-packed from hedge to hedge with flowers that the Mole had to most strongly resist the impulse to fall to the ground and roll in them.

"O!" he said. "O! O!—O *my!*"

"Perty, en't et?" said the Harvest Mouse, grinning broadly. "Got five o' these left still. Here and yonder, a tidy piece of owd yard. An' when I goo on, all of et will be gooen' to the nature-people, signed, sealed, delivered. They'll look after et, 'cos they cin do et. Even if they don't hev noo money, neither!—An' *him*, there," (a derisive nod, distinctly Ferret-wards) "he will just hev to goo on ploughen' round et, woon't he?"

"O, but you have *fritillaries!*" exclaimed the Mole, in raptures.

"Yis. We call 'em sulky-ladies in these parts. Perty."

"You've got vetches! You've got cowslips! And bird's foot!—O! And *orchids!*"

"We got the meadow-saffron, too. Coomes in the fall."

The Mole knelt wonderingly at the edge of the haze of purplish-pinks and pinkish-purples, and whites, and yellows, blues, and oranges. "And what are *these?*" he said. "—And *these?!*" He touched a little flower made like a fan of tiny trumpets, all in shades of orange. Butterflies were jigging around it, and all across the meadow beyond. "I never saw *this*, even in my Valley. Truly! I never saw this before!"

"Doon't know the half of 'em myself," said the old

mouse. "Et's nivver bin ploughed. Not in my time. They say et's nivver bin ploughed—not *ever*. Just scythen'—like us allus did, back of July, when the seed-heads are well set. I can't do thet noo more now, though. 'Tis a rare lot too much for me. They hev to coome an' do et.—I show 'em how!" He laughed his thin, high laugh.

"So it's not all quite gone," said the Mole to himself. "Not everything is lost." And as he stared on in amazement at this small field, enclosed as it was on all four sides by walls of greenery, his memories of the world he had known rose through him one by one, like boulders.

Eventually—though the Mole did not want to leave it, ever—the two animals walked the short distance back across the pig-field to the road. "Where you a-gooen'?" asked the Harvest Mouse. "Down to the shore?"

The Mole hesitated, and met his gaze. "I—I'm not sure," he said. "The shore ... Yes—s'pose I might. Silly not to, after all that pedalling."

The old animal looked back at him, sensing now, as if with the very air beyond his whisker-tips. His gaze flickered, as so many had, to the Mole's jacket and waistcoat which by now, like their owner, had seen better days. He opened his mouth to say something, but the shriek of an over-revved engine interrupted him. With a self-protective instinct both animals withdrew to opposite verges, the one to his dogs and secluding cottage-path, the other to his cycle and panniers. Moments later a small *motor* snarled between them without deceleration, a blur of ratbaby-fur-cut inside it.

The old mouse looked weary: he was hanging heavier upon his sticks now. "You coome this way again, now, bor—you knock on my door!" he said.

"O, I will!" replied the Mole heartily. "Most certainly I will!"

And so they parted. When he reached the place where

the tall thorns ended, the Mole glanced back towards the house, one end part of which was visible here over a garden hedge. In the centre of the garden, in a depression, lay a tiny pond in hourglass-shape, crossed by a rickety timber bridge of apt dimensions: to one side of this, a single low column of water blurped erratically. A few rows of peas and cabbages stood beyond, with a frame for runner-beans half erected. The rows were a bit on the weedy side, but the Mole smiled with pleasure at the sight of them.

"Why, but he could have been a boy when I was—when I was—O, but what *do* I mean?—the age that I am now, of course!" he thought. "It's all so very odd. I might have *met* him! Not that I'd ever have come here, if I hadn't been along that tunnel."

So the Mole pedalled on across the sandy country, and later in the day he entered into what proved to be a great forest-zone of straight-as-post plantation pines. But what stayed with him, floating on the surface of all he saw like a reflection in dull waters, was the memory of cloud-shade drawn suddenly back to reveal a fallen starscape of purplish-pinks, and pinkish-purples, whites, and yellows, blues and oranges on a narrow plot of earth. More than once, too, it was as if he could hear the old mouse's voice as he said to him again, "Et's the truth, now. I wor a prince amongst these fields, bor. In my day."

CHAPTER FOURTEEN

THE RIDDLE

The Mole did spend some time near the coast. He found his way to the centre of the plantation-forest, setting up his camouflage tent well away from any track or ride in one of countless long, symmetrical rows. It was not a wholly unpleasant spot: thanks to the trees' height, and the fact that they had been thinned, the sunlight could penetrate down to its grassy surface in dappled, needle-edged patches. This became his base camp—for four nights, no less, as it turned out. From it, he went off each day in different directions into the surrounding country, framed as this was by salt water on three sides: as well as the sea to the east, two broad tidal estuaries lay both north and south, neither of them more than six miles from his hidden tent.

The Mole was not searching now—just looking, less would-be settler than tourist by default. Once, in the brightest sunshine, when nobody was about, he even went so far as to put on his Shaydes. For whatever reasons of his own, he delayed visiting the shore itself until the last day. The sun that morning was shining out of a blue sky streaked by remote, wind-shaped cirrus: far beneath them, the Mole found himself following an unfrequented, silent lane across an expanse of grazing marshes. Ahead of him was a row of oddly shaped small houses, many of them timber-clad and all heavily roofed and grit-sealed against offshore gales. They looked to the Mole like an encampment of their own that had somehow hardened into permanence, standing spaced out widely along the top of what proved to be an immense shingle bank. The extent of this was only clear to him once he had climbed it: in both directions it stretched evenly away towards another far horizon —one where the sky made contact with both solid land and water.

Close to, the ocean did not frighten the Mole as he had expected. It lay under its blue sky that morning as a great neutrality, bearing no message either of encouragement or otherwise. It told him neither to go nor to stay, neither to take off his shoes and paddle nor to keep them on and walk: it minded its own business. Perhaps some other animal in the Mole's plight could have drawn meaning from it, come to some fresh view of things. But as he sat there on top of the warm shingle, looking steeply down to the waves over sea-built steps in the stones, the Mole's mind was as empty as it had been, sometimes, when he stared into the embers of the fire in his own grate.

There were oystercatchers about, and their plangent penny-whistlings, penetrating the distances, did call up in him some faint desire to reply in kind. Gulls too came close overhead, occasionally blocking out the sunlight for a flap-shadowed second, but all he could hear in their cries that morning was "CAR-park-CAR-park-CAR-park-CAR-park!"

He had brought his old Hollowmew's map with him on to the shingle. He wasn't at all sure, but perhaps here—next to this great full stop on further eastward movement—he might find it easier to decide where he should go next. Yet what could the map tell him, after all? It was just a lot of lines and place-names. Nothing on it said *Mole-Nomads: Look Here First*, or *Moles Especially—Avoid!* The sea wind was far too gusty for him to be able to open out the map, so he pored over it in sections, scanning the tiny, italicised village names for want of any better information. Some in Suffolk still appealed to him: Kettlebaston, for example, which at one stage on his journey he had narrowly missed. He searched hard for a "Teapottingham" or an "Ailby Motherton" in the same vicinity, but did not find one. There up to the north west, though, Drinkstone sounded faintly promising.

A flip and three folds brought his attention down to Kent, where Underriver stood out as a name that seemed to call him, and never mind the fact that he had nothing but the most serious doubts now about any of those serpentining threads of blue denoting actual rivers, or the valleys that they wound in. Five minutes and much folding later he had got himself round to the middle of the country, where in short succession he spotted first Hinton-in-the-Hedges, then Barton-in-the-Beans, then Coton-in-the-Elms.

Could the names of places be trusted to indicate their present character? Much, as he wanted it to be so, the Mole was sceptical. Yet Hinton-in-the-Hedges must have kept *some* hedges, he reasoned, or how would anyone ever find it? And Barton-in-the-Beans, whatever else, must have *soil* suited to the bean-rich garden. As for Cotton-in-the-Elms, who knows? It might be a centre (even as a museum) for the vanished craft of tailoring.

But, then, this was an old map, he reminded himself. And if place names *were* descriptive, then might not its modern equivalent now be covered with names like Grimlittle Boxlands, Hulking Shedfields, Greater Greystuffing, or Much-Whitethings-Beyond-The-Wolds? For a few terrible moments, as the gulls flapped out the sunlight and the waves sucked pebbles along the shoreline below him, the Mole was seized by a desire to get himself to *anywhere* in the

country where the mad grand architects of Weaselworld
had yet to arrive with their plan for all possible futures, if
only to give witness—solitary, mute, but comprehending
witness—to its beauty before the machines arrived.

The moment passed, and the Mole browsed on. There
was one name especially that his eye kept coming back to.
This was Finchingfield—from here, some forty-five to fifty
miles west, and a little bit south, back in the county of
Essex. Surely, he thought, a village called *Finchingfield* must
have something about it of the world-before? There might
(might there?) be fields there—proper fields? Though it
was probably too much to hope that there were finches in
them.

He stared out at the flat-rule rim of the eastern sea, and
wondered. There was still perhaps one part of him tenu-
ously attracted by the long-lost security of the Rettes'
house, where at least he had had a wardrobe he could call
his borrowed-own. *Should* he go back there now? Admit
defeat? Beg Mr Rette to take him back under his wing until
he had worked out some better plan?—But then, the Mole
reasoned, what plan might that ever be? And, after all, what
was there to prevent him from working out something here
and now, by this great wet full-stop? Especially, of course,
if it made no difference?

"You moles are resilient creatures." The Mole recalled
the Badger's words so clearly it was just as if, in that
moment, the big animal had come to sit next to him on the
warm smooth stones. "... You get through, for the most
part, don't you? ... Come what may? ..."

"S'pose so," said the Mole, and nodded grimly. He
snorted with resurgent determination and molesque trucu-
lence, picked up a pebble and hurled it seawards. "Come-
what-may! Come-what-may-not!" He turned back to his
map. "Very well then, Mole.—Now. It will be *Finchingfield*
first. Then—if that's no good—over to *Underriver*. ... But,

how? O, there *must* be a ferry, there—across to Gravesend?
If there are any ferries left at all! Then, hmmm ... Back up
again? This side of London? Not *round* it ... no—no! Then
... *over* to Hinton-in-the-Hedges, and *up* to Barton-in-the-
Beans and Cotton ... oh, I see, *Coton*-in-the-Elms, and after
that—if there *is* an 'after that'—then West—West—
WEST! That's the plan, Mole. That's all the plan you need.
Chin up, now. It's May, you have a bicycle, and you are in
England. What more should any animal need to know, after
all?"

There was that sea horizon again, as flat as it was non-
committal as it was flat. But now, a few hundred yards up
to the Mole's left, he did catch sight of a message on the
waters. A raft of scum was riding the waves there, its foot-
deep mass of yellow foam spreading then retracting,
amoeba-like, surfing each wave-crest before it was drawn
out again on the undertow. Every half minute or so it got
close enough to leave a narrow kiss of yellow on the shingle, with bits breaking off and flying short distances land-
wards. Why, the ocean itself was one of Weaselworld's
dustbins! So thought the Mole as he clambered back up the
shingle bank now.

At the top, between two of the clapboarded houses, he
saw a small area of blown sand mixed evenly with mud—
smooth, soft and damp-looking. It was quite untouched,
and when he turned back for one last view of the ocean he
could not resist leaving a single, neat mole-print upon it.

The hot weather had arrived in earnest now. From the start
of the Mole's journey, the weather had felt noticeably cool
only in the occasional showers and storms he had encountered, and he was beginning to wonder if these had been
anything like so widespread as he feared at the time. When

he turned inland again that Thursday (he was *sure* it was Thursday) and passed into another, more southerly belt of the clay country, he saw groups of stag-headed oaks of no great age standing along the most naked lanesides. So, too, in each of the canopies of surviving small woods he biked past he spotted the barkless dead-white finger ends of trees—not elms, by the shape of them, but other familiar types instead. It did seem as if by now—the random charity of storms aside—the trees in these parts must be living off the dew alone. Once again, and the more so the further he got from the sea, the Mole's instinct was to look for water wherever it could be found. But it was only in the river-valleys that he found it.

More than once he saw ploughing (ploughing, in *May?*) with clouds of dust, not seagulls, rising and falling behind the tractors. Streams were simply dry—in one village he saw a goat tethered to a grassed-over stream-bed, nibbling at Jack-by-the-hedge—or could boast nothing more than pockets of standing water whose oiled-rainbow surfaces broke into patterns as the May blossoms fell on them. More than once, at picnic times, he mistook the sound of the wind in the rattling-paper leaves of nearby poplars for that of running water. The dry earth of unsurfaced tracks had been crushed by fat tyres into something resembling a brown talcum powder, and the once shiny-new paintwork of the Mole's bicycle was now permanently dulled by an even film of much the same stuff.

He found duckponds where yellow-flag irises were flowering out of the cracked and nearly dry clays of the pond bottoms, and not a duck to lay claim to them; and in the hot middles of each hot day a haze shimmered above the vast cultivations, distorting the shapes of whatever lay beyond. Even the brambles were turning up their pale undersides as if in admission of defeat and sweet woodruff, where he saw it once, lay under the trees like lank green hair. For a single day—it was Friday, he was *sure* it was Friday—the sun was hidden behind heavy, ridged grey cloud—rainless cloud from which came nothing but an isolated pattering of large, warm, useless drops to damp his fur. And everywhere, everywhere, cloudy or sunny—faintly here, overpoweringly there—was the strange, seaweedy smell of the void.

The Mole would not admit to himself in so many words that he sensed impending disaster in all this—how could he? But what he sensed in all this, nonetheless, was impending disaster. Nature herself was gripped, not only by the relentless clamp of this tyrany of cropping, but by an unabating solar presence—the Great Friend turned somehow (and by what actions?) to enemy, or something disturbingly close to it. Again and again—when he was traversing the flour-dry soil of some off-road detour, or dodging the black bubbles of tar that would crack against his tyres as he hit them, or when he saw the stuck-closed blooms of some roadside flower weeping black liquid of another kind—he found himself begging the rain to come and bring the world back to normality, to *life*.

Near lunchtime on his third day westwards, the Mole found himself descending a gravelly, deeply indented track into the valley of the little river Box, a tributary of the Stour, which itself marks the border between Suffolk and Essex. The landscape here was, suddenly, almost hilly, with short but also steepish slopes on either side of the stream. Behind him, to the north, was much the usual prairie upland, across which marched a double line of massive cable-concertina-skeletons. But in the small valley ahead of him there were *field*-sized fields, rimmed with belts of trees. So here he stopped, tucking himself into a narrow strip of woodland just above the track with his bread rolls, tomato, and tin of sardines. (It was a day of luxury.)

The tree-belt he sat in was not of much interest in itself: a few oaks, Scots pines, sycamores—several of these dead—with an understorey of elders and brambles, and dog's mercury flopped over exhausted between them. Yet as, meditatingly, the Mole studied this spot, he did begin to wonder what else it might produce if it were given half a chance or less. What stores of seeds of all-but-forgotten plants might still lie dormant in the ground beneath those papery brambles? How *might* they begin to spread out again from here—yes, even here—if things were only a little different in the lands beyond?

Grasping at this moment of non-pessimism so as not to let it pass too quickly, the Mole went on to contemplate his experience of the void itself. For didn't he have to admit that even in this territory-of-absences, for all his sense of loss, there was still *something*? Maybe it was no more than the shape of the land surface itself: its subtly unpredictable swellings and crestings, and the ways these were duplicated in the lines of the crops as they raced on past him at whisker-level. This was the beauty of deserts, perhaps, or of some great grass plain of Asia as Parco Molo himself might first have seen it.

... But, well ... yes, he thought. There was something else too; he could not deny it. He had met it most clearly in the evenings, when the sun was getting low, and the same elusive, curious sensation would come drifting back to him, not out of the fields but as if from far beyond every one of their distant horizons. It was a sense of some question—some riddler's conundrum—being posed as if directly to him, the Rootless, the Troubled, the Wandering Mole. Yet each time it had happened, he recognised now, not only was he quite unable to make a reply: he could never so much as guess the nature of the question in the first place.

Near the centre of the timber-framed field he was over-looking there stood a single small tree. It was a field maple, rising out of a dimple in the hill-slope fringed by a circle of nettles. While he had been thus ruminant, the Mole's eye had returned more than once to this tree and its ball-like spread of fully opened pale May foliage. There was something striking there, in the way the tree's shadow fell away so blackly beyond the foreground of nettles. It seemed to him that within this circle there lay another shadow, or deeply-shaded form. The green barley around it blew, and stood, and blew, a current moving erratically through it, much as if some solid but invisible hand were swiftly taking one after the next in a narrow channel of dry brush-heads and shaking it from beneath.

As the Mole was pushing himself up to leave, his gaze fell once more on this shaded channel of wind-made-visi-ble. He sat back again for a moment, focusing his attention on the fluvial drivings of the gusts through the crop, and the mysterious randomness of each variation on the theme. He looked again at the maple, and its blacker-than-black understorey. Then his eyes widened. For there *was*—*wasn't* there?—a form within that shadow! There—*there*—the outline of something unquestionably solid, whose move-ments were just as slight as they need be for a figure sitting supported by a young tree's trunk, and blowing—softly, patiently, without display—on a set of pipes? Could he not see—there!—the backward sweep of curved horns, the broad and muscular shape of a back like that of no known animal, the outline of a pair of raised, shaggy limbs—

And wasn't the music—O, so faint as to be almost beyond hearing, yet still in some way present in the land-scape—wasn't the music sounding in the most perfect syn-chrony with those Aeolian currents through the barley—yes, the same, ever-present chemical barley—as if controlling them, or reproducing them? Or both at once?

The Mole stared now, his eyes quite probably wider than those of any mole in creation, waiting for more—some additional movement in that inner patch of blackness—that would confirm that what he thought he saw was what he saw.

But as he watched and waited—over one, two, three minutes, more—the wind died back very slowly, or moved elsewhere. As it did so there was a change in the shade amongst the nettles, no longer moving themselves. It was as if two hands had sunk down, holding between them some form, resembling pipes.

"O my," breathed the Mole. "O ... *my!*" He waited one moment more; looked back one more time. Then, in seconds, he had found his way back to the gravelly track, well out of sight of the field, and was repacking his things with far less than the usual degree of efficiency before crunching off, half on the saddle and half off it, down the slope to the river.

Did the Mole think again about this experience as he continued on his travels? The answer is yes, but also, no, since whenever he did recall it—and that was frequently—he would put it out of his mind again immediately. One thing above all he knew he could not afford to do, and that was speculate. Far better not to try to make any sense of it at all. But for all his efforts he did still arrive at a thought that could not be stopped from surfacing in words, and surfaced not just once but many times more during the rest of his journey: "It was as if he was waiting. Just waiting. For something to change."

But the Mole himself, he could not wait—he couldn't—and he span on westwards, and a little bit south, just as before concentrating his mind on the practical, down-to-earth decisions of a long-distance bicycling journey.

Since the very beginning of his travels, the Mole had hoped against hope he might be able to find some old country inn hidden so far away from things down its back lane that it had been little touched by change: an inn whose dark little tap-room still resounded with the cackling laughter of a covey of weatherbeaten ancients comparing the heights of the peas in their pightles over pints of house-brewed tuppenny ale. Surely, he had thought, at least at the start, *that* sort of place won't have changed much?

But in what Mr Rette liked to call "the real world", the Mole found different. Most of the time he got no further than his first sight of the car parks—those ever-present shining lakes of glass and metal that seemed as a matter of course now to frame pubs on three sides out of four. If possible, these looked more blighted still when *motor*-free, with the old building stuck there in its sterile little enclosure of tar or potholed gravel, divided up by clumping kerbs and dotted by great green bins and stunted junipers wilting in their bisected barrels.

The magical old white-fenced orchard gardens were vanished, with outdoor drinkers condemned to pokey little enclaves of beaten grass on which they were further contained inside the crudest kind of bench-plus-table, made like a trap you had to climb into. From there they had nothing left to do except survey the rev-heavy jockeyings of *motors* departing and arriving, like judges at a ballroom competition. Yet if the two establishments the Mole had so far visited were anything to go by, it was little better inside: in neither had he lasted much more than five minutes. The first had been a big, boldly mock-Tudor place called *The Firkin Wonderful* ("A Good Olde British Pub In The Pub-U-Like Group"), which sat squarely next to a traffic-lights on a Hertfordshire crossroads. The Mole had been drawn to it by its oddly *non*-fake leaded windows, but once through the use-chafed swing doors he was stalled within three paces: by the confusing layout—the place opened in all directions, and seemed to have everything but a bar; by the urging babel of half a dozen chalked-up food lists; worst of all by the *sounds* coming down at him from the ceilings.

Not to be put off—at least, not yet—he had gone up to a low board marked *Puddings Of The Day*. Here, anyway, was a subject in which he did not have to feign an interest. This read:

> Death by Chocolate
> (Standard Portion)
>
> Death by Chocolate
> (Double Size!
> Take Someone Else With You)
>
> Torment by Trifle
>
> Tachycardia by Toffee
>
> Martyrdom by Meringue
>
> Chocolate, Toffee and Treacle Squidgy-Pudding
> Cake FILLED with our
> glorious firm-but-oozing Chocolate and
> Molasses Sauce
> and crunchy-but-sticky Chocolate Buttons.
> Served with triple cream!!!

More disturbed by this than tempted, the Mole moved swiftly on into a maze of dim-lit interlinked spaces with changing floor levels and little balustraded balconies where animals could be seen eating, seated at all the styles of farmhouse chair known to history, and some others that were not. Here, from the black-but-*black*-beamed ceilings a hideous noise was raining down: the Mole could make out something along the lines of "Eyewanna—eyewanna—eyewanna—eyewanna—eyewanna—reelyreelyreelyreely—reelyreelyreelyreely—reelyreelyreelyreelyreelywanna ..." The voice, he guessed, was that of a female: whether hedge-hog, vole or Mindanao moonrat he would have to leave open. But why, he wondered, *why* might *anyone* want to imitate the sounds of some far-too-long unpleasant moment—in a Clearway crash, perhaps, or in some great sea-battle—where metal screams for yard after yard along the surface of metal?

The Mole peered into the ceiling shadows with newly sophisticated eyes. *Could* these sounds be emerging from that little black box, hanging there in that dark corner like a bat? He strongly suspected that they were. And hadn't Mr Rette told him—more than once, by now—that voice-con-tortions of this kind were known here as "singing"? Not that this made sense any more than did the singing itself; this, obviously, was all done in foreign languages.

He moved on into the next crowded cave-space, with wailings in another mode raining down on him from box to box as he passed. These were matched by the chill tin-klings of a piano that might itself have been turned to ice, and a remote and insistent clashing, as of bin-lids in a dark ravine. The wall-recesses in this part of the build-ing were stuffed with books, giving it the feel of a chaotic secondhand bookshop. But not one of the customers was looking anywhere near them, let alone reading. At ran-dom, the Mole picked out a volume from a shelf nearby.

It was a copy of *The Poet At The Breakfast Table* by Oliver Wendell Volmes – not one of the Mole's favourites, as it happened, but famous in his day. There were another two copies of the same work on the very shelf where he had found it. So what Justin Rette had told him must be true, he thought sadly: in the too-late world, books were just things to be used in pubs, to show that "You can eat in this bit"—always assuming you were prepared to take the risk.

But it was now the Mole experienced a moment of what might pass for revelation. He had spotted a fine specimen of a stone hot water bottle of his era standing on a curious, hearth-free mantelshelf. From this, nostalgically, he was doing his best to wrench it (it had been firmly glued in place) as a bat-box directly above his head was putting out what first he heard as:

> "Yanevuh sed gudbiiiy
> Sumwan tel miwiiiy
> Ditch hafta goooww
> Leemawurl socollll ......"

As generally happened, this and allied opacities (amongst them an emphatic "Yoora nudda loan, Yoora nudda loan") were reiterated many times, as if the singer were so obsessed by them that he (or she) could not bear to drag himself (or herself) off to bed. For no especially obvious reason, the Mole found himself focusing on the words (... this hot water bottle *would not* come off ...), then puzzling at them, and puzzling more deeply, and then more deeply still. By the time of the third—fourth?—repetition ... no, but could it, *could* it be possible? ... he had begun to understand them. —Could he? Was that *really* his own language being used here? Were those really plain old English words as he had once known them, being vowel-drawled, smudged and distorted, as if the singer had downed three glasses of potato wine in a single gulp?

The Mole raised a distraught paw towards his brow as a new song began, and a stridorous drenching of "Ahh lur-rrvvv yeeeww, beh-beh, wohh yeahhh"s began its march towards infinity. He looked about him at the crowd of animals, some blazing in pools of white light, others all but invisible in the shadows, every one of them, it seemed, deep in conversation. Might all of *them* be talking in this style, even as he watched? Might an animal be *expected* to use this new way of speaking, even at the bar (when he found it) in such a place as this?("Quaar-turrr uvv ahh pahhnnt uvv Mahhlldd, beh-beh, wohh yeahhh.") The thought was too much. Hot-furred with panic, the Mole beat a swift but dignified retreat to the doors and the outside world.

The Mole's second less-than-triumphant foray had been into a pretty, clematis-draped cottage pub in a village on the Cambridge-Suffolk borders. He should perhaps have been put on his guard here by the place signing itself as "Restaurant-Pub", or by the fact that the proprietor—a weasel in dinner-jacket and spotted bow tie—stood outside the homely entrance, apparently to see in the evening's guests. But it was far too late by then, and the Mole dove inside, if only to escape the Weasel's horrified look of enquiry at the sight of his cycle clips, which, obviously, were still in position.

Inside was just the kind of low-ceilinged, small-roomed place the Mole had dreamed of finding, but for the fact that every one of its worn deal tables was demonstratively laid for dining with multiple cutlery, napkins, wine glasses in three sizes, ornate candle-holders and more. On the sides of the ceiling beams were chalked wordy appreciations of "recommended" wines, and one bottled beer, with an injunction to "Try Ozzie's Little Perkie (all his own work) or a Habanera Buena-Vista Slam Bang!" A menu on a blackboard advertised *mignonnettes* of monkfish, sea-bass *sortilèges, lorgnades* of lobster and *quarterons* of quail, *chiffoniers* of venison served with goat's cheese *cruches,* and all at the most astounding prices. As the Mole gaped at this, a salad floated past him on a servitor's hand: it seemed to consist entirely of purplish lettuce overlaid with sliced strawberries.

The Mole looked around the most immediate of the tiny rooms where animals of style—if not what he could honestly call smartness—sat squeezed together at the various tables, elbows miserably crunched down to avoid friction with their neighbours as they dined. The conversation was largely muted, a genteel low hubbub, but some harsher voices did break through in fragments, momentarily fixing the Mole's attention:

"... Oh, no!—No, no! She's getting an MRE pension now, you know. That's *plenty.* Take it from me! ..."

"Of course we do have to focus on *branding the portfolio.* It's the *repertoire drinker* we are after, like everybody else—I mean, that area of *leisure-spend.* You know, the highest-grossing ..."

"... I was talking to *David* the other day."

"Oh ... OH! Not—*the* David? I mean ... not—*that* David?"

"Ha, ha, yes! *The* David. *The* David.—David and I ... *David and I* are on really *quite good terms* nowadays ..."

To the rear of the place was a small recess containing four very high, modern-looking stools arranged against a tiny curve of planking that must, the Mole deduced, be the bar. Not to be put off—at least, not yet—he approached this and waited for the young ferret beyond the planks to finish polishing glasses and acknowledge him. This took two minutes. When the animal did turn round, he said, "Ah, sir. Yes. So sorry. Will you be dining with us tonight?"

"Um—no. Don't think so, thank you very much."

"You might just like to try one of our starters?" urged the Ferret, as if sensing hesitation.

"Well, I—um—I was hoping to order a quarter pint of Mild," replied the Mole. "And, O—if you had one—a pickled egg?"

The Ferret froze very slightly, looking at the Mole as if with newly-adjusted vision. His gaze flickered up and down the visitor's not entirely dust-free, oddly period clothing. "We don't do—ahh—'quarter pints', sir," he said, in a low tone that suggested some kind of sacrilege might have been committed.

"O.—O. Well, I suppose I could manage a whole half pint if I had to. I am bicycling, after all! Of—um—Mild?"

"We don't DO 'Mild', sir."

"O. O dear. Nor, um—pickled eggs? I suppose?"

"No, sir."

"Once more the Mole felt himself flushing hot beneath his fur. "... Onions?"

"No, sir."

"Bless me. That's a shame, that is. O, well. Right you are.—G'day."

With that he turned, looking for nothing but the low door beyond, from which he burst at some speed past proprietor, dinner jacket, spotted bow tie, and second horrified look of enquiry.

By this present stage in his journey, as he moved on westwards into the centre of northern Essex, the Mole had decided to admit defeat and go into any rural pub he could find, just so long as it was quiet (and *not* traduced as "Restaurant-Pub"). "Otherwise," he thought, "I shall never go in one at all."

So it was that on the very morning following this resolution, he happened to be going down a backish back-lane, about a third of the way between one village and the next, when he came on a concern sited in just such a spot as he might have hoped. It was called *The Honest Hodsmal*, which seemed promising too. Otherwise, though, it was much the usual vandalized place, its old brick frontage half covered by a huge flat-roofed greenhouse whose panes were held together by a lumping, style-free whitestuff frame. The grey chippings car park had been recently extended, with a channel bulldozed to slightly higher land on the edge of the void beyond. Three white vans—two large, one small—were parked close by the greenhouse entrance.

Even now, the Mole may have harboured some lingering faint hope he might be able to step into a country pub in the too-late world and hear the sound of country voices. No sooner had he pushed open the stiff bar door of the *Honest Hodsmal*, though, than he knew it was not likely to be here.

"… Ooohh yeh," someone was saying. "Yeh-yeh, i's the on'y way intit? No time fer none uv that rubbish now. Cost a bleedin' *carpet* uvverwise. 'S tradish'nul now anyway intit?"

"Wot, tradish'nul—"

"Yurh, i's yer Tradish'nul Sixties-American. Intit. Open plan like. No fences annat ter bovver wiv. Jus' grass like."

"Jus' *grass* like. Ter park the car on!"

"Yeh.—Yeh. Asswot a garden's *for*. Intit."

"Asswot *I* say, Henry—asswot *I* say, mayt."

The bar inside was done in winegum and deep turquoise. It had a window-box, a games machine and a convector heater all running off the same multi-plug. There-was a cigarette machine too, and a spider-plant, and the pale oblique-cut tree-trunk tables were very, very varnished. The bar-side was covered in blackstuff and buttons like a kind of tilted shiny mattress—such of it as the Mole could see, that is, since in front of it, in a row, there sat three extremely large dormice, each of them nearly as round as an orange. The conversation faded to very little (or more exactly, to nothing) as the Mole came

round the door, but he bade all these present a bold
"G'mornin'" and went straight up to the accessible angle
of the bar.

The publican himself was a stoat of some stoutness, and
was possessed of a luxuriantly dangling Mexican mustache,
with a duckbilled cap to overshade it. He sported a long
and necessarily capacious black tee-shirt with a line drawing of monsters and the words "Prohibited Planet" jagged
across the chest; his trousers stopped, dangle-threaded, at
the knee. The fur of both his arms had strange, ugly
designs burned into it, one of them showing a female stoat
in a bathing costume. He did not (the Mole thought) look
very well.

"Yussmay?" he said.

The Mole paused, poleaxed by standard confusion. May
he—what? ... He may ... Yes, but *what* may he? And why
had it sounded like a *question*? In mounting panic he considered leaving, re-entering, and trying the thing over again.

"Wot'll it be, then?" said the Stoat, sighing, with slightly
exaggerated patience.

"... O!—O! Yes! A half of ... you don't have the—
um—the Mild? By any chance?"

"Mild? Yeh. Half?"

"Yes, please. And a—" Next to a small board reading
*Leak Soup, Scampi Pasta, Jackit Spuds With Baked Beans or Tuna,
Chicken Ticker Marsala* the Mole saw a big jar—of a really
quite familiar kind—three-quarters full of *pickled eggs!* Joyfully, he ordered one. He really felt quite hungry. (It was
the cycling though—he always felt quite hungry). Looking
along the back of the bar, he added, "And a packet of those
Fifteen-O-O Crisps, please."

The stout Stoat turned slowly to him, like a bellbuoy
rotating on a wave. "Fifteen-*oh-oh* crisps?" he echoed, with
slightly less slightly-exaggerated patience, his eyes wandering momentarily towards his other customers.

"Um. Those—there." The Mole pointed.

"Oh—*these*," said the Stoat. "The Scuttlers' Plain Old Original? The Scuttlers' Down-To-Earthers, with fifteen per cent more in each bag?—*For* the period of the special offer?—These?" He grasped one, rather too tightly, in a plump paw.

"Yes.—Please."

"'Corse, er …" said the Stoat, as the Mole was making his way to a seat. "Comin' back to that uvver fing, Darren, I mean, you know uz well uz I do, I'm not a big drinker myself any more. Who is these days? Eh? I never get frough more'n six pints in a night now. When did I, since I bin 'ere? *Never.*"

The Mole sat with his back to the window, near the bar, thinking he would at least be in a good spot to get into a conversation if the chance came up. From here, he had an uninterrupted view of the three dormice—it could hardly have been otherwise—whose array of short-sleeved work-shirts, blue or white, were all more than generously filled by great furry tummies and blobose waistbacks that settled against the insides of the material like bagged liquid. The belly of the middle mouse over-hung his yawing trouser-belt like some great soft coconut bursting with milk, though the upthrust bush of his tail was sadly stunted.

"Wul," said this animal. "Time fer anuvver? Make it a pint of Piyey, Henry, if you don't mind."

"Old-Piebald-Pig?"

"Yeh. An' a Hedgeplasher's Scrunch. As it is approaching scrunchtime."

"Iris! One Plasher's, if you please, for the mal here!"

"Gotter get meself ready for the road," said the order-placer.

The animal to his left nodded morosely. "'s all the over-taykin' intit, Darren."

"Oh *yeh*. Oh you got to overtayke.—Aincher? You got to. You *got* to."

"You got to."

"You *got* to."

"I mean, I wooden respeck meself as a mayle *of* the species, if I diddunt overtayke."

"You gotta get up front," said the mouse-to-port reasonably.

"*Oh yeh*," responded the first, as if the proposition had now been definitively framed. He moved forward, embracing the bar-front buttons with his great belly. "You got to show 'em *hoo* is *hoo*. Us of the Vans *is* the ones who is Up Front. Intit."

"I tailed one bleeder up 'ere," said the right hand mouse.

"An' when you say *tailed*, Mor'imer—"

"An' when I say *tailed*, Leigh, I *mean tailed*. Bleedin' pathe'ic slowcoach 'edge'og. Stuck right on 'is stump, I did. Nine inches, all the way up. Gave 'im a freebie. —I mean, come *on*, eh? If 'e can't do sixty on the straight—"

"—Sixty-five on the corners!"

"—Speshully the blind ones!"

"—Shouldn' be on the road, should 'e?"

"Should *no*' be on the road."

A serving hatch opened. "Right, Darren," said the landlord. "One Hedgeplasher's Scrunch, to your orders, sir. Jus' like the plashers used ter scrunch 'em."

"Pore ol' sods."

"Pore ol' sods. Pore 'ol sods like they were. Wottever it wuz they got up to. Bet *they* diddunt get no pickle wiv their Cheddar. Eh? Sittin' out there in their culverts, wiv the rain pourin' dahn?"

"We've moved on since then, Henry."

"We have moved on, Leigh. No daht abahtit. Though of course—that said—i' is a shayme the way i's gone."

"'I' is a shayme, 'Enry. You say right, my mal. 'I' is a shayme."

All four animals were wearing what the Mole had come to call standing-shoes: those hideous objects he had first thought might be used for sport but which were—he now understood—used only for standing on street corners, sitting on benches, and the occasional bit of walking about. All three pairs, neatly raised up on their barstools, were very white (and orange, blue, black, red and etc.) and *very* clean. "They will never get the earth on those shoes," thought the Mole wonderingly. "Never!"

"You aht fer th' day, then?" said the Stoat, filling in a silence, his glance falling on the traveller's cycle clips.

The Mole did not realise he was being addressed until he caught the stoatly gaze. "O.—Ah. Me. Um—yes. Well, more than a day, really. I've been pedalling about for weeks—"

"Weeks, eh?"

"Weeks and weeks.—Weeks and weeks and weeks!"

"Blimey," said the mouse-to-starboard, turning slightly. "S'prised you 'ad the strengf to ge' frough the doower."

"Yeh," agreed his immediate fellow. "Strong spring on tha' doower." All four animals laughed uproariously.

"I'm not much of a fitness fanatic meself," said the landlord, as if revealing some previously hidden truth. "S'pose i' is quite nice though, is i', out there on a bike at this time uv year?"

The Mole hesitated. "O ... yes," he said. "All the—blossom, and things. Nothing like travelling under your own steam!"

"'Ow far d'yoo come then? Frum where yoo started—"

One by one and very slowly, as the Mole was explaining, all three dormice turned to look at him, a gaze of all-too-familiar horror deepening across each round face.

"I used ter ride a bike once," said the Stoat, with perhaps the most vestigial shade of regret in his voice. "When I wus younger, like. I did too, Leigh, an' don' you snigger none or you'll 'ave ter go an' count yer whiskers.—'Ad ter give it up, of *corse*. All the traffic—"

"All the traffic, 'Enry."

"All these vans abaht—"

"All these *bleedin' vans* abaht!"

"Couldn' do i' now, could'jer?"

"Nah. Nah! You got ter drive now."

"I' is a shayme, though, intit. The way i's gone."

Somehow, then, the conversation drifted away from the Mole and the subject of cycling, allowing him to get up, glass in hand, and take a closer look at the rest of the bar. A number of black and white photographs hung against the be-turquoised paper, the biggest of which showed a group of old or oldish animals dressed in flat caps, worn tweeds and corduroys, with a couple of females to the rear in neat belted raincoats. All stood, very serious, hands clasped together, round a big table on which rested a vase of daffodils and a lighted oil-lamp: the glow from this rimmed the faces from below. Stuck to the glass was a cutting from some old magazine. It read: "And a rousing song to finish off a jolly evening, with folk-singing just as our forefathers used to know it. The song has passed from one singer to the next, but now it's 'Time, please!' Hands are joined around the table and *Auld Lang Syne* prepares all for the parting of the ways."

Other photographs of a similar date and style showed each of the singers individually or in pairs, seated with their glasses of ale on simple benches or chairs. One old fel-low—wearing a hat whose shape suggested it might have been designed for forcing rhubarb—was framed sitting in front of a tiny, cross-glazed window. And there, the Mole realised, was the very window itself, right next to the pic-ture, though everything else around it had changed.

Another cutting opened: "Chairmal of the evening is Peter Molekin, and he hopes ..." But the cracked and yellowing paper ended there, though the Mole could see from one remaining edge that it came from a magazine called *Pictureplay*. To his right, above the fireplace, two stiffly formal dancers were shown with the caption, "The mals who dance. The fiddler strikes up *Jack's The Boy*, Percy Hoggett and one-eyed Liney Leverton dance their famous hornpipe in the narrow bar. Mr Bunbury is the fiddler, and for the next entry he changes to an accordion ..."

Well, well, thought the Mole, breathing out hard. He raised his glass to his lips, but did not drink. Well, well, well. There it was; he could not deny it. He had found his old gaffers in a pub, after all—in one shape if not another.

"—'Oo'd've oddsed i', eh?" said the barmal as the Mole went back to his seat. He was nodding towards the photographs. "They were still doin' all tha', right 'ere in this pub, up till—wo'?—twenny years ago? Assright!—A small handful, uv corse, as i' then wuz."

"Twenty years ..." said the Mole, looking back towards the nearest photograph.

"Iss place wuz *famous* fer i'. Seein' as they wuz the on'y ones still doin' i' anywhere round 'ere. As we do 'ear."

"Wot, you still finkin' uv that promoshun uv yours, then, 'Enry?" asked furball-the-first.

"*Oh yeh.* We got to do i'. Now we got the carspace? Got ter get them dahn 'ere *summow*.—Eh? Good fer the business, Darren. Good fer the business. May 'ave ter chaynge these tables, too. Make i' a bi' more tradish'nul, like."

"Wot, not yer Tradish'nul-American, then?"

"No, not yer Tradish'nul-American, Leigh, no. In this case. More sort of Tradish'nul-*Tradish'nul*. We might 'ave a Speshul Evenin'. Every fird Fridy in the munf or wo'ever. Ge' 'em all dressed up in the old cloves like, yeh. One uv those ol' girls is still alive today, I 'eard. Don' s'pose we'll ever ge' 'er dahn 'ere now though."

"You won' ge' *me* dressed up in old cloves, 'Enry."

"We might no' be able to find any to fit you, Mor'imer, if you don' mind me sayin' so, mayt, so don' you worry abaht that, eh? Nah, but wot we need" (here the Stoat's eyes roamed towards the Mole) "... wot we need, really, is to ge' the ABC dahn 'ere. Intit. Ge' the ahtside world in? Ge' some *cov'rage*, right? Ge' the place known for iss, wot-yoo-call-'em, Old-Time Resturrashuns. There's enough bleedin' 'istory rahnd *'ere* ter be goin' on wiv!"

The Mole had finished his half of Mild by now, and his pickled egg, and his crisps, so he bade the four round animals farewell and left, only to be stalled inside the greenhouse-entrance by the slipping of a clip. He had stopped next to the building's original front door, and on the wall here he saw another picture—a painting, or more exactly a reproduction of one, which sunlight had slowly bleached down to a slim range of blues and peacock-greens. It had also been burned through at its centre, most likely by the inspired application of some drunkard's cigarette. But none of this did anything to alter the strength of the Mole's reaction when he saw it.

The painting was one of those anonymous Victorian pastorals done in a style that threw details such as stones in the foreground into focus, but generalised and blurred most of the foliage. It showed a small, winding, reed-fringed river, a hump-backed stone bridge, a flock of sheep on the road with behind them a young shepherdess, still crossing the bridge and pointing to something. There were birds in flight, a tiny child playing at the water's edge; and there—beyond perfect flower-stained meadows—a perfect, round-capped row of what could only have been elms.

Perhaps it was the effect of the Mild, but within seconds of seeing this picture the Mole's eyes had filled to the brim with tears, which quickly formed rivulets along the black fur of his nose and dripped to the tiles below. He felt himself swaying—internally, if not in reality—the emotion

itself swaying up through him like some compelling tide of
insight, one to which he alone in the world was party. He
took a step towards the painting, grasping its fake-gilded
frame in both hands. Then he laid one of his paws flat
against the surface.

"This is where I belong!" he whispered. "This—here—
a place where ..." He could not hold back a sob. "Where
you didn't have to *know* about ... All this. Where you did-
n't have to *know*.—O! Let me back! Let me back!"

He gripped the frame again, staring and peering, almost
as if by so doing he might find some stairway on to its perspective—one that he could climb. But, even as he was
doing this, the greenhouse-door behind him was opening
quietly. A strangely familiar voice—itself full of emotion
and anxious surprise—said, "Mo ... Mu ... Mr—Mu-
Mo-ah-le. ...? Is it—*is* it you? It is you. It *is* you!—They
were right! At last!—*At last*! In the eleventh hour, the fifty-
ninth minute, the—the thirty-third second.—Oh, thank
Pan for that!"

Mopping his face as best he could (he could do little
about the floor), the Mole turned in amazement to see
none other in the world than Mr Gordon R. Rette. He was
looking more than usually haggard, and stood as if poised
in mid-dither, half way between the Mole and the open
door. "Just—er—excuse me—just—one moment," he
said, and half-ran back into the car park. "It's *him*!" he
shouted. "It is him! Well done, mals. Right this time.
—You cracked it!"

Beyond the glass, two very large, muscular and black-
suited rabbits in Shaydes nodded unsmilingly, and sank
back into the front seats of an immense black car. They
remained, waiting and motionless, with all four doors wide
open. Then one of them pulled out a Deracitel.

Justin Rette had arrived back from school only moments before his father's car pulled in at the front of the house, complete with one small passenger plus panniers, tent, maps and bicycle, one half of the latter dangling loosely from the boot. "*Mole!*" he shouted with pleasure, emerging from the front door. "Hey! Great to see you, mal!—Did you find it, then?"

As may perhaps be guessed, the Mole was already out-stripping all normal levels of confusion by several degrees towards Absolute. "... Hello ...? ... Justin ...?" he mumbled feebly.

"—But did you *find* it?" repeated the young rat.

The Mole stared vacantly. "... 'Find' ...? ... 'It' ...?"

"Like you said in your letter! You remember?—England!"

" ..England? ... England. My letter ... O.—O! In my letter—the one that I left?—Yes.—*England*." The Mole paused again, looked at the sky, and scratched his head. "—Um, well. I ... You know, Justin, I'm not sure, to be honest. I really don't know. I do hope I didn't. I do, most seriously.—But even so, you know, I'm rather afraid that I might've."

PART THREE

In Farawaysia

Without a conquest you cannot have an aristocracy . . .
George St Bernard Shaw

Oh I believe in yesterday . . .
McRatney/Lemming

CHAPTER FIFTEEN

A VISION OF AEROPLANES

The Mole was not looking for explanations. Nor, as it happened, was he *looking*: he sat now with his eyes squeezed tightly shut. Above all he was not looking—or even turning his head—in the direction of the round-ended, bulge-framed slot of a window next to which he found himself trapped. Even if he had allowed himself a further sight of what lay around him, no one on this Earth or off it could have begun to explain to him how—just a little less than forty eight hours after he had humped his way along his last East of England dust-track—he could find himself seated inside a long, luxuriant, faintly vibrating and curve-walled carriage—a carriage running not along rails, nor tramlines, nor on a road, nor even on a waterway, but (he squeezed his eyes yet tighter) … but … it wasn't possible, he knew that for sure … but—flying?

FLYING?! How could a *train* ever FLY!? Yet the single glimpse the Mole had had out of the window when the sun came up (and then went down again a moment later) (a point he flatly refused to contemplate) had revealed to him the most stomach-sinkingly moan-inducing perspective ever known in the long history of sinking stomachs—one that was simply beyond imaginable: down, down, down, DOWN on to what did most horribly resemble the tops of clouds ...

The Mole's problem—an old problem for him by now, but freshly, even stimulatingly, presented to him here—was that the perspective along the inside of the "plain" (as Mr Rette had inexplicably named the machine) was little less disturbing in its way than what might or might not lie beneath it. For here—arranged ahead of them across a broad expanse of shell-pink armchair seats on cygnet-grey carpets, with much trimming at the edges in hard gold braid—there sat groups and gaggles of impressively needle-toothed animals. Most of their species, or possible species, were quite unknown to the Mole; but all of them, he was convinced, must have weasels for second cousins. When they spoke—and they were doing so increasingly, now, since breakfast had begun to be served—they spoke, by and large, in the most confoundingly peculiar range of not-quite-English accents.

An airborne mole is, or was, something of an existential oxymoron—an observation the Mole might have made himself had he only been master of the jargon. The thought that beneath this floor at his feet there was now nothing at all—not even so much as the dozens of occupied floors of an impossibly tall City megalith—nothing but an incalculable amount of empty air between himself and the embracing soils of the planet surface: this thought was enough to reduce the small animal to a persistent-jellificatory-state bordering on the liquid. Thus he sat now, as he had done for most of the past three hours, in the deepest of jellied silences, gripped by a terror so insistently mortal that his ribcage was moving barely enough to let him breathe.

"What may I get you for breakfast, sir?" asked a widely smiling female animal (species: indeterminate), in a voice of gentle reverence. Her uniform was the shade of a ripe Victoria plum, a fact the Mole ascertained through a three-percent squint of politeness. "If you would wish it, we have the full English breakfast, including very fine devilled kidneys, in honour of our guests, with kedgeree to follow? Or you might prefer smoked salmon with eggs Spanish-style? Or manta-ray in Mornay sauce? Or New England oyster stew? Or if you have an appetite this morning, we have a chef's special of powerfully spiced Wyoming free-range chicken in a dark peanut béchamel …?"

"—Mmm …" said the Mole heroically, breathing as he did so. "Mmmm ..!"

"Just—coffee, I think," said Mr Rette, grinning horribly. "—For both of us, yes. If you don't mind. Though it all sounds very nice, of course. Oh, er—and could I have a plain bread roll perhaps? No, no butter. Thank you, ha, ha."

"—Lovely girl," he said to the Mole a moment later, testing for signs of talpic consciousness. But his travelling-companion's vision range had once more declined to zero.

The Mole might have stood a slightly better chance of dealing with all this if it had happened more slowly: over a period of ten to fifteen years, say. But in the single day he had spent at—or more exactly, in relation to—the Rette base-camp, he had been whisked at speed from one place to another with barely time to speak: first to a St James fur-barber, where he had been most intensively scrubbed, and groomed, and combed, and loathsomely scented; then on to Saville Row where he had been lowered into an already three-quarters-constructed charcoal-grey suit that was pinned up and virtually completed while still on him; thence to a Wigmore Street optician where he had been fitted (or more accurately, disguised) in a pair of Antonio Immolio-Santoliquido square-to-oval slimline hornrims. Now, on his left wrist, he also sported a strap-on pocket-watch: this, Mr Rette had informed him, in a tone border-

ing on the mystic, was a genuine Rolonn-Rolof. His dis-
guise ran even to the nature of his undergarments: these
included a pair of nearly ankle-length Melvin Schwein
"Desiderata" boxer shorts in sheerest Chaoping silk.

This transformation completed, the Mole might have
walked past the armed guards of any corporate tower or
installation in the world with barely a flick of his (as he
heard it) eye-dee card, also now carried, so fully did he
seem the coolly thrusting young mole executive—at least,
so long as he did not speak or move.

As to *why* he was seated here now, in this bolted-down
airborne armchair, if he had tried to explain it to himself
at all he would not have got much further than to put it
down to his habitual bane, consideracy. Mr Wyvern-Toad
had expected him to be there, apparently—yes, and very
much expected it. And Mr Rette had obviously been distraught to the point of imminent collapse at the possibility he might not be. And as things stood, well, how *could* he
have let the animal down?

All his attempts to find out where they would be going
had come to nothing, too. In the one brief moment when
he had been able to speak to the Toad at all, he had replied
simply that he should not worry himself about the matter
in the slightest. "We will be everywhere and nowhere!" he
told him. "Much more in the air than on the ground. Just
think of it, Mr Mole, as a little trip to Farawaysia, eh? An
expedition—an expedition! To the airs of the south
Atlantic!" So there it was, and here he was, in Farawaysia.
And all of it without having taken one of the "magic pills"
Mr Rette had offered him to calm his nerves on their last
night on the ground. (Mr Rette himself had taken four in
one swallow.)

One of the less insistently disturbing, but nonetheless
really quite disturbing, and widespread, things the Mole
had noticed about the too-late world was that it hummed.

It hummed buzzingly, for example, in the Rettes' kitchen. It hummed very quietly, but also whiningly, in the Toad Tower, outside of the Toad's own office, which was wholly silent. It hummed *almost* soothingly, but even so insistently, inside this airborne projectile, after the fashion of some far-off, ceaseless Thrumming-of-the-Spheres: sole evidence of the fact that all present were being lobbed across the planet's middle atmosphere at a speed the Mole would certainly never want to know. In all its ubiquitous forms, rather like a good butler, this humming seemed to be suggesting that whatever went on where *it* was present would, could, and indeed must go on just the same forever and beyond all questioning.

So it was that when the Mole thought he heard a new deepening in tone of the hum-du-jour, arising as if at his left side, then growing in volume, the change was arresting enough to achieve a small miracle: he opened his eyes and—against every dreg of instinct left in him—looked through the window for the second time. And there—no, but there, *there*, how *could* it be?—floating at his left paw like some gigantic, black and *rigor-mortis*-stiffened shark-with-wings, riding the atmosphere above an ocean of cloud, was—well, but what was it, though? What was it—what?!

The Mole grabbed at Mr Rette's left lapel, and then his fore-arm, from which Mr Rette detached him again immediately. "Ggggg—!" he said, pointing with anfractuous arm in the general direction of the black shark shape. "Ggggg?—Ggggg?!" And in a higher-pitched, imploring tone he added "Mmmmm!!"

"Mr Mole ..." whispered the Rat through locked back teeth. "Calm down! Please! It's the *refuelling* jet. For *backup*. You understand?"

"Ggggg?!"

"We won't need it! Don't worry! I don't suppose for one moment we'll need it." (Here the Rat's tone became a shade more introspective.) "... Not unless there are *major* glitches, which is unlikely. Or some of the snafus get catastrophized, of course, or vice versa. Which is possible. Er ..."

"Mmmmm??"

"—No, really! Just—you know—just hang in on there, Mr Mole.—*On in* there!—Got it?"

But the Mole seemed unencouraged: he was pointing at the sinister black outline just as he had before. The Rat looked at him with the expression of one who fears, indeed knows, his words will be as so much drizzle on a sun-baked rock. "Great gnatblacked ...!!—*Friendly*. One of us? A 'friendly flyer'?" Here Mr Rette went so far as to flap his hands twice, in the style of a tweety-bird, and grin.

The Mole relaxed just a little, allowing his gaze to rest on the curve of empty seats immediately in front of him. But within thirty seconds, his urgent clawing grip was locked once more upon the Rette-suit worsted, and his wandering arm was pointing as before.

"—Oh, *those* ..." responded his keeper, sighing and passing a paw across his brow. "They've just caught up with us for a while as well. Don't *worry!* There must be some reason. They usually follow on behind in pairs, in my experience. They're just the Security. McMinc Security?—There are a lot of Very Important Animals on board this plane today, Mr Mole. *A lot.* Wouldn't want to get shot out of the sky by anyone, would we? Major, *major* impacts on World Trade if we did, ha, ha, I didn't say that!"

"Mmmmm?!—Mmm—mmm—mmmm ..!"

"For Pans—*Please!* Keep your moans down! I didn't mean it *would* happen! I mean, come on—look at them. Those things can only have come out of the factory the week before last! Typical McMinc, of course. Sneak-bombers, hey? Third-generation Winglock Sneaks, no less. Up-to-the-wire slam-dunk hard-ball-splatters, that's what those things are! *Nothing* could get past *them!*" The Rat's gaze drifted outwards. "... Though why they are all flying ... Oh, bl—!"

"Mmmmmm?!—Mmm—mmm—mmm—mmmm ..."

"No, no ... that's all right. That's fine ... just fine. You see? They're splitting up and falling back now. Ha. Just some technical thing, I knew it. Have a sip of your coffee, it'll make you feel better. Possibly.—Go on. Go on!"

Still uttering low-level moans, the Mole reached out for his cup with a groping paw.

"Will either of you gent'mals care to take a Jackouzel before the Meeting commences?" The beautiful animal was back again.

"—Er, no. No, thank you," said Mr Rette. "We're wonderfully relaxed as it is."

Blind terror or no, the Mole did realise that a meeting of some kind was to be held up here in the air. Thanks to Mr Rette's earlier urgent attempts to, as he put it, "bring him up to velox", he also knew that crucial decisions were to be made today in this carriage—decisions that could go a very long way towards cementing the future of "World Trade" and the role in it of the various corporate giants represented. He had even been included in introductions to some of the participants, as he had stood numbly on the afterglow-or-dusk-lit infinities of some flat and suspiciously non-English space last night, or morning, in the transition between the looming and taper-snouted murk of Mr Wyvern-Toad's own Wealden Plunderer (named *The Espansiva*) and that of Mr Mydace McMinc's exactly like-sized Velociraptor (*The Inextinguishable*).

This was to be—Mr Rette had explained—a pared-down, main-player Aerial Summit. More precisely, it was to be a *pre*-Summit Aerial Summit, since the organisations concerned—allies and rivals alike—were hoping to agree "informally" a joint strategy by which the Summit proper—the forthcoming World Mystery Consortium, scheduled for the autumn of the year in Houston, Texas—could be steered in their favour.

The aim of this spirited campaign group was straightforward: to stimulate and, over time, vastly increase the use of the internal combustion engine, and the consumption of petrol, around the world—this in the face of a growing body of scientific evidence (and of course, the Rat had not been able *not* to mention this) suggesting that same world's climate was being driven rapidly haywire by, as it happened, the consumption of petrol, and the use of the combustion engine. To this end the participants had only recently formed themselves into a new alliance known as the Blacktop Consumers' Coalition.

Amongst the many high-flying corporate representatives on board this morning were Mr Gulf Gopherit of Mexe-Con, Mr Chuck Hogwood of Schmerzler, Mr Hundt Baskervole of Foredo Motors and Mr Strobe Volebrush, deputy CEA of General Armaments. Also airborne were a number of other luminaries closely associated with their host, Mydace McMinc. They included Mr Warren R. Bitt, multi-multi-billionaire and Market seer, upon the breath of whose word the fortunes of entire phalanxes of corporate activity could be made or lost overnight; PR-mal Mr Harmony van Sleek of the ReMind Agency, and his British-born colleague Mr Sidney "Wes" Sleazel; Professor Matt Mustrak, Researcher in Chief at the McMinc-funded Slyde Research Institute; Mr Bing Lemmog, Deputy Director of Globobank, the world's largest and most powerful bank, along with a number of deputies from Europe and elsewhere; and Messrs Hartz and Martz "The Mart" Martenson, joint heads of the Burgerburg burg-burger chain and the *Toyz "For" Pupz* franchise, and extranational shopping mall developers. British-headquartered multicorps were represented, amongst others, by the redoubtable Mr Humfrey Wyvern-Toad of Toad Transoceanic and his three close colleagues Messrs Clutchfund Stoatdegrave, Gordon R. Rette, and Mole, and by Messrs Neville Gnasheram and Iain Grubhogg-Hedge of AnglosaxOil. There was more than a little truth in Mr Rette's observation that there would be major impacts if this particular private jet were ever to fall flaming from the skies.

As to the conference host himself, even in the Mole's distracted gaze he stood out as in some awful way remarkable: an elderly mink, slightly stooped perhaps, but with nothing lost of the intensity of his distance-penetrating stare, or of the personal magnetism of earlier years. His barking laugh was that of an animal who knows himself to be not only at the centre of events but actively, moment to moment, generating the stuff of the inner sanctum he occupies. Just as his much-honoured father, Mydace McMinc I, had done, the old mink sported a pair of rimless *pince-nez* which rested miraculously at the tip of his short, brown torpedo-snout, never slipping from it even when he was at his most animated, his hard little green eyes rising above the lenses in conversation like dark moons escaping a joint eclipse.

It had been McMinc Senior, back in the last days of the nineteenth century, who bump-started the family fortune, frozen footed in the deer and coonskin uniform of a Yukon sourdough. His often repeated dictum—"Every cent I made up there, I got it out the ground with my own two paws. And I played it fair!"—was still on his son's lips even today. Though whether the first McMinc could have said quite the same of his entrepreneurial operations in the six hectic decades following his return from Dawson City, or whether the second could ever have made such a claim throughout his working life, was open to question—in theory, if not in practice.

With the vast wealth from his Klondike lucky strike behind him, Mydace McMinc I had quickly established an old-style extractive, industrial and agricultural empire incorporating, amongst other pursuits, lumber, shipping, cattle ranching, South African diamond mines, and Mississippi cotton and Central American sugar plantations. But from the start there had been one commodity that had lent a Caesarist stability to this far-flung network: oil. Mydace McMinc I had established his oil interests as early as any other entrepreneur in history, so much that even by 1912 the Supreme Court of the Federation (which not only cared about such things then, but still believed it had the power to influence them) ordered the monopoly held by his company, Ensign Oil, to be broken up in the public interest.

Yet a mere two years later, a new branch of the old tree, smelling just as sweet by another name, could be found getting assistance where most needed from the nation's military in Tampico, Mexico, where, for whatever reasons, it was not safe to sink oil wells without ordinance. A few years later, on the China coast, a similar diplomatic mission was overseen in similar style by the very same General. By the time Ensign's prospectors arrived in Saudi Arabia in the early 1930s, the company's bulldozers had been able to move in with barely a soldier in sight to destroy the orchards and the settled ancient communities of the oilfield lands and disperse their culture to the desert winds. Barely a Bedu passed through there in the early years who did not hear predictions of vast personal wealth impending, sometimes direct from the lips of company representatives. Yet even the sheikh who claimed the right to sign away the concessions to the land received no more than a few tens of thousands of dollars for his betrayal.

By the late 1950s, the name of Ensign Oil had vanished for good, replaced by what was now the globally familiar

"Exxit"—symbol of the giant Exxit Oil Corporation. And it was this company which remained at the driving heart of today's incomparably larger, more elusive and multi-faceted McMinc Inc, a transnational of such power and territorial penetration there was not a chief politician in the western world—not even, it was said, the President of the United States himself—who would not jump to the receiver when he knew Mydace McMinc II was there on the line.

Over the decades, McMinc Inc had absorbed many thousands of one-time rivals of every style and shape, either shutting them down the next day—the normal practice—or rebuilding them as submissive faceless units of the patrimony. The old mink's tactics in this field won him the nickname of "The Gannet", the most recent swimmer of significance to enter his expansible gullet being another North American oil giant, Movit. The combined annual income of Exxit and Movit alone was now said to be greater than that of the united Germany and the Iberian Peninsula together (excluding the Basque Country, but including the Balearic Isles in a good tourist year).

Mnemonomous readers may already have noted more than a few correspondences between Mydace McMinc's career and family history and those of Mr Humfrey Wyvern-Toad. It is also the case that whilst, so far as anyone knew, no openly heated words had ever passed between the two animals, most of their exchanges did tend towards the chainmailed end of friendly. More than once they had been observed at meetings such as the one to be held today, watching one another with warily assessing eyes, each like a championship player on the Centre Court poised to block moves his opponent may not yet have thought of making.

Based on the most impartial estimates of his share options alone, and with the enigmadillions rounded up for convenience, Mr McMinc's alleged personal fortune now stood in the region of nine hundred and ninety-nine obfuscatillion, nine hundred and ninety-nine crypticrillion, nine hundred and ninety-nine arcanatillion dollars. But since no one knew for a fact what he was worth, opinions were divided as to whether his fortune, on paper or off it, outstripped the Toad's. The burning issue between them, though—as unmentionable as the size and uses of a private expense account—was whether one or the other of their two shifting empires would ever prove absorbent enough to engorge the other. It was a sure thing that, if such an event ever did take place, there would be one more obfuscatillionaire to add to the global unemployment totals at nine o'clock on the following morning.

Another half an hour went by, and during this—for a few breath-deprived hearbeats at a time—the Mole began to peer sideways out of the window by him. It was not that he had overcome his terror—far from it—but as so often in this age of machine-made possibilities, the dreadful new perspectives opened up to him had their own potent magnetism, drawing his eye back and back as surely as the view down off a riverine cliff, or into a marl pit, will draw the eye of any passing picnicker. And though it still felt madly, *madly* wrong to be looking at the clouds not as Nature intended but from, as it were, the backstage angle, that did not make them any the less beautiful, hiding all the world as they did under their undulating eiderdown of whites smudged over greys.

But even as the Mole was beginning to get himself just a little used to the grandeur of what he saw, the view began to alter, with veils of mist whipping close past the aircraft's wing and then vanishing again in a fraction of a second. Holes started to appear in the clouds beneath him, revealing the most bellyachingly moan-inducing new perspectives

down, and down again, to what could only be the surface
of the Earth itself. The little burrower's mind, already
severely challenged, grasped out for some measure of distance, size, or perspective that could help him make sense
of what he saw. For weren't those distant, shadowed, fis-
sured crags and drop-drop-*drop*away slopes beneath them—
peppered as they were with isolated, sand-like grains—a
range of hills? But no—no!—no, O no! They weren't *hills*.
They were *mountains* (he covered his eyes, then peered
aghast once more), *mountains, great towering* mountains, their
vastness disguised by the distance in the sky above them of
this insanely airborne first-class smoker! And those
"grains" weren't tiny rocks at all: they were *boulders* the size
of barns or bigger! ...

"O—o—o— o—o—o—ooooohhhh!" This moan
earned him a vigorous Rette rib-nudge, though the sound
would have registered less than 0.1 on the Moanster scale.

Of course, with such a view, the Mole could not now
stop himself from looking, if only in bursts with moments
of recovery. And as he did so, the non-possible towering
mountains drifted back to his left, to be very gradually
replaced by lesser heights, some of these clad up to their
crests in forests. Yet here and there, and there beyond in the
furthest distances, the forests had been plucked away to
leave nothing but a dusty-looking goose flesh. And there
now, directly below him, the sides of two long parallel
ridges had been cut open in sinuous, chasmic black strips
that seemed to run on for miles: the frayed, black-grey
edges of what could only be spoil heaps reached out
towards the farmlands on both sides as if straining to
engulf them. In one place nearby, then another, the very
mountain peaks themselves had been sliced off and discarded like the tops of boiled eggs, and in their place lay
flat, creamy-looking pits. And the rivers in this country, he
saw, ran black as ink. In the ribboning chasm-strips, bright

objects moved, coloured points in a mobile design, tinier than the toys of ants: they might have been machines. There was a haze everywhere, too, that did not look like fog or mist and the rivers here, and further out where the wing-tip pointed, pulsed black as ink, and again there black, and there, and through the centre of some large town, black as any ink.

Within twenty minutes, the Velociraptor and its entourage had left all sight of mountains and hills behind them, climbing up into a sky as brilliant blue as any the Mole had seen. Under this, every detail of the ground below was visible. Beneath him now lay a great flatland, rolling away in all directions for—he couldn't begin to guess—hundreds—thousands?—of miles. The surface of this expanse was shifting strangely, the faintest of oscillating patterns coming and going on its surface. It was divided up with absolute symmetry as if by some dictatorial zealot living in dread of the slightest hint of singularity, on a deadly-repetitive layout of squares and rectangles based on a grid of roads running straight as a tomb builder's plumb-rule. The patterns recalled what the Mole saw when a sharp breeze was playing in the fur of his own forearm; and, observing this, he made sense of what he saw.

For this land was under crops—and what could these be but wheat, or barley?—set at uniform distances, away and away towards the very horizon of the planet. With newly sinking heart, the Mole recognised as he least wished to that the great, *great* voyage he had made across the East of England, all those weeks' travelling, might have been fitted into ... he couldn't guess, he couldn't begin to guess! ... some insignificant corner of what stretched beneath him now. There below, Mr Pottidge-Pherytte's perfection of regulation-cropping had been realised absolutely, unconditionally. Beyond it, there was nothing left to hope for or imagine.

The Mole was just about to withdraw under a pair of padded black eyeshades, given to him for night-flying. But an anxiously-confident young weasel, slippery-suited as the rest, approached Mr Rette and informed him in a cleric's voice that the Conference would open in ten minutes: guests were invited to make their way forward to the Conference Chamber.

A moment later, Mr Wyvern-Toad turned into view from a seat cluster three yards in front of them, where he had been talking to Mr Gnasherham. "To arms, Gordon!" he said, beaming, and, raising a wry eyebrow, "... Mr Mole!"

The Water Rat turned to the Mole for a moment. Then he turned away again. He did not say a word, but what he thought was writ large across both tail and whiskers: "Nothing *good* can come of this."

CHAPTER SIXTEEN

THE MALL IS ALL

The Conference Chamber of the *Inextinguishable* took up the entire central section of the immense aircraft, having at its centre an oval table falling just short of perfect circularity—even this space could not quite accommodate that. Close above its marbloid surface hung a large covered lamp —also oval, and made in the style of a light for a billiard table—whose brilliance fell only so far out as the seat-places at the rim. In the centre of the table, on a white plinth, and with low-level lights arranged around it, stood a globe on which the continents had been embossed. Its subtle gleaming drew the eye: it had been finished in beaten gold.

As the Mole was led—more than a little loose at the knee—towards his own named place he realised, with not-quite relief, that this part of the "plain" was without windows. He was just about to sit down when two objects resembling very wide rolls of wallpaper began to unfurl themselves on opposite sides of the table, down the outward-sloping walls. Immediately they stopped moving, the planet Earth appeared again immense on each, parts beautifully obscured by banks, spatterings, standing whirlpools of cloud. At his seat now, the Mole peered and peered again from behind his confusing spectacles: these pictures did have the look about them of something almost real.

The style of the table lighting did little to increase the charm of those present at the meeting. The light bounced back on to the undersides of their faces from the white table surface and the papers lying at each place, throwing the tops of snouts and heads into shadow, projecting devilish little points of light into gloss-black eyes, and limning the already brilliant whites or yellow-whites of many a set of fangs.

Mydace McMinc scuttled in through the shadows to stand at his place in half silhouette, a cheroot doubly impaled in his mouth, in front of one of the tall sloping screens. All stood as he picked up a short glass, raising it first to the gilded globe before him and then in a sweep to both of the screens. "Gent'mals," he said, "I give you— The Territory."

Each of the animals at the table (barring one, who was confused) raised their glasses after him, and drank. "The Territory! ... The Territory!" went up the snarling, growling, barking, but immensely civilised cry. The tip of many a damp nose glistened there now, like rose petals in a heavy dew at sunrise.

Whilst the Conference was reseating itself, laughing and joking in low voices, a secondary circle of aides and others took shape beyond it in the shadows. The Mole turned to Mr Rette for illumination: he could find out, at least, what some of these strange beasts *were*. But Mr Rette had got only so far as to explain, through the most gritted of teeth, that Mr Bing Lemmog (with his grey-brown fur and stunted tail and red, red eyes) was indeed a southern bog-lemming by birth, and that Professor Mustrak (with his striking auburn mane) was, indeed and in fact, a muskrat with an ancestry in the northern marshes, when the host to the gathering spoke again.

"Okay," he said. "To any I have not said this yet—welcome to the party." The light glanced dimly off the low-reflective surfaces of his antique eyeglasses, and as he spoke his white whiskers flickered at the corners of his face like fragments of some Renaissance princeling's ruff.

"Oh ... Mydace ... Sorry to interrupt so soon!" It was Mr Wyvern-Toad. "Ha, ha."

"Humfrey!" said Mr McMinc, staring through his grin. "Good to hear from you!"

"Yes ... ahh ... at the risk of causing complete chaos—we don't want that—"

"We sure don't!" said Warren R. Bitt, and everybody laughed, almost to hysteria, at the precision and wit of it.

The Toad bided his time. "I simply felt that we might have *more* of a party if the seating plan were just a little less—what should one say?—oppositional? All the Brits and colleagues over here, all the Yanks and colleagues over there? All the Japanese—oh but, now, where *are* the Japanese?"

When the laughter subsided again Mr McMinc—genuinely pleased, it seemed, at the mood of this opening—snarled back, "Yah, sure Humf! Mix it up a bit, huh? Just so long as we don't rock the pandanged aircraft!"

"If I could suggest—where could we begin? ... Oh ... If I could swap say Mr Mole, here" ("Mm—o—o—o—o!" moaned the Mole through closed lips) "with Mr Gopherit, for example? And then, Mr Rette, with—ah—Mr Baskervole? Next-but-one? And on, like that? I'm sure we'll all feel a lot more like, to be sure, the friends we all are here.—Yes?"

This game of unmusical chairs completed, the Mole found himself sitting between Mr McMinc and Mr Harmony van Sleek (with Mr Rette not untwitchingly beyond him), whilst on the far side of the Mink—due to a certain imbalance in the numbers—those of the American contingent still sat much as they had done before.

"Okay, well I guess I can just run straight on in here," said Mydace McMinc. "It's not as if anyone here hasn't read the script. Or written it. Hah!" (Deep bellysnarling laughter.) "And, boy, do we have some great scriptwriters working on this. So. On the BCC front we have guarantees—solid guarantees ..."

"Solid, Mydace," said a young mink from the outer circle, clenching his tail very hard as he did so. "Solid as a goose-egg nugget. Ashes-on-the-roses, month-end, latest."

"—that the US government *will not sign* any pandanged mallet-headed 'treaty' with *anybody* on emissions. Yup. Finally. They came good. Cut emissions, you cut jobs. Cut emissions?"

"*You cut jobs!*" responded a chorus, in and out of the shadows.

"Emissions *are* jobs," said Mr Gopherit, in the *basso profundo* of one-hundred-per-cent conviction.

Mr McMinc nodded. "Even the unions go along with *that*. And we got the Blacktop Consumers' Coalition together just in time to impress that rather obvious fact on our—somebody give me a name for 'em, boys—our 'colleagues' in government?" (There was more muted, half-serious laughter at this remark.)

"Government has to know—hey, *every* government around this planet has to know—it's all goin' to go right on." The old mink opened his hands, and shrugged. "It's all goin' to go right on, just like it did before. Tough, huh? Animals are goin' to go out there in the morning, and *get* in their cars, and *turn* those keys, and drive. *And drive.* Am I right? or am I right?"

"Wall Street relies on it," said Warren R. Bitt. His personal assistant, Ms Sunni Bunnidust, a fellow-jackrabbit, stared at the backs of his long, broad, black-tipped ears with the gaze of one who worships only wisdom.

"Now there's an animal who was born with his eyes open," said Mydace McMinc.

"It's a moral obligation," said Schmerzler chief Mr Hogwood, his strong-jawed, belligerent face searching for some imagined opposition beyond the brilliance of the table. "To consoom."

"Now that is the *truth*," said Mr McMinc, and a light barrage of "Yups", "Yeps" and "Agreeds" went the round of the oval. "And no bunch of chowder-headed, flap-jawed 'scientists', so-called, in any outside-funded institution *anywhere* is goin' to prove anything to anybody that links our franchise—our on-goin' *planetary franchise*" (he threw an arm out towards one of the screens) "with all these hoo-hah 'climate changes' they keep singing about." A note of ferocious threat black-edged these words. "Hey, mals. I'm kiddin' with you. Am I kiddin' with you?"

"We now have—er ... effective and extensive cross-discipline counter-research," said Professor Mustrak. His broad face bore a smile fixed upon it by Nature, so that it was impossible to tell if he was smiling, and his big, thick tail waved in the shade behind him like a drowning poet. "—Of the most *helpful* kind."

"Darn tootin' we do, Matt," said the mink-in-chief. "You mals up there at the Slyde have done good work there."

"Our research *shows*," said the Professor, "in summary, that to burn fossil fuels in quite large quantities—in point of fact, in very large quantities—is ..."

"Good for the *planet*?"

"Good for the *planet*."

"But—um ..." said a small, low voice, from a point almost exactly two and a half feet to the left of the Conference host. Even in his current state of in-flight agitation, the Mole simply could not help himself. He had to speak out—he just had to—when he heard what seemed like nonsense spoken. ". . . I mean, you know, if you don't mind me askin'—is it true?—That?"

"Oh!—No. . . . No!" said Mr McMinc, and laughed his penetrating laugh. "It's not *true*.—Well hell, who knows! Maybe it is true. Maybe it's true and maybe it ain't. All it has to do is look true—right, Matt? And we know you're always the number one guy to get *that* nailed."

". . . Er . . ." replied Professor Mustrak, slightly compressing the top sheet of the notepad in front of him. His smile now looked as if it had been starched across his face.

Mr McMinc frowned. "Frankly, Mr . . ." His eyes refocused slowly on the small animal seated next to him. "—Do I know you?"

"Mole," said the Mole.

The old mink stared at him for a moment, and his gleaming round green eyes narrowed very slightly behind their lenses. The end of his tail curled out an inch, then contracted again. "Well," he said, the very faintest hint of a threat in the air. "And how are *you* today, Mr Mole?"

"O.—Me? O. I'm quite well, thank you very much. Apart from being up here, of course."

"Good . . . good. Normally, you see, Mr Mole," (and here the Mink's gaze drifted away across the centre of the table in the general direction of the Chief Executive of Toad Transoceanic) "we don't bother discussing itty-bitty details like that one you just raised, you catch my drift? I'm just a tad surprised you don't know that. You got to get your bugs in a row there, Mr Mole."

Mr Rette added a final touch to a well-observed small sketch of a rat-skull and crossbones on his notepad. "*The centre cannot hold*," he said, inaudibly.

Mr McMinc turned back to the table. "Okay, now. On the D-reg initiative, what do I know you don't? We're not gonna call it that, on the notepaper. 'Deregulation'?—I don't think so! No no no no no *no*." (There was another wash of complicit laughter and the baring of many a set of well-made dentures.) "What you got on that, Harmony? You got a headline for us?"

Mr van Sleek, the animal to the Mole's left—a black-footed ferret whose pale cream face-fur was boldly patterned around the eyes by a burglar's mask of black—extended his long neck and scanned the table as if for running prey. "We got a vanilla, Mydace," he replied, in a voice that seemed to move along on well-greased wheels. The Mole could not help noticing that whilst this animal's suit was indistinguishable from the rest, his shirt was much the colour of his eye-patches and, what is more, the collar was *buttoned down*. "We were thinking along the lines, 'Multiplexial Conducement In Franchisisation'? We still maybe need to add a vowel or two there. But it has that slant of dullness?"

"It's in the right space," said Mr McMinc. "—Hell, I'm not sure *I* understand *that*." (Laughter, teeth.) "That's good, Harm. That's good! But among friends, now, I think we'll just stick with D-reg. 'Regulation'?" (He spat out the word.) "We don't need it. Do I hafta say it? We don't want it. It's that thing governments did to tie business down. 'Environmental' regulation? Ball and chain. 'Animal rights', 'health-at-work'? Ball-and-chain, *big* ball-and-chain! We're *way* beyond that now, that was day-before-yesterday. Tomorrow, *we* regulate." He raised an eyebrow, and met the gaze of his colleagues with the very faintest of grins. "Ohh ... where the need occurs, mals. Where the need occurs! *We* decide when. The Market decides." He slapped both paws on the table. "The *Mystery* decides. In the upcoming century—the upcoming millennium! But for the Mystery to be free to decide, we *need* these Deregulation-Regulations. ... Okay, some of you will not yet know Tom Finqueret, Legal Advisor In Chief to McMinc as of two weeks ... Tom ..."

An animal sitting just far back enough from the table for

his face to be lost in shadow—his species once again obscure, at least to the Mole—said, "We're nearing granulation on this. I think I can say, goability is close. It's in the meat-safe." Several others sat behind him, in deeper shade still. "Where the rubber meets the road is: when we put it out of reach. Up, up. Where governments can't go."

"Yah," said Mydace. "That's the picture. We need laws (*our* laws) to eliminate 'laws'. We need powers to remove and transfer 'powers'. But while we're still down here in the engine room, we're just goin' to have to keep those kid-gloves on, yes, okay, I'm sorry—persuade, persuade, persuade. *Our* animals to go on their committees. Our animals to *be* their committees, whenever, wherever. Tomorrow we *are* the government, pandangit! Now that' ain't such a bad idea! No such problems over there in the UK, huh, Humf? We need more governments like that."

Mr Wyvern-Toad grinned back. "Oh, we invented the idea, Mydace. It just took a little while to get it up and running. A reliable historian would bear me out in that, I think."

"Never been a one for history, Humfrey," said the old mink, the golden globe hovering for one moment in both his lenses. "Always preferred makin' it, huh?—Persuade, persuade, persuade ... We'll call it ... Harm?"

"We have a select portfolio on this one, Mydace. In order of current preference, we run: 'Detrusionary Concord'?"

"—Hm." Mr McMinc stroked musingly at the long, oily black guard-hairs on one of his cheeks.

"'Defenestrative Euphony'?"

"Ha ... ah."

"'Supinitional Reciprocity'?"

"Hu ... uh. Go on.—Go on."

"Okay, finally, I blush to say this one, but—'Downward Harmonization'?"

"*Downward Harmonization* ... No, I like *that*, Harm.—I *like that*.—Gent'mals?"

A series of grunts, nods, "Yehs" and "Yups" ran swiftly around the oval of faces.

"There's still a place in the world for poets—eh, Harm?"

"Oh, you're too kind, Mydace," preened Mr van Sleek.

"Okay," said the old mink. "We agree?—We agree. That is the first job of the World Mystery Consortium, next Houston. You bet your *tail* it is! The WMC achieves that goal: 'Harmonization'—Downward. First stage of many future stages. To where *we* want to go. We take off the ball and chain. The world does not *need standards*. It *needs Trade*. This little planet is getting smaller," said Mr McMinc, staring about him over his small round lenses. "We all know that. Every day that comes, we all of us have to fight harder for the primary resources to conduct business. Oilfields? Opencast? First-growth forest? All the stuff still standing in the way—all those spider's webs, all those 'checks and balances'—they have to go. They have to *go*. We have to be able to fight bare-knuckle—whenever, wherever."

Here the Mole, good at sums of the simpler kind, put an available pair of twos together. "Um ... Sorry, Mr Mink, but doesn't that mean—pardon for interrupting, but—those rivers we went over—"

"—Rivers? ... Rivers. *What* rivers?"

"—flowing black—"

"Ohh ... *Oh*.—Kentucky, huh? I guess. Is that what you mean? What about 'em?"

"Well—won't *all* the rivers be flowing black, at the end? Or most of them? If you can dig up everything just where you want?"

"Not if the citizens living near them pay to keep them clean," said Mr Baskervole, leaning towards the Mole in a conspiratorial style.

This brought forth another bout of raucous, pink-gummed laughter from all sectors, into which—grinning himself—Mydace McMinc flung the following, silencing remark: "Let's say the words, huh? Why not? Corporate World Government. Let's put a handle on it, that scenario. *Corporate World Government.* That's the endgame. That's the third act. That's when they start throwing the wreaths."

"—but ..."

"'But' *what*, Mr Mole?" hissed Mr McMinc.

"Well—that is—O! *Blow* it! If there *aren't* any rules—you know—what will there be left to guvv'n *with*?"

The old mink turned fully towards the Mole and bit hard into him with his unsettling green-eyed gaze, holding it on him as if he wished to mesmerize him into silence. But the Mole did not back down, nor look away. After a moment, Mr McMinc too began to laugh, in a hoarse, scathing, sandpapery kind of a way. "Hell, Mr Mole!" he said. "I just can't figure if you are an apple-knockin' clover-kickin' Herkimer-Jerkimer gully-jumper fresh up from the boondocks or a goldarned, pandanged genius!" He fell to laughing once more, and the table (barring two who merely smiled) joined him. "*Dagnabbit*, boy! That is the point! That is the *point!* Corporate World Government *is* government liberated from rules. And the tailline on *that* is—government-without-government. And that's not 'government-without-government' as your much-respected To-We Party likes to have it, a.k.a. '"government"-without-government-but-with-in-parentheses-(government)'. This is *zero*-g-g. *Zero-zero*. If you follow that?"

"Um—"

"The American people—the most sophisticated elec-torat in the whole pandanged world—" went on Mr McMinc," what do they want most of all from their politicians? I'll tell you Mr Mole. They want *Government That Does Not Govern*. —Governments? Hell, they'll just be facilitators!

They'll create the conditions to let it all happen, sure. Then: they hold the line. They police the consoomership, they keep things sweet. They keep the roads open. We're talking the End of Politics here, Mr Mole. 'Ethical' governments? Well of course here in the States we don't have that problem, but if you can find me one about the place—okay, fine—they are just going to have to damned well *de-ethicize*. Lickety-split! Ethics and the Mystery? Oil and water, Mr Mole. 'Society', now—"

"—That difficult word," said Mr Wyvern-Toad.

"'Society'—whatever the hell it may be, Humfrey, that's right, if you can stick a pin in it for me—is there for just one thing: to serve the needs of the Mystery. Not the other way round, boy. Regulations? Forget regulations! We need to open up an oilfield? We need to do it. Forget what's there first. Forest? Tribesmals? Shepherds? Farmland? Villages? *Forget* all that! We need trees for furniture? Fine and dandy, we cut down that forest. We need new grazing for our cattle? New cultivations for coffee, tobacco? We need new lands. We need to cut *down* that pandanged forest. We have to be able to go on moving outwards. *Indefinitely*, you got me? So, whadda we do?" (He shrugged, bringing his claws together in a little Gothic arch) "We set up the World Mystery Consortium. And at this very moment in time we are building the W.M.C. into the big one. *The* Big One, Mr Mole: a Court, no less, that will stand above all other courts *on this planet*. Any government stupid enough to stand in the way of the aims of Business with its 'environmental', 'animal rights' laws, all that cabbagehead claptrap?—Hey, we take it to that Court. We take it there—we sue it for its *fur*. We take that government to the cleaners and back again. Because, why? Because—sorry guys—its laws just happen to stand in the way of the highest end of them all; our right to do business as we wish."

"It will be a fine, fine thing," said Mr Finqueret." All

decisions made behind very locked doors. Accountable to no one but itself. Meetings held, naturally, only at secret but *secret* locations—"

"Maybe we'll get it its own fleet of jets, sure. And staffed of course exclusively by corporate lawyers. (You wanna put your name down now, Tom!) And it will be able to wipe out laws.—*Laws*, you get it? Wherever—any country. Biggest to the smallest. No higher power. No higher *power*."

"... Not, of course, that your own government is too keen to get in the way even now, Mydace," observed Mr Wyvern-Toad.

"Sure, Humphrey—sure. But we could still use the time and money we spend lobbying Congruence on other things. We got tens of *thousands* of trade organisations, we got sixty thousand lawyers, pandangit, all of them with their meters running, we got ninety thousand lobbyists—they *cost*. That's a hangarload of moolah we can put into other things.—But, yeah, they stayed in line on emissions, you bet your tail they did. Ninety-five to zero on that, O-*kay*! Now that's political wisdom. We go on. Just like before. We pollute—oh, just a tad, just a tad—and we keep on getting' those subsidies to go on doin' it. And we get what we shoulda had outta them when the sun came up—Corporate Responsibility."

"*Voluntary* Corporate Responsibility," said Mr Gopherit, all attention.

"*Voluntary* Corporate Responsibility," echoed Mr McMinc. Anything that needs doin' when the chips are down? Hey.—The Mystery decides. What makes more sense? Huh? The *Mystery* decides. Think about it. What could be simpler?"

"Well, I just don't think it's ri-i-ii-!!" Out of nowhere, the Mole's sentence had been violently shaken loose as floor, table, and the chair he sat on seemed to drop away from him by a distance of one to two feet, with his own self following on in close pursuit. It was not just he who moaned: as, wide-eyed, he carefully re-established his relationship with the closed world about him he saw several other animals, Mr Rette included, gripping hard at their chairs and table-edges.

"Air pocket," said Mr McMinc, shrugging. "*Big* 'un! Can't miss 'em all, I guess, even in my Raptor. Now— Bing—I wanted—"

But a young animal in uniform had come up out of the shadows and bent to whisper in the magnate's ear. Since he had chosen the ear lying on the Mole's side, that same mole was just able to make out his words. "Captain apologises for breaking in on the meeting, Mr McMinc, but wants you to know it will be necessary to follow a more easterly/stroke/southerly course than first planned, for the rest of the voyage, due to a much earlier-than-expected arrival of Hurricane Clarabelle along latitudes west. Delay of approximately one to one and a half hours on scheduled e.t.r. Miami, current estimation."

"Yeah, yeah, yeah. Fine, dagnabbit! What the hell!" growled Mr McMinc, waving him away.

"H—h—h—h—," thought the Mole, not in any way untremulously. "H—h—h—h—*hurricane Clarabelle*?"

"The point, you see ... Sorry, Mydace, but may I *just* come in here, very, very briefly?" said Mr van Sleek, turning to the Mole. "I feel the most—weird—desire to unpack all this a little more for—er ... well, for our friend here? Mr Mole? Take it right out of its suitcase, you know? Give it to room service for a re-press?"

"*Mr Mole* should *know* all this from Pudunk," said Mydace McMinc. But even this long-time case-hardened old fighter was not, it seemed, totally unsusceptible to the miraculous effects of the Mole's presence, for immediately after this his expression melted into a grin and he said, "Hell's dweebs, Harmony, you go right on now. Talk away!

Why not? We got all the time in the world here! We can stay up here ten days if we want to!"

"You see, Mr Mole," said the Ferret creamily, releasing the scent of azaleas from his fur as he turned to the small overseas guest, "what actually happens in the world is not the point here. That, you know, is very rarely the point. What counts, Mr Mole, is the *Reality Leverance*. Hit that on the button, you got it taped, you got it wired! And—er—here, of course, is where we of the ReMind Agency, and our numerous—our legion—partners and associates worldwide, have a certain importance, if I may say that."

"But ... but ..." said the Mole. He was getting back on to breathing form by now. "If ... if animals are doing things that other animals don't want—"

"—then we make them *think* they want them!" responded Mr van Sleek ecstatically. "—Or, of course, if that's non-productizable for any reason, we make them think the—whatever—isn't anything like so big or so widespread as—" (he broke off for a moment, laughing in something like embarrassment) "it, er, it, er, may be. Mr Mole, animals *want* to think things are better than they are. (... If I can use that word, 'better', here, without risking a value judgement of some kind.) They need that. They *need* it. And we in Reality Leverance have built up, in very short order, a ludicrazee-dollar-a-year industry right on the back of that fact! There it is behind you" (he gestured in the direction of the tall screen and its imperceptibly rotating planet) "—the ReMind auditorium. Animals might not like something? Hey, ReMind will make them think different. We get our material out, all routes, television, radio, the labyrinth, the press, campus noticeboards, oh, jungle drums if necessary! They don't even know their opinions are changing until they've changed. And *then* they don't know! It's beautiful."

Mr Sidney "Wes" Sleazel, Harmony van Sleek's recently

appointed British colleague, sat at Mr Rette's left paw. He too may have come under the pull of the Mole force-field, for at this moment he struck his forehead fulsomely and cried out, "Oh gee, oh gee, oh *gee*, Harm! Hot biggety-buggety! Oh, hot biggety-buggety-*bug*! It's *byuddiful*!" At which point he struck his head again, and several of the animals around the table coughed.

"Back where it started," said Mr van Sleek, "—pioneer days—they used to call it Appearance Management. We at ReMind, we call it many things; we have a portfolio, sure we do! We call it Perception Proctorship. We call it Sleight of Thought. We call it Nutri-Think. Different days we call it different things."

"*Hot bug* ...!" said Mr Sleazel, breathing heavily.

More than once along the difficult road of the past few weeks, the Mole had heard things of a similar kind. He was no more impressed by them than he had ever been: the difference now, perhaps, was that he was a little better prepared to say so.

"We do not police opinion," said the Ferret, as if this might be something well beneath his dignity. "No need for *that*! Our task is simply to ... steer it, gently, but with a firm, sure hand. So that, over time, like some great oil tanker turning around a spillage—ah—it finds its own true course, in the direction we want it to go. It's a game! It's a *game*.—Oh, a very, very serious game!"

"But it's just more—sorry to say it—" said the Mole, "it's all just more fibbing, isn't it?"

"'Fibbing'?" echoed Mr van Sleek blandly.

"He means—we don't use the word," said Mr Sleazel, who seemed to be in a state bordering on hyperventilatory ecstasy. "Oh, Harm! Harm! This is such a barn-burner, Harm. This is such a sockdolager! It's a ring-tailed snorter, Harm, it's the bees' own eyebrows! He means ..." (he sobbed) "... we *lie*."

"Several low cries of "Oh!" were heard from around and behind the oval, and there was not a face at the table, except perhaps for those of Messrs McMinc (inscrutability: grim), Wyvern-Toad (inscrutability: artless) and Rette (inscrutability: terminal), that did not express deep shock. "*The wheel is come full circle,*" muttered Mr Rette, neatly rounding the end on a thigh-bone as he did so.

Slowly, wonderingly, in fly-eyed rapture, Harmony van Sleek turned to the Mole, half rising from his chair as he did so. "We lie!" he cried. "It's true! It's true! It's what we do! We lie, we lie, we lie, we lie, we LIE!"

The two Proctors of Perception leapt from their seats simultaneously, clawing at their ties as if they had been nooses, and fell into one another's embraces. "We lie, we lie, we lie, we lie, we LIE!" they screamed, and laughed, and wept. "—OH!" cried Harmony van Sleek, almost dancing on the spot as he spoke. "Oh, Pan, Pan, *Pan!* This is so much better than therapy!"

Mr Volebrush stared in deepening horror from the other side of the table. "Great guns!" he said. "Wha-a-at is going *on* here?"

"You'd be dead, Harm," snarled Mr McMinc in a very low voice. "You'd be *dead.* We'd deep-six you quicker'n a chameleon does lunch. We don't pipeline Re-Mind day-by-day outrageous amounts of lettuce not to mention additional large wagonloads of curly kale for you to start admitting you—"

"Oh yes, Mydace!" burst in the Ferret. "—Yes! Yes! *Outrageous* amounts! *Wagonloads,* yes! We are *ludicrously* overpaid for what we do! We should pay *you!*" he cried fulsomely, though a kind of cadaverous ghastliness had now begun to mingle unaesthetically with his state of exaltation, not unlike cold, grey cistern-water trickling into a luxurious suds-filled bath.

"*Jumpin' jacksnipes!*" said the old mink, his mouth wide

open. "This is ... er ... this is—" The gathering's jaws gaped with him, the abstracts "McMinc" and "indecisiveness" making for another existential oxymoron—and a disturbing one, or so it seemed.

But, of course, the Mole had no compelling reasons for thinking the patricians of Weaselworld did not behave like this at every meeting they held. And so—being, as ever, deeply curious despite himself—he went ahead and asked another question. "You shouldn't be doing it at all, if you want my opinion," he said. "—Don't suppose you do. But I don't understand what it is you *do* do. When you do it."

The senior partner in Conceptual Nutrition turned with wide-eyed, pleading gaze towards the old mink, shaking his head as he did so. His English colleague, seated, simply sobbed, his sobs making a remote low echo in some metallic angle of the Chamber's outer reaches.

"Oh, what the hell!" growled Mr McMinc, stretching as he spoke. "—Go on, Harmony—*go* on! Why not?"

"What w-we ... d-do ..." said Mr van Sleek, his vocal wheels seriously depleted of lubrication now,"—what w-we *do* ... is *paint* what is not so very, ah ... ahhhh ... 'sensitive'? ... (ha ha) ... in every shade of planet-loving green that nature dreamed of, and then some. Never mind about what Exx—no!—No! ... MexeC—" (he groaned, broke off, but only for a second) "—*this* oil company, or *that* ... oh Pan, Pan, Pan ... may be doing, right now, to whichever bunch of tribesmals it is in whichever Western-African or, you name it, South American oilfield? Or the forests and rivers out there these tribesmals are said to own, er, own, do own, I have no reason to doubt *do own*?—Mr Mole, Mr Mole ... Do I have to do this? Couldn't we just do coffee someplace? Coffee and maybe a donut? Two donuts! We ... we ... we point elsewhere. We point *loud* elsewhere. That five square kilometer seal sanctuary a company's started way up there in Alaska? Showpiece stuff. 'Look *this* way, guys!' We do the

TQ-MOPs, we make the videos, we pound the press with flyers. 'Look over *here*—here!—here!'"

Ashamed at what he thought he was being told, the Mole looked down.

"Great Western Nuclear Depositories," said Mr van Sleek, regaining a little fluency as he landed on what may have been a slightly less embarrassing example. "They want to go on building new dumps for radioactive waste in the desert? Sure they do, sure they do! So what do we do? We *change their name for them.* This is where you need the poetry. You with me? The word power? We make them over and they come out, *Ecosphere Havens.* A whole new hairdo, baby. Ecosphere Havens, ain't that cute? They build a new dump—a *haven*, you get it?—but there's one of these klutz rare-breed things on the patch?" ("There always is," said Mydace McMinc.) "You know? Some *tortoise.* Won't be crawling round there much longer, leastways if it doesn't want to glow in the dark. So: GWN move the slow-movers way down the valley, and we do the coverage and we call it (and we had to work at *this* title), we call it 'A New Home For Our Endangered Pals'. We get a company cuddlebug to do the voice-over, you know the kind of guy—your type, you know? Nice-type guy. Dress him down, but down— check shirts, jeans, not too tidy, make him look the regular kind of guy. We cut the tortoises walking to the *Ode To Joy.* Beetvolen? He shoulda been working for us."

"It's what you do," said Mydace McMinc, stubbing his cheroot, hard.

"We paint things green. Oh, *oh.* We paint things *green.* One contract we had early on, the San Andreas Electric? Their Paradise Canyon nuclear installation? They cut down a few trees. Just one mountainside, y'know? Bush-league stuff. But they wanted it kept profile free. So they call in Re-Mind, and we said okay! Paint the whole pandamned *mountain* green! The freeway was thirty miles off, who was

going to know different? It took one heck of a lot of hard
gloss paint, nearly half-a-million litres. Two coats, with an
undercoat first and major sanding-down and filling. Hey,
but now, Mr Mole—*that* is Reality Leverance!"

"Oh, Harm, Harm ..." wept Mr Sleazel. "It's just so
byuddiful, Harm ...?"

Mr van Sleek's gaze roamed the Milky Way of feral features in an aberrant, staring fashion, resting, very uneasily,
on the Deputy Director of the world's largest bank. "Now
Mr Lemmog here," he said conversationally, (at once choking out "No-oo! ... No-oo! ..." much in the style of a
medium at a seance) "—Bing ... Bing. Ha, ha, ha. How ya
doin', Bing? Forgive me ...?—Bing, now, see, he wants to
pump several jillion dollars into RNZ's latest piece of real
estate down in Madagascar? (No..oo! *Please*, noooo ...)
—Okay! Fine! It's gonna take out half a forest there—what
is that, Bing? How many square kilometers was that?"

The bog lemming leaned forward around his host's
sharp profile to stare at the squirming ferret with acetylene
eyes on full blast, though even as he spoke his expression
softened visibly. "Mr van Sleek, I hardly see the relevance—I hard ... I ha ... We ha ... we'd have to gress the
dats on that. If you want a ballpark figure, it's—oh, what
shall we say?—"

"No, forget it, Bing, truly—" interrupted Mr van Sleek.
"Truly—don't concern yourself!—The fact is, Mr Mole,
it's one helluva lot of forest. There's going to be a bit of a
mess made? Opencast? Big holes? *Big* holes. New roads,
waste dumps, workers' shanty towns. You get the picture.
So they call in Re-Mind, and we apply ourselves to the
Sleightwork with our usual across-the-canvas assiduity. At
the end of it, RNZ is what? Hey! It's one of the world's
front-running conservationists! Because, why? Because
RNZ is only taking out *half* the forest! The *rest* of it they
leave alone!" The Ferret laughed, hysterically and in isola-

tion, after the style of a spot-lit mad scene from Grand Opera. "So ... 'Madagascar Rain Forest, very, very rare breeds of monkey (and etcetera, etcetera) SAVED by Caring Mining Corporation!' Oh, the world, the world ..." (a strangled sound broke from him here) "... the world is in such very good hands." Opening his trembling paws to the assembly, Mr Van Sleek slumped back into his seat and complemented Mr Sleazel's sobbings with his own.

"... Yup," said Mr Lemmog pensively, sitting back in his chair and looking up at the shadowy space above the hanging light as if mildly entranced by it. "Do one thing; say the opposite. Number-one working principle. We all know *that*."

Mydace McMinc turned slowly to observe the animal next to him, his canny, hardbitten old face amingle with disbelief and the blackest of suspicion.

"Sure, sure!" went on the Lemming, fixing the Mole with his red, red eyes. "As you all know, we of Globobank, we too ... *lie* ..."

At this, the clutch of aides gathered close behind him broke suddenly, like undammed water, into a mournful chorus ("Ye-es, ye-es, ye-e-esss!—We lie—we lie—we lie—we lie—we lie!") against which the broken sobbings of the two conceptual nutritionists rose like solos in some bizarre oratorio of involuntary confession.

Mr Lemmog opened his hands accommodatingly. "And if it does get noticed, that's fine, that's just fine. We have the technique for that. We say—we always say—'It was a mistake'. And we say 'Hey, anyway, guys! That was *then*. This is *now*.' Then we go on doing what we did before." All belligerency vanished, the Deputy Director of Globobank looked around the faces of his colleagues with something akin to tenderness, his gaze ending on the Mole. "Ohhhh ..." he said," ... I see it now. Now I *understand*. This truly is wonderful ..."

Mydace McMinc's eyes switched sharply from Mr Lemmog to Mr Wyvern-Toad, whose eyebrows were raised in a look of the deepest, the most simple-minded puzzlements.

"The point is, Mr Mole," said Mr Lemmog, "we of Globobank also make a very far-reaching, scientific application of the techniques of Sleight of Mind. And when you look across our program, *boy* do we need to!—*Uh*—uh ..."

"Well all I can say," responded the Mole, "is you should jolly well be ashamed of yourselves."

"—*Ashamed* of ourselves?" replied the Lemming, his face an early Cubist portrait of conflicting emotions. "No, no, no! Mr Mole, you got that, wrong, sir, you got that wrong! We're very, very proud of the way we do things. Are—er—aren't we, girls and boys?"

A chorus of wailing and sobbing "Yes-oh-yes"'s rose from the shadows. "Proud! So proud! So proud!"

"But—"

"—What do we do?" said Mr Lemmog, anticipating the subtlety of the question. "Ahh ... if I may, Mydace?" The Bog Lemming pointed with a delicate small hand to the button at his place at the table.

"Sure, Bing!" responded the old Mink, grimacing. "You just make yourself at home, now!"

The Bog Lemming tapped briefly at a narrow black tapperboard that had risen magically from the table to greet his paw. "We of Globobank have one rule above all others, Mr Mole," he said. "*Thiyyunk biyyug.*" (His southern origins may have showed through here slightly.) "*Everything* Globobank finances is very, oh, so *very* biyyug! We do not thiyyunk small, Mr Mole. 'Small' is not on the menu."

The turning world faded almost imperceptibly from the two big sloping screens to be replaced by an overhead image of a seemingly endless, many-mile-wide stretch of water framed by parallel mountain ridges. Music making heavy use of trombones blared brashly from the blackness, calling up in the minds of some present a fuzzy mental picture of blonde-furred flying horse-females bearing the bodies of heroic warrior businessmals towards the portals of an exclusive and well guarded heaven of many golf courses.

"Okay ..." murmured Mr Lemmog, having tapped this racket into silence. "We don't need any sound here, I guess. We pulled this particular smoothserv, Mr Mole, as it happens," he explained. "Went for the cartoon version with Bunnys Bug doing the commentary instead. More homey." ("It was one of ours," lamented Mr van Sleek, sobbing afresh into a well-soaked handkerchief.) "But this may give you a clearer picture. These, Mr Mole, are the types of Major Development Project we finesse, worldwide, across the whole broad prospectorate of the Underworld. Here, India, the Sarmardar Valley project: the biyyugest—*the* biyyugest dam-project in the history of animalkind! When it's finished this beauty" (he gestured towards an enormous structure now on the screens) "will have bump-started the construction of 3,200 dams, no leyyus, in this region of India A-lone. That's covering several thousand kilometers of river valley along forty-one tributaries of this great river, a river that is itself 1,300 kilometers long. And who financed this?—That's right, *two full years* before the Indian Government's own 'Environment' Department passed the project as sound? Globobank, Mr Mole! Globobank."

The Mole looked on with ever more educated eyes. Horrified and despairing he might still be, but surprised? No longer.

"And *here* ..." went on the Bog Lemming. "—Here, we see the Sinmowgli lignite and coal-fired power plants project, six of the one, six of the other, and counting, into which the G-Bank has injected already in excess of 2.5

stupendodadillion, loaned at a (he snorted; it was not a laugh, exactly) very attractive rate of compound interest. The related coalfields—opencast, of course—established over, I forget the figure—hey, well, *hundreds* of kilometers of virgin territory? Biyyug, Mr Mole, that *is biyyug*."

The Mole stared at one screen and then the other in the vain hope it might reveal something different, as one image succeeded the next of inconceivably vast, green-rimmed stretches of mountain valley buried under billions of tons of water, Leviathanesque greystuff dams themselves as high as foothills, gigantic industrial complexes whose rows of chimneys and looming, maw-like cooling towers belched out sky-filling volumes of gasses, steam and flames. Giant concertina skeletons strode out from them across the landscape in every direction, and on all sides towering rock crushers pumped out further pillars of dust, grey-black or yellow-white, with tone variations between the two.

He saw fly-by pictures of entire provinces that might once perhaps have been husbanded or forested, lying scabbed and scurfed into something like an animal's hide in an advanced state of mange. Huge pits lay there now, inside the grey rims of which machines moved, and hacked, and scraped, and where—defying all logic—small clustered townships of huts were also visible. Then the picture changed again, and he saw symmetrical rows of parallel-slot docklands, all done in greystuff, in under-construction deepwater ports. And all of this he witnessed, in one drifting image after another, as if from the detached, demiurgical viewpoint of a young winged god with money in his pockets.

"We were talking emissions earlier?" said Mr Lemmog. "This project here?"(More looming towers.) "This project alone will eventually pump out something either side of 120 million tons p.a. of cindron athsmoxide. Think of *that* in terms of jobs!—Now this ... er ... is Cameroon ..." (A sky-wandering image down on to the top of a pristine, hypnotically beautiful tropical forest) "—Like a home movie, ain't it? Only one little logging project on the books here presently, taking out timber from an area *just* the wrong side of Alabama. (Jobwise? You compute it.) And here ... Gabon ... logging, again ... the North Amazon basin ... logging, forest clearance, resettlement programs ... Malaysia ... yeah ... Indonesia ... Mr Mole, need I say it? Globobank makes biyyug impacts! Bi-i-i-iyyyug impacts!"

The Mole had no choice except to fall back on the 'but' word, using it three times in succession as he struggled to give shape to some sort of sensible comment. "... why?" he asked. "*Why* do you make all these great big things?" Yet another dam appeared, the viewpoint-helicopter catching a reflection of itself in its vast flat surface. "Why all these *dams?*"

"Now let's get just one thing clear here, Mr Mole," said Mr Lemmog coolly. "Globobank does not build these projects itself. Globobank *finesses*: we make loans to the Governments and private consortia concerned, according to our criteria. They use them to hire-in project ratcheters and justifiers ... ahhh ... more normally known as 'Environmental' Consultants, who prejudge each plan so as to ensure it will go ahead." (Another "Whaaa-a-at is this?" arose from miscellaneous table-points at this.) "Then they hire-in the contractors—ah—from our own fine country, *and* from Europe, Britain especially, to oversee each project. And to buy in the equipment needed. All of which *we make*, of course."

"But—why?"

"Isn't that a good enough reason?"

"Well—"

"... Okay, Mr Mole, if you're going to push me on this, okay, sir, okay! You would not, for example, want to see hundreds of millions of hard-pressed animals in these struggling countries going without piped water, would you?

Of course you wouldn't! India alone has an unknown number of thousands of villages—uncountable, very probably. They all of them need water. Right?"

"But ... what about the animals in the villages in the places that get flooded?" said the Mole, staring agitatedly at another inland sea that had once perhaps, been a fertile river-valley.

"Oh. Ohhh. I do think it is a little unfair of you to ask me that, I sure do, Mr Mole," said the powerful banker peevishly. "But—okay, okay, *okay!* Their villages are, naturally, destroyed."

"*Destroyed?!*"

"You bet your tail they are. They have to go. There is a certain element of...of...small-scale displacement involved. Oh, eighty thousand here, a hundred thousand there ... Sometimes, as of practical necessity, at the point of a gun ... quite often, ha ha ... at the point of a gun. Guns. Not *our* guns, of course! Great Pan, no! As I said, Globobank merely finesses. Since Independence, India alone has moved, we hear, some twenty million PMIs (that, er, that's—er— Project-Modified Individuals? PMIs? Handy little acronym, if you ever needed one.)"

"So—um—what you mean is, you are driving all these poor animals out of their homes in—one lot of villages," said the Mole, drawing an invisible diagram on the table in front of him, "to—get water to *other* animals, in, well, another lot of villages?"

The Bog Lemming stared back at the Mole, his earlier sense of wonderment having now, it seemed, quite left him. "Mr Mole," he said frigidly. "It is sometimes necessary, in order to save a village—here," (he held the village of his hypothesis invisibly, in the palm of one hand) "to eliminate another, or others, in the ... what shall I call it? The Greater Elsewhere?" (With his other small hand he waved these villages away, "holding" the first until his point was made.) "That's just how it is in this world."

In his mind's eye now the Mole pictured the Village of his own memory, and the old pump that had stood in the centre of the green there bringing up water, year in, year out, for as long as anyone could recall. "But—what if— what if every village had got its *own* little supply of water?" he asked. "Then you wouldn't need to drive *anybody* out."

"You'd have to be gosh-danged clever—"retorted Mr Lemmog hotly, looking about him as if for support. "*Gosh*-danged clever—to find a water source for every village in the *Underworld*! Ha ha! Ha, ha, ha! That *is* a somewhat naïve, a somewhat destructive, kind of an approach, sir. A little way pre-Pudunk, if you do not mind me saying so. And in any case, if every village in India or wherever had its own well or dingswizzled little D—I—Y reservoir, what in Pan's name would we of Globobank have left to do there?!"

The Mole groped on, as if for the light of a glow-worm on a pitch-black summer night. "But your—um—their dams, they do *work* all right, do they? I mean, they do get more water to the animals who need it?"

"Hell, no, Mr Mole!" responded the Bog Lemming, as if only stating the glaringly obvious. "The dams don't *work*! Didn't I already say that? No, no, no, they don't *work*, not— ahh—substantively, not definitively. Not *as dams*. Whether they *work* or not is not in essence, at any stage, an issue with which we of Globobank concern ourselves. The dam gets built, and mostly it ends up irrigating a few per cent of what was claimed for it by the Ratcheters. No, no. They are very inefficient, mostly, these dams. The Reports always say they'll get water to the villages, but come *on* now. Let's not play stupid. Or there are other glitches. The Sadbagheera Barrage? Sure, that one did get water to tens of millions in cities this side the Pakistan border. Only problem is, it took it away from tens of millions on the far side. Mr Mole ... that's how it *is*."

"—Well," said the Mole squarely, "if you are going to go around destroying animals' homes all the time to build them, and destroying forests, *and* turning the countryside into a lot of moth-eaten great holes—perhaps it shouldn't be. Perhaps you should stop."

The Deputy Director of the world's most powerful bank stared at the Mole with the roundest of round eyes. "... Stop? ..." he repeated weakly, and another wailing and gnashing of teeth arose from the shadows to his rear, wordless and shrill as the cries of oystercatchers adrift along the black-beached shores of hell.

"Wall Street relies on this continuing," said Warren R. Bitt mildly. "If it stopped, it might not be able to take the strai-i-ii-!!" Again, every animal present found himself unceremoniously lifted from, and dropped back on to, the chair he sat on.

"Air pocket, goldurned, gangdanged *air pocket!*" growled Mydace McMinc, gasping slightly as he did so. "What the hell are my pilots *doin'* today—roundin' up the dadblamed things for the corral?"

Mr Rette added another small bone to what was now an impressive small charnel-house piled upon his first skull-study. "... *and by a sleep*," he breathed, "*to say we end The heart-ache and the thousand natural shocks Rat-flesh is heir to? ...*" Another moment of turbulence sent his pigment-ink designer pen shooting off the paper. "*Or ... tum-te-tum ... te-tah-te-tah ... by opposing,*" he whiffled, "*... End them?*"

But Mr Lemmog had not yet, it seemed, quite given up on the Mole. "Mr Mole," he said, and there was a note of near-desperate pleading in his voice now, "you *must consider* the purity—the clarity—of our Reality Leverance on this. Okay, so we may have had to ask a few tens of millions if they just wouldn't mind moving someplace else. Okay, so the logging projects may have taken out a few million square kilometers of forests in places Johns Doe and Bull have never heard of! Okay! But you have to look at what the *public sees*, sir! It doesn't *see* opencast. It sees global programs of *Enviro-Compassionate Resource Stewardship*. It doesn't *see* forced resettlement. It sees *Paradigmatic Agricultural Land-Use Programs*. It doesn't *see* rainforest logging. It sees *Perpetuatory Snail-Sensitive Planet-Management*. It sees our much, much smoothserved Earth Endurance Fund—a masterstroke of my own devising, as it happens—which, with a staff of one (plus a secretary, part time Wednesdays and Fridays)gives out, in fact, *very* small amounts of funding to 'conservation' projects whilst, meantime ..." He looked at the Mole hopefully. "You get the drift?"

"Oh, the E.E.F.!" mourned Mr van Sleek in a strangled contralto. "It's exquisite! *Exquisite!*"

"Today, sir—thanks to wholly fabulous acts of Higher Mindsleight by all of our Departments working in concert—Globobank has emerged, I believe, as the World's Number One Deeply-Caring Conservationist: the only one of its kind the planet needs. This is major, *major* Mindsleight. Meantime—and I do say this, sir, I do say it, despite the truly zerksome obviousness of the remark—business as usual. Huh? Business as pandamned *usual?* As a T.T. mal, you should be *proud* of this achievement!"

"I am not proud of it," said the Mole gravely. "I am very ashamed for you. And I don't understand why you're not ashamed yourself."

"Kk-kk-kk-kk-kkgggg!" gasped Mr Lemmog, his eyes popping now much as if some invisible hand had been tightening on his windpipe. A moment later he sucked in air, then positively exploded. "*Damn* it, animal! Pan damn it! Pan damn it and you! You know exactly why! You do not need to ask! No one *ever* asks that!—Because I *can't possibly afford to be!!* None of us could! None of us could be in this game ... this *game* ... and stay sane for more than ten minutes if we began to ... Ah!—Ah!! ... if for one moment we admitted ..."

Thin and cracked as a Dust Bowl fence post, Mr Lemmog's voice tailed away into silence as, once again, a dreadful semi-asphyxiated wailing rose up from the shadows. Like others before him, the powerful banker slumped back into his chair, one small paw pressed hard across his eyes.

"Quite a burnout rate here today, Mr Mole," observed Mydace McMinc cautiously, but also perhaps with something bordering on admiration. "Hey—Bing. Hey! Hey!—Get a grip there. Smarten up now."

"Really, gent'mals!" said Mr Grubhogg-Hedge, from the relative safety of a table-end. "I do think we should be addressing matters a little closer to the day's agenda."

"I second dat," said the Martenson twins, leaning their big bear-like frames forward around the collapsed lemming as if to get a better sightline on this anarchy-breeding mole. "You gotta understand, Mr Mole," said the nearer of them (who was Martz), "—huh? Why should *I* want to talk to dis animal? Because I want to, I guess. Dat's fine, okay. Dat's fine. What you gotta understand, Mr Mole, de tail-tip on de tailline on dat is, like Chuck dere said: *every* animal on dis planet *must consoom.*"

("Konn sûme?" puzzled the Mole.)

"Hey, Mr Mole," said the twin beyond. "Why is de American public da greatest public in da woild? Huh? I'll tell you why. Because in America—"

"—In America," continued Martz, "you kin sell *anytink* to *anybody*. Jus' so soon as you got your smoothservs maxed. De American people—"

"De American people," said Hartz. "Dey *want* to buy! Hey, what else is dere? Shopping. Dat's it. Life's a Mall."

"Dey want to *buy*," said Martz. *Toyz "For" Pupz*—dat's us—dat is where it starts. You give me a child—better still, you give me a baby—let him loose in *Toyz "For" Pupz?* I will own dat child inside one half hour—"

"I will *own* him," said the brother. "An' once he is mine, I will keep him till he's grown. He'll know only *Toyz "For" Pupz.* He'll see only *Toyz "For" Pupz*—"

"—He'll be my sweet little donkey, and he'll come back and back and back to me until he's old enough to go out dere alone into da Wider Mall. *TFP* is, you could say, rolled all into one convenient package, da potty-trainer an' de Alma Mater for every young consoomer of da western woild—"

"Yuh! Where dey learn how to choose between whatever we offer them to choose—"

"—an' whatever *else* we offer dem to choose. From where, years of patient nurture and groomin' later, dey emerge full-fledged, ready to soar out dere in whatever sophisticated Consooming-Relationship dey find demselves. (Jus' so long as it's with us, of course.)"

"Animals don't *want* a million different little shops all selling dem little bitty pieces of dis an' dat!" said Hartz, his muscular tail swiping at the shadows in much the same way as his brother's.

"—Not knowin' where to go an' get what dey want or if da guy'll stock it when they get dere. Dey want *choice*—sure! But da choice dey most want?"

"Da choice dey most want is da same choice, Mr Mole. Da *same choice.* Deep down, most animals want to know just one thing—you tell him, brother—"

"—Dat *tings are always goin' ta be Da Same.*"

The two Martens called up their tapperboards from out the mystic tabletop, and tapped. As before, the Earth misted away, to be replaced twice over with images of a circular, pale brown object patterned across with little creamy spots.

"*Dis,*" said Martz, "is de Boigerboig Big-Bag Bunnybite

Boig-Boiger, regular size, as it is seen, sold and consoomed in any an' all of our 2001 outlets (and counting) in Australasia an' along da Pacific Rim out as far as Tongetabu. Okay."

The image jumped very slightly, and the colour-temperature also changed, but the subject now on screen appeared otherwise identical to the first. "*Dis*," said Hartz, "is de Boigerboig Big-Bag Bunnybite Boig-Boiger, regular size, as it is seen, sold and consoomed through Iceland, Scandinavia and Finland, with penetrations into Latvia and Estonia and points northeast to date to Novaya Zemlya south. See da difference?"

The Mole squinted in deepest incomprehension. "Well ... no," he said.

"*Dat's because dere ain't one!*" boomed the two Martens joyously and in closest synchrony.

"Wherever you want to go on dis planet, Mr Mole," said Martz, "whichever da country, whatever da climate, whoever's runnin' da show dere, or havin' a war wit whomever next door, you go through da portico of a Boigerboig Boig-Boiger Bar, you'll get da SAME ting. Regular *means regular*. Four ounces exact, shoulder-an'-trimmins globo-beef, a bun of plain white bread made to our secret mini-inputs recipe, dat is always *exac'ly* ninety-eight millimetres in diameter, an' topped wit' pre-cisely thirty-seven sesame seeds of da same colour, dimensions an' factor-of-chew per bun."

"O—dear."

"*Dat* is reliability, Mr Mole!" said Hartz. "*Dat* is Quidditatory Customer-Confidence! From one day to da next, one year to da next, one *generation* to da next. At our current but improvable rates of development, we have one-point-two-nine Boigerboig Big-Bag Bunnybite Boig-Boiger Bars openin' around da woild *every single* day an' night dat comes to us. It's such a fine ting, dis, such a great ting, we are even now tinkin' of foundin' da woild's first Boiger Museum—

in Cleveland, Ohio, where it all started—to record da whole, glorious story for dey as come after."

"How—well, um ..."

"'Interesting?'" suggested Mr Rette, as he touched in the rope on a little study of a gallows.

"I kid you not, Mr Mole, dey love what we do out dere," added Martz, with fervour. "Oh, dey love *us* out dere! Dey want to be like us! Dey want to *be* us. Wherever—wherever."

Breathing heavily now, the more distant of the martens tapped again. "Upmarket, we have da Fingelgurker's Quality Steakmeat Restaurant-Chain," he said. "*Dis* is what you get when you order our regular twelve ounce T-bone with fries an' side-salad in Santa Monica, or Shawinigan Falls. An' *dis*—" (as before, there was a change-free change) "is what is set upon da Fingelgurker identi-table in Aragon, Oporto, Châteauneuf-du-Pape and Montepulciano. See da difference?"

"... no ..."

"*Dat's because dere ain't one!*" repeated the Messrs Martenson triumphantly and in tandem and, inclusive of the vigour of their tail-swipes, just as they had before.

"Walk into the lobby of one of our Mahanga Paradise Luxury Hotels in ..." said Martz, tapping, "Cairo ... Budapest ... Edinburgh ... D'Entrecasteaux Island ..."

"See da difference?"

"Fraid not."

"*You* know *why!*"

Between gritted teeth, Mr Rette had just succeeded in swallowing an armstretcher of a yawn. "*Life's but a walking shadow ...*" he breathed, "*a tail Pulled by an idiot, full of pain and fury, Signifying ...*" His pen meandered in a twisted tail-like line.

"But ... Okay ..." said Martz, coming very slightly off the boil here. "We have to say dis too. Sure! Some days, da

Consoomer wants other kinds a' shoppin'—it's his right. It's his *right*. Some days, he wants 'Variety'. Some days, he wants 'Multiplicity Of Choice.' But still, how does he want it?"

"He wants it all under one roof!" cried Hartz jubilantly.

"So ..." (more tapping) "... we give him: Da Mall."

("Maul?" ventured the Mole in his thoughts. "Mawl? M'awl? Morle?")

Now the screens were filled by a cheese-after-midnight nightmare in which a giant hallway—high and curvingly-roofed, and lit by spherical lamps on filigree stems, and with palm trees isolated here and there in white pots—fell away from view to the remotest of vanishing-points. On either side were shop fronts with boldly-displayed name signs: the nearest was a *Pasta Shack* eating-house whose frontage had been daubed blotchily, like a prop flung together for an end-of-term play, as if to suggest something old, rustic and, possibly, Italian. The concourse itself was thronged with animals moving like drones in a hive, upon each of whose faces was imprinted the same expression of tameness, biddability. Some plumper specimens sat drooped in isolated "armchairs" let into plant-fringed little islands in the flow, clutching multiple bags and large balloons decorated with store names and symbols.

"So. Dorking ... Sri Lanka ..." The scene changed, to the extent that the species of those present differed. "Singapore ... So it goes, Mr Mole. What you see here is IT. Da ting itself. Da Paradise of Poichasin' Power dat will in time come to enrich de lives of animals in every city— every town—on dis planet. For every animal, Mr Mole," (and here, somehow, the Marten's tone conveyed both piety and threat at once) "—*every* animal—must consoom."

"Yup! An' here *he* is!" added Hartz, tapping onward. "De *Turbid Consoomer*, envisionated here in a Transocietal Market-Analysis-Based Digitalo-Teleautograph. Da most

advanced form of life upon dis planet! Da high point, Mr
Mole—da high point of animal evolution as a whole."

The screens bore what was to the Mole, if to no one else
present, an appalling sight. A strange being—stylised
somehow so that it was neither vole nor lemming, rabbit
nor woodchuck, but a horrible blurred concoction of all of
them and many more besides—stood smiling abjectly outward, as if pleased, with eyes in which some artificial
sparkle of "life", not *life*, was visible. The creature was
dressed in a sloppy shift imprinted with—and again, here,
some sort of trickery had been used—a universal logo,
which pulsed continuously between one brand-name and
another. On its head it wore a standard duckbill, similarly
imprinted, whilst its lower half was clad in bulging, shapeless trousers and a pair of standing-shoes, variably bile-
chevronned. Over its ears it wore narrow black earmuffs
linked to a box at its waist, and here too was clipped a
Deracitel with a picture of an animal on or in it. The creature stared outward in thought-free pleasure, changing gen-
ders, species and appendages in an overlapping flow. Of all
the ghastly things the Mole had seen in this world, this was
the worst yet—the most crushing, the most desolate. In
this image of life-in-death, or death-in-life, with its flaccid
smile and unseeing, unquestioning eyes, all hope—all idea
of hope as the Mole understood it—had been calculatingly
stamped out.

"*Animal Economicum*," said Martz "The Mart" Martenson
proudly. "An' dis ..." (more tapping) "... is where he lives.
Or where he would like to live. Da far an' glorious shore for
every Consooming Animal who does not make dat final,
damn-near impossible leap into da Economic Stratos-
phere."

The creature vaporized into an image of a house—one
that was no less manipulated and generalised, detailed and
vague. In spirit, though it was always much larger, this

immediately called up in the Mole's mind memories of the sterile, Nature-repelling ranch-bungalows he had seen on his travels. On the large expanse of bricked-over ground in front of it, a series of snarling, silver-grilled and most intensively hornet-stung shoeboxes transmogrified. There were never less than three on screen at any one time.

"Dis is de woild we woik towoids," said Hartz. "De All-Consoomin' Final Grand Consoomer Shakedown."

"An' *dis* is what we are up against in our fight," said Martz, his fingers active. "What you could call—between friends, huh?—de enemy territory?"

The screens showed a rapid, captioned run of images of actual, not synthetic, animals: Inuit deep-wrapped in furs on an Arctic ice sheet; Saharan Tuareg on camels, their blue-stained faces all but lost behind the folds of turban-veils; animals in berets seated with their coffees outside an ancient, shuttered *Café de France*; bare-furred animals with paint-patterned faces paddling a dugout along some remote jungle backwater in Indonesia; animals in vividly coloured cloaks and feather head-dresses dancing against cloud-snagging Andean peaks; animals—the Mole gasped in dismay, for, yes indeed, these were badgers, otters, hares—seen at rest in the low light of their humble English burrows.

"Dis is a key growth field for us today," said Mr Martenson, H. "Correct-Consoomership-resistance-zones. Out-of-Consoomership-subsistence-lifestyles. What brings all dese guys together? Dey don't need us, yet. Or dey tink dey don't. Dey still do it their way. Dey don't shop. Or dey shop, but only in places dey shouldn't. Dese animals are pre-Mall. Now Mr Mole, you hear me on dis—all dat has got to *go*. We are goin' to get to dese mals, however far out in da rhubarbs dey are, an' we are goin' ta get dem *addicted to shopping*, jus' like da next mal."

"... But, bless me!—Wha—?"

"So here is *dis* guy," interrupted the closer marten, and the screens showed a jungle animal carrying a spear and wearing very little more, "stuck in his stinkin' bug-ridden swamp enjoying tings he hasn't *paid* for?—Oh, *ohh*, dat is so wrong! Dat is so *wrong*. Dis guy, he can live offa da land still? Offa da *land*! He's independent. He's got no overheads. He pays no taxes, he don't buy *nuttin'*—Pan, dat offends me!—whatever he needs (whatever he *tinks* he needs) he gets from da *trees*, an' da *river*, an' maybe from a coupla little fields or whatever out da back of his village? Now, Mr Mole. All *dat* has got to *go*."

"O!—No!"

"You get him to want *dis*," (a shift to a shift) "or *dis*," (a picture-Deracitel) "an' you got it nailed, you can reel him right in. He wants dem? Sure he wants dem, soon as he's been smoothserved. He jus' don't know he wants dem yet."

"He has to curl up in *shame* if he don't have dat Schwein-logo shirt," said H. "Oh, *oh*, so unglacial, dat! He has to not be able to look his people in de *eye* if he don't have dis month's pair of Shrikes! He has to see himself de only way worth doin'—as da sum of da parts he is lucky enough ta own."

Martz Martenson turned to the Mole, and winked. "But he's got ta be able ta pay for it, too—right? An' to pay for it, he's got ta forget da nuts an' da berries an' come on in, like a regular kinda guy, to his First Real Job—"

"Loggin'?—minin'?—"

"Turnin' boig-boigers in a Bunnybite? Get him on dat ladder of Consoomership—bottom rung, okay, bottom rung—he's ours. Sure, it could take two, three generations, even, in da deepest pockets of resistance. We play da long game, Mr Mole! But finally, dis guy's kids, or his *kids'* kids—if da woild lasts dat long—dey'll end up where dey shoulda bin all along. In *Toyz "For" Pupz*. In da Malls. In da Paradise of Poichasin' Power. An' when *dis* guy (A Bolivian *campesino* in full fiesta costume, waving condor-wings against a dark mountain) "has got to be *dis* guy" (the universal Mall-mal, in shift) "—hey! Dat has got to be paradise, right, am I right?"

"It is a noble fight," said Hartz Martenson soberly. "A grand an' a noble fight, an' we shall not rest in it. Dat is de End Of History, Mr Mole. De only end worth havin'. No more wars! Tink about dat. Why should *he* go to war against some other guy just like him, who's doin' de only ting dey both want to do already—shopping? Who'd ever—ever—want to start a revolution (an' against what, for Pansake?) in a *Mall?*"

The peerless logic of this argument had communicated itself to the gathering, and a round of spontaneous applause broke out around the Conference Chamber, to which the two big martens responded by rising, grinning broadly, and nodding. Only the Mole (and, as it happened, Mr Strobe Volebrush of General Armaments) did not clap.

"I like a bit of variety myself," said the Mole dejectedly. "And—and it's nice to do things for yourself." But it seemed that no one heard him. Out of nowhere, a memory came to him of a spot amongst the voids of eastern England: one of the places where he had most missed all he had once known as countryside—the husbandry, the horses, the working animals singing in the fields, the hedges and the flowers beside them. The picture imprinted on his mind was that of rows of sterilised, waving wheat, all of a shape, all of a height.

CHAPTER SEVENTEEN

MCMINC ON METAPHYSICS

"Sure, we'd end up keepin' some of it," said Mydace McMinc, breaking in on the Mole's reverie in a style so relaxed it was almost chatty. "Sure we would. There are some serious attractors here, nobody's missin' that. At the Entertainments Sector end? *The McMincWorld Jungle Tribes Experience?* Sure: 'Lived for YOU as once it was lived for real, in the Steaming Heart of the Wild, Wild Jungle.' *The McMincWorld Old Italy Experience*: 'Wander the streets of Ancient Italian Hill Towns and revel in the idyll of an all-but-forgotten Europe'. Maybe we set up whole chains of Culture Conservation Reserves, with the natives to play themselves. (We organise early, to keep out actors' unions.) Safari trips ... Luxury hotel complexes ... No doubt about it, it could be big. It's got definite Mystery potential."

"I used to live in a hole myself, once," replied the Mole desperately. Well, he had to say *something*. "Never happier, to be honest. ... No, no, I mean it."

For one fleeting moment, the eyes of Mr Gordon R. Rette and Mr Humfrey Wyvern-Toad met across the glowing pale surface of the oval.

The Conference Chamber was now very silent, and

remained in this state for a good thirty seconds. "Did *he say* ..." asked Mr Gopherit hoarsely, "did *he say* ... he lived in a *hole?*"

"O, you know, a long time ago," answered the Mole bluffly. "—Nothing like it, you know. It's really very jolly. Nothing like a nice little hole of your own. Your own little garden. Can't be improved on. Nothing *like* that first taste of spinach in the spring!"

Warren R. Bitt addressed the Mole with his mild and wide-eyed gaze. "Surely, Mr Mole," he said, laughing decorously as he did so, "you're not suggesting that living in a *hole* is in some way superior to—great Dane, the entire range of sophisticated lifestyle-potentials available to us in our present advanced state of civilization?"

This query was rather too sweeping and wordy for the Mole to cope with. "I just ... I just wonder what makes animals most happy," he replied.

"'Happy'?" said Mr McMinc wizeningly, staring at the Mole as if he had that moment confessed to personally authoring the Animalist Manifesto. "What has *that* got to do with anything?"

"Well—" Once again, the Mole met the old mink's belligerent, gleam-eyed gaze full on, puzzling as he looked at him. "Well, for example, Mr Mink—if you don't mind me askin'—what makes *you* most happy?"

Mydace McMinc clutched hard at his unique silk tie, and then at his heart. He stared, and wheezed, and made small but futile snarling sounds from the raised back corners of his lips. "I—will—*not!* ... I—can—*not* ... You have no ruhh ... no ruhhh ..."

"This is outrageous!" shouted Mr Volebrush, half-rising from his chair with others following suit. "Sir, you have no right to ask the C.E.A. of McMinc Inc—of all animals on *Earth*—a question of that nature! Mr Wyvern-Toad, sir, will you *please restrain* your colleague here, so we can get down to business? Let's get some *openage* here. We have a great deal to discuss here today!"

But, still staring horribly, the venerable mink was already waving a trembling, intemperate paw at his associate from General Armaments as if to tell him to sit right down, and shut right up. "I ... I ..." he said, and as he did so the baleful, talpicidal stare on his sharp small face melted into something that could almost have been mistaken for a child's smile. "Well gee, Mr Mole," he said. "When I get out there on that river—sure! On my estate up there on the Aroonook? Haven't been able to get myself up there the wrong side of two years now, dang it! Oh, it's a prime stretch of water, Mr Mole. Shallow, gentle flowing. You can see those ol' sockeyes on the bottom, the water's so clean. You got to look hard though: they kinda—hide themselves away against the stones. Oh, and the colours up there in the Fall! You can take a boat out, sit there with a pole, ride the water. While the whole day away ..."

The Mole returned the magnate's gaze with sad and, up to a point, comprehending eyes, and sighed.

"—But *dagnabbit!*" snapped the old mink. "No one's got time to live like that any more! Bless my preferentials, I sure as hell don't. I got one or two other prioritizations on my mind, any one time. Somehow, goin' fishing never seems to get firstcased into McMinc Mission-Of-The-Moment Modus Operandi Modules, can't quite say why!—What? You want to live your whole life like that? All of the time? Jumpin' jacksmelts! You'd have to be runnin' the whole dadblamed *world* to live like that now!"

"—And—ahhhhh—excuse me there, Mydace, but ... That wouldn't conceivably be a component of your current MOM/MOM? By the remotest chance? 'Running the whole dadblamed world'? If you don't absolutely mind one's asking?" This point of order came, laughingly, and in the most conversational of tones, from the C.E.A. of Toad

Transoceanic, who sat now just a little farther back in the shadows than he had done previously.

Slowly—very slowly—with the disbelief of the board player who has been looking everywhere but at the impending checkmate, Mydace McMinc refocussed his gaze on the silhouetted amphibian. "Why, Pan damn you, you—slimy animal!" he snarled. "You set this up! You *set this up!* How in Pan's name did I not see this coming? Why you dirty … you *dirty rat!*" (Mr Rette flinched here, just hard enough to spoil the blade-line on his guillotine.)

But the Toad gazed back with a look of impenetrable puzzlement, saying nothing.

Mydace McMinc sustained his incendiary stare just one more moment. Then he said, "Well, Humfrey … Mr Mole …" and in so doing he became, apparently, as relaxed as any animal sunning himself on a warm rock. "No one on this flight—I do believe—is arguing the future of the globe ain't corporate. The only question we gotta settle is, just how corporate is that goin' to be? How Corporate is corporate?"

"… By which you mean? …" said the Toad, his expression unchanged. "One is so easily confused."

"*You* know, Humfrey. Pandangit! *You* know! Just how many company-networks the world is goin' to need, at the end of the day. At present we have—what is it, now?—seventy thousand of us, plus? 'Supra-nationals' … 'Vanquinationals'. That's more my style. Every one of us big and powerful as a nation-state, or bigger, but one hell of a lot more difficult to locate on the face of this planet. If you did happen to have outstanding business with us."

"*They seek us here, they seek us there* …" smiled the Toad.

The old mink nodded. "But who says we can't improve on that, Humfrey? Who says we can't do something else here? Something, ohh—simpler. Deeper? Subtler! Let's call it a—" (he described an imaginary sphere-shape with his paws) "Transcendentional? Not 'a'—no. No ... '*The*' Transcendentional. Look at it organisationally, Humf, come on! This makes only sense here. Corporate World Government is the long game, you bet. So, hey, who's going to *need* more than one super-super-corp to keep things on the simmer? Think of the savings on staff and paperwork!" ("That's a point," said the Toad.) "Think of the scaledown in mixed-message-glitchup-potentials! Not to mention executive-showdown-policy-disimprovement-snafus. Big is beautiful, right, Humphrey? Very, very, very big has got to be the *Armageddon*-wowser. I know you see it, Humphrey, I know you see it. No further structural improvements possible—going forward. The Global Franchise. Now that, Humf—*that* is Free Trade!"

"Well, I do have to say it, Mydace," responded Mr Wyvern-Toad, beaming from without his shade. "It is most extraordinarily flattering of you. In fact, I hardly know what to say in reply. You are—I can only assume—suggesting the final responsibility for occupying this ulti-mate—ahhh—'transcendentional' corporate position should fall upon the humble (but, of course, most capably world-bearing) shoulders of one's own modest enterprise?"

"What are you, animal?" bawled the old mink, like a street-market trader facing an undersell. "NUTS?!" But then—controlling his rage almost immediately—he went on, "Naturally ... Humphrey ... that role can and must fall to one organisation alone. Come on now, I don't have to tell you that. There is one and one only hypersynergistic vanquinational, one only *Universe*-class corporation, with the flexibility, the versatility—the *evolution*—to shrinkwrap an entire planet! One only with a C.E.A. of the Vision necessary to guide it along its overwhelming course of partnership through-absorption, toward the ultimate.—Hell, I don't need to say the name, Humfrey. *We* are The Future."

"Odd, Mydace!" purred the Toad. "One had rather believed, you see, that *we* might be The Future. We do, after all, control a network of companies, worldwide, so vast and darkly inscrutable that only two of our executives, myself included, know the precise full scope of it."

"We have a network of companies, worldwide, so vast and darkly inscrutable that only *I* know the precise full scope of it! We exist—in the ether. We exist—in the Labyrinth. We exist as digits! Animals, plant, servicing, transit—three years, outside, *everything's* goin' to be done for us, or for the guys who are doin' it already. Try lookin' for us then, Humf!"

"You intrigue me, Mydace," responded the Toad, colouring almost invisibly. "I will say that much. Call me old-fashioned but, ether or otherwise, we have plans in train to build a new world h.q. so high, those occupying the uppermost floors will have to have the oxygen pumped up to them to keep them conscious."

"Good for you! *We* have plans to build a new world h.q. so high, the mals on the top floor will need crash helmets to stop them knocking their blocks off on the pandanged *moon!* Just so soon as we've swallowed key competition and nailed the degirth." (The final word here quite spoiled another well seen skull.)

"Ahhhh!" said Mr Wyvern-Toad. "Ahhhh! Ah-hah! I *see*, Mydace. Yes, I do see. And, er—how, now, exactly, might you be thinking of doing that? If you don't absolutely mind one's asking?"

"I DO ABSOLUTELY MIND ONE'S ASKING!!" yelled the elderly mustelid apoplectically, rising unsteadily to grip at the edge of the big oval table. "... And the answer ... No! No!!—Pangang the gurngolding—! Durngurn the bangangling—" He broke off, staring and gasping in a passion of inner conflict.

But then Mr McMinc relaxed once more, smoothed

back his snout-fur, and after a moment's hesitation, resumed his seat. There was a pulsating silence of more than ten seconds, in which many a dangerous jaw could be seen hanging open in dismay. "... The answer ..." he whispered, "... is ..."

"... is? ..." prompted the Toad, whose eyebrows were by now almost detached from his forehead.

"Okay, OKAY, pandamn you!! Gene manipulation. We know we're way ahead of you on that. Way ahead—"

"Mr McMinc!" breathed Mr Finqueret in an awed and fearful voice, as gasps came from the shadows behind him.

"Way ahead! In this last four months we've gulleted six, seven of the planet's biggest seed distributors. Oh, you'll know about it, sure you will. It'll come up on the screens. SeedWorld? ExcluzaSeeds? They're us now, Humfrey. Top, top secret but, yeah—we McMinced 'em. Sorry about that, 'old boy'."

"Mr McMinc," persisted Mr Finqueret, "none of us is yet in a position to—"

"Shaddup for pansake, Finqueret! Can't you see I can't *not* tell him?" spat out the Mink dyspeptically. "—We're negotiating for so many more it'd make your tail curl if you had one. Get the picture, Humfrey? Pretty neat, huh? What seeds they got—they're McMinc seeds now. Hey ... sorry, guys. We keep 'em, or maybe we write 'em out the story— that's out for keeps, compree? Buy one get one free, 'cos tomorrow there ain't goin' to be none. We're talking cremation here. The new gene stocks our mals got manipulated? Sorry there, guys, we call the shots there too, didn't you know? Piece by piece, it all goes over to McMinc. Country by country: McMinc GM Seeds, McMinc GM Foods. Worldwide Patents applied for *and granted*, yesterday, in the one country where patents are goin' to have teeth. So what does that mean, Humfrey, old boy? It means McMinc owns the farmers. Utah to the Ukraine? Zanesville to Zanzibar!

They use McMinc or they *don't use*. They plant MCMinc GM or they *don't plant*. We run the whole precinct, on a minimum-*minimum* labour basis. 'The McMinc Tomato'? Two years, outside. Who needs more than one? 'McMinc Wheat'? That's it—the one and only. 'McMinc Barley'? Ours, not yours, baby. McMinc rice—cocoa—coffee—beetroot—pomegranates—cloudberries. You name it, McMinc'll do it. It's just like these two fellas said, Humf. Everything in this world is goin' to be The Same. The gorgeous, gorgeous McMinc Same! 'Local'? There ain't goin' to *be* no local. 'Local'? That's McMinc. Oh, McMinc shareholders are goin' to be so deep in McMinc Clover they won't be able to see the pandanged *sky!*"

"It's exquisite," wailed Harmony van Sleek. "Exquisite!"

"And that goes for England too, Humf. Just in case any of you mals have any doubts on that. *You English* are goin' to grow what we give you to grow, you're goin' to eat what we give you to eat, and be thankful. And show your thanks in *terms!*"

The Toad was in no hurry to reply. "... Fascinating, Mydace," he said. "Give credit where credit is due, I have always believed that. But, ahh ... Ahhh ... I *think* you used the word 'swallowed' back there, at some point. Is that right? In relation to—one does have to ask this—not, to take just one of many possible examples, Toad Transoceanic, say? You do have a strategy for that, I'd guess ... First moves, MOM/MOMS, that kind of thing?"

Mydace McMinc seemed to be choking now on words he did not want to utter. He snarled and growled, and snarled again, turning his eye on every animal near him, the Mole not least, as if a part of him was contemplating lunch on the bone.

"A—er—plan, of some sort?" nudged the Toad.

"We don't *know* yet, damn you," said the Mink quietly. "That's the truth. You're still just that little bit too vast and pandanged darkly inscrutable. Maybe ... We think ... Maybe you'll lose parts of your Armaments-Servicing Sector first? Yeah. We think they might come over—kick-start the counter-flow. That first small current in the—the counter-flow ..."

The Toad moved forward so that the light fell directly on his face. His eyes were blazing too now, with an uncharacteristic intensity. "*Thank you* for that, Mydace," he said. "Nice of you to let me know. We will look into that—who knows, you may be right. There may be problems we've been missing. Nothing that can't be fixed, though—wouldn't you agree, Clutchfund?"

Already in the process of tapping at a small device he was holding, Mr Stoatdegrave nodded.

With a movement of feline dexterity the Chairmal of Toad Transoceanic stood, kneeled up on to the table, leaned out and, to a cry of low horror from all around him, plucked the gilded globe away from its spindle. "You want to play games with T.T., McMinc?" he said. "That's fine by me! Just don't think we haven't the players to give your team a hiding!" With that, he kicked the globe as if it were a football, to send it tumbling directly towards his rival, who collected it in his arms, snarling now in a rage of such ferocity it was almost as if he had reverted to the condition of his remote ancestors.

"Predate! Predate! Predate! Predate! Predate!" screamed Mydace McMinc as he threw aside the gleaming sphere. "Every territory on this planet will be *ours*, you four-flushing cabbage-faced webfoot!"

"Colonize! Colonize! Colonize! Colonize! Colonize!" returned Humfrey de Buforchy d'Etanguy Wyvern-Toad, in a tone of rapacity barely distinguishable from the Mink's. "We English will still get there before you, Mydace— we always did! And I don't think I need descend to your level to make that point!"

Many animals from both contingents had risen to their feet by now, as if instinct was calling them forth to join the standoff along national, tribal—who knows—*speciesial* lines. Once more the two war-cries were sounded, by many voices on either side. It is difficult to say where this might have led next, had not the *Inextinguishable* at that moment run into a third meteorological cliff-face, and the most formidable yet. This so arrested the aircraft's movement that every standing figure found himself staggering heavily sideways, as if in the style of a musical with a zombie theme. The lights flickered, the satellite-view Earths ghosted queasily on their screens, and the globe of beaten gold rolled away into a shaded corner of the Chamber like the child's toy it had become.

"Gent'mals, please!—Please! This is turning into a farce!" said Warren R. Bitt, in a shocked low voice. "Wall Street *cannot tolerate* instability of this kind."

One by one—cowed by this reminder of fundamental truth, and with much po-faced straightening of ties and jackets—each of the standing animals resumed his seat. The Toad and the Mink were last to sit: each continued to face the other down across the oval, eyebeam to blazing eyebeam. But at last both unlocked their stares, and sat at once.

Oddly, though, one animal present was not yet silenced (nor did the Mole himself feel the slightest responsibility towards Wall, or any other, Street). He was looking towards the huge image of the Earth as it floated, restored once more, on the sloping screen behind him. A number of things had been puzzling him about it, and in this long moment of embarrassed silence, seeing no reason not to, he thought he might find out more.

"Why, um—could anyone tell me—why it looks like that—just there?" he said. He was pointing towards the centre of the top part of the South American continent. In several places here, bizarrely, the land mass seemed to be glowing faintly, rather as does a scattering of near-dead embers on a bed of ashes, traces of orange-red pulsing across its otherwise completely static brown-grey surface.

Mr McMinc bared his gums—he did *not* want to answer more questions of any kind. Then, as ever, he half-turned in his seat and responded sullenly, "That's Brazil. It's Brazil. How is it you do not know this? Brazil is burning— sectors of it. The Amazon?—The *Amazon.*"

"*Brazil* is *burning* ..?" repeated the Mole ungraspingly.

"You can see it from space sometimes. The satellite picks it up. It's big, yeah. It's big."

"'Big'?" The Mole could not begin to picture the scale of the devastation. After all, he thought, Brazil must be bigger even than Oxfordshire and Berkshire rolled into one! His imagination recoiled from it. Hadn't he seen enough devastation already with his own two eyes, not just in Oxfordshire and Berkshire, but in Hertfordshire and Cambridgeshire, Essex and Suffolk? Still he asked, "But *why*?"

The old mink shrugged wearily. "Logging ... agricultural development programs ... burgermeat-grazing forest clearance ... The usual stuff, Mr Mole. The usual stuff!"

The Mole stared at the unsettling, almost-living image and his heart sank to somewhere slightly groundward of his shoe-leather. "Now I understand why Pan is so weak," he said, in the low voice of one who has just for the first time accurately reckoned the overwhelming odds-against. "The Earth—O, I can hardly say it—the Earth itself is dying. It is *everywhere*, isn't it? All these things you do, all this destruction." He looked around the assembly, from face to silent face. "And it is you animals who are the murderers."

"You could maybe find a coupla others, Mr Mole," said Mydace McMinc drily. "One or two, you know? Round about the place? Be fair, now."

Frowning, and staring very hard at the tip of his pigment-ink pen, Mr Rette coughed and covered his eyes.

"This mole guy is a pandamned *shrub-hugger!*" snarled Mr Gopherit. "He's a slug-nuzzler! He's a pandamned pond-scrapin' *bog-noser!* No company mal *ever* talks like that! Who in hell let him in here?!"

"Mr Mole," said Mr McMinc, completely ignoring this. "I am the head of the world's largest—hell-fire and damnation!!—*one* of the world's largest transnational organisations. As the round-brilliant diamond drillbit at the driving point of this great machine, *I see only* the size of the dividends we pay to our shareholders. *I see only* the position of my group of companies in relation to other—comparable groups. *I see only* what the Mystery shows me. 'The Earth is dying'? What does that mean? The 'Earth'—what's that? It's a diagram. It's a satellite picture. It's my resource-field. Period. Even if it was dying, what the hell difference would it make? We shall go on, just as we have always done, till the last eyedropper-full of oil has been pumped, the last hairsbreadth of ore has been mined, the last pandamned tree on the planet felled, if necessary. Because *we*, Mr Mole, have the Mystery. We *are* the Mystery."

The old mink was staring at the Mole now with a defiant, wounded righteousness, as if unable to comprehend how anyone might have come to question the principle of what he did. "We have a right to do this," he said. "You get me, now? We have a *right*. That's what Democracy is, Mr Mole! That freedom. *Our* freedom. To do what the hell we must, wherever the hell we want to do it, and keep this great machine ticking over. This machine? It's the most beautiful thing. The most beautiful thing. You gotta kill a world to keep it, if that's what we're doin'? Pandangit, that's fine by me."

"One last spin of the wheel!" cried Mr Wyvern-Toad. "Then to perdition! Think of it, Mr Mole, as a kind of … creative destruction?"

"But—how will animals be able to *live. Anywhere?*" demanded the Mole agitatedly.

"Maybe they won't!" snapped Mydace McMinc. "... Yeah, who knows? Maybe they won't. I guess there'll still be enough islands to go round for the—uh—the big league to run at least one apiece. I myself own an archipelago."

"I, too, own an archipelago," said the Toad warmly. "In effect. Distributed around the world, you know—sensible, one feels, in the current climate. Two of my islands are over four miles in diameter."

"Three of *mine* are over *five* miles in diameter," retorted the Mink. "And one of them has a mountain over three thousand meters!"

"One of *mine* has a blue-water lagoon!" replied the Toad.

"I myself own four islands," offered the Bog Lemming, still in stricken tones. "And as of this present time I—ah—have been in negotiation for a fifth. With a reef."

"I am in the market for a ninth island myself," said Martz Martenson. "I am so," echoed his bother. "Although, due to current fluctuations in the value of my stocks, I may have to make a choice between it and the Van Gofer."

Mydace McMinc's eyes wandered from the table, and if they were focused at all now it was on some imaginary point far beyond the darkened wall of the Chamber. "... Yeah," he said. "We'll get another fifty years, I guess. Forty, any-how." He looked on beyond the darkness one moment longer, then he said, "But, hey! Mr Mole! Turn up the air conditioning and forget it, mal! This is what you *do!*"

"It's what you do," echoed the Water Rat, very quietly, with the nod of one who understands.

"—Even if the nozone layer docs pack in," said Mr McMinc, "we already got that covered—hey, Matt?"

"We certainly do, Mydace," responded Prof. Mustrak. "Minkmark Physochemicals (Belgium/ South Africa/ Sri

Lanka) has the prototype for what we can futurise as one hundred per cent UV-resistant filtration sheeting."

"*ArtSky*," said Mr McMinc. "That's what we're goin' to call it, right?"

The professor nodded. "It's featherlight, rip-proof, fantastically strong, a perfect midday sky-blue in tone. And it has its own internal lighting braid."

"—You get that, Mr Mole? Along with the earthquake-proof pylon grid we're designing for it, all any stupendo-dadillionaire will have to do is fix it up over his chosen island—islands—and hey, it's aced. It's in the bag. Freedom of movement? Sure! Any time of the day or night. Billionaires—they may have a problem. But the—heh—the AAA-list? Tell me when you got news."

It was necessary for the Mole to pause a moment, digesting the possible meanings of this, few though they might be. "But ... but what about everybody else?" he said at last.

"Hey, Mr Mole, Mr *Mole!*" replied Mydace McMinc. "We're goin' to need Security. We're goin' to need engineers, transit personnel, domestics. That's a whole bunch of jobs. Beyond that—" He shrugged. "It's always been a tough world, brother."

This last remark put paid to the Mole's battle-weary attempts at debate. He said no more for the rest of the meeting, which—as a result, no doubt—progressed smoothly except for the occasional burst of candour, rampant from one side of the table especially. But he did not give up thinking, and what he saw—what he could no longer avoid seeing—was that Weaselworld was doomed. Though he may never have sat in such a meeting as this, the Badger had seen the truth: Pan would have his revenge, when, after the last, crushing insult had been dealt to it, his domain collapsed around the perpetrators. Weaselworld would kill itself as surely as the last leaves fall from the trees in November; and perhaps all that mattered now was whether enough would be left after it was gone for a new kind of world to build itself from the wreckage. The Mole saw one other thing, too: this disaster—this unimagineable cataclysm—would be brought about by nothing more than an attitude of mind.

Sitting on there in his place at the table, the Mole felt he must do something, anything—anything he could think of—to try to change the course of this ship of fat-heads for whom Nature herself was enemy, slave and expendable bullion. He had tried reasoning, to the best of his ability, and where had it got him? And the *Mole School For The Transformation Of Young Weasels*, where they might, per-haps, over time, have been taught to think differently, was quite beyond his powers and resources. He stared into the shadows, hoping even as he feared it that this hurricane they were busy flying round might have the good sense to change direction and come their way. Or might he pre-empt it, by rushing to the driver's cab (in his mind's eye he still saw the craft as a kind of train), overwhelming its occupants, and single-handedly steering the prime movers of the Blacktop Consumers' Coalition into the storm's engulfing heart? Yet even if, somehow, he did this (where exactly *was* the driver's cab? ...), would it really make so much difference to the wider weasel-destiny?

A little over twelve hours later, the Mole found himself inside the Conference Chamber once more. Along with most of the rest of the passengers, he had retired to the guests' cabins to try to get a few hours' sleep before land-ing, but the elusive, churning vibrations inside his pillow had kept all chance of that at bay. So he got up again, and wandered ahead through the long section of seat-clusters where some animals lay snoring, looking for a space in the machine in which he felt anything like at ease.

The white oval stood just as it had in its pool of light, though cleared of papers now, and with the golden globe discreetly restored to its central axis. The two huge leaning screens also remained open, and on them, twice over, the world was turning too slowly to see.

The Mole sat down in what might earlier have been his seat, or that of the Chairmal of McMinc Inc. In so doing, he pressed one of the buttons controlling the tapperboards, and the small register of little black squares rose up before his nose. What *were* these things, though? Would he ever understand? He fumbled inside his jacket (it had so many pockets), into which he had transferred the small and by now badly battered ring-bound notebook he had bought on his travels to use as a diary. Most of this he had filled with scrappy notes to himself about items of shopping, and directions, and maps, and where he packed what in which pannier and, somewhat futilely, things to tell Ratty. But a few pages did survive in which he had managed to jot down some impressions of his journey, and he now had exactly one sheet left unscribbled on.

He pulled out the pencil and poised it above the paper. But—O, where to begin! After a little more poising, he put the pencil down again. He had written two words: "I", and "don't". In a half-curious kind of way he stared again at the grid of tapper-letters and numbers and then, experimentally, tapped at one. Nothing happened. He tapped at another. Nothing happened once more. He tapped at five, six, seven letters, then numbers, then letters. The same nothing happened a third time. The worlds turned and did not turn, just as they had done before.

"Don't seem quite to have got the hang of—" He tapped one more letter. After the fourth nothing had followed its appointed course, a strange low soughing sound could be heard in the shadows at the front end of the Chamber.

Curious, if still only in a muted kind of a way, the Mole
ambled towards the sound to find that sheets of paper—
paper of immediate usefulness to an animal hoping to
diarise his impressions of any world—were, by much the
usual kind of magic, appearing out of a long dark slot.
There was a lot of print on their back sides. But the front
of each was still quite clean.

"O—well," he said to the empty room. "Most kind."

Having neatly stacked his sheets on the table, the Mole
stood, musing once more. He would write now ... he *would*
... if only he were not quite so tired. His eye strayed to the
nearer of the screens, and then he walked towards it. Could
that possibly be—no, but *could* it be England, and the
rest?—that vulnerable-looking little cluster of land scraps
up at the right, stuck out at the edge of a land-mass so large
it bent out of sight round the curve of the planet? In the
great space of ocean spreading up to the north of it he
could pick out a few details. One tiny-looking island, and
there, to the north and east of it, a faint sprinkling of yet
tinier white shapes. These were not clouds: he could tell
that straight away. They resembled a shower of snowflakes,
seen at a certain distance—through one of the windows of
Toad Hall, perhaps. He raised his paw towards them, as if
touching a part of the screen on which they floated might
make them more comprehensible. But they were way out of
reach.

"Not easy, sleeping on these things," said a voice. The
Mole looked back into the shadows, from which slowly
emerged the form of a ragged-looking water rat.

"The hum kept me awake," said the Mole.

"Oh ... Sorry. Had a nightmare myself," said Mr Rette,
snuffing.

"O—O dear."

"I dreamed—it could have been a documentary. Can't
get it out of my mind now. 'Kennylands' was a tower

block—that's right. But it was huge—went up for floor after floor, which was fine, but no use, because it was sinking down into a—I don't know—great pit of quicksand, or something. And I was running up the stairs with all the other animals, getting higher and higher up as the place sank lower down. Some animals were just staying at their desks, working away. As they would! It went on and on— oh, staircase after staircase! And there were announcements coming from somewhere—one of those close-to voices that sounds as if it's right inside your head. 'There is no cause for alarm, there is no ... The building is not sinking!' That kind of thing. And the place seemed to be sprouting new upper floors, but I got tired of running up to them, and woke up. Ha ha. Ha ha ha. To find myself here."

"Dear me!" said the Mole. "Are you all right now?"

"I'm fine." The Rat shuffled away, his paws sunk like pipe-wrenches inside the pockets of his packaway silk dressing-gown.

"Would you like a—" The Mole looked about for a kettle and hob. He had nearly said 'cup of tea'.

"I'm fine."

"Mr Rette?" said the Mole after a moment, in which he had turned back in fascination to the sloping screen. "Do you know what those things are? Up there?—Those snowflakey things?"

The Water Rat squinnied, standing on his toes to do so. "Hah," he said. "Huh."

There was a long pause.

"*Do* you know?"

"Yes," said the Rat. "Yes, I do. Or I can guess."

There was another pause, of similar longevity.

"What are they, then?"

"They're icebergs, Mole. They're icebergs."

CHAPTER EIGHTEEN

A LA RECHERCHE DES TROUS PERDUS

During the working week that followed his return from Mr McMinc's aerial summit, the Mole's presence was not required at Toad Transoceanic. The weather was good, and he got into the habit of going off again each morning on little walks, much as he had done before his cycling journey. He was slightly better equipped now, carrying with him an ancient rucksack (found, as ever, by Justin in the garage) into which he would stuff a flask, a sandwich, and a paperback copy of the *Complete Works Of Wagtaile* which Mr Rette had lent to him from his own bedside shelf. He also carried some of the sheaf of scribbling-paper the McMinc jet had so kindly disgorged for him, though he rarely got around to using it.

Much as before the journey, too, he saw very little of the Rettes themselves. Mrs Rette was away at some posy ham (as the Mole had heard it: she had said ... but the reader may guess what she said) whilst her husband's day at the office seemed to have extended almost to the point where it conformed to his worst fears and met up with its own tailgate in the middle of the night. The two animals did exchange the occasional muffled greeting in the brief

moments when they happened to be in the same room or
nocturnal passageway together, and these were just long
enough for the Mole to notice a new quality in the way the
Rat met his eye: if he had had to put a word to it, he might
have called it shamefaced.

On his first day off, the Mole had walked a short way
along the river before turning up the hill into the beech
woods. On the Tuesday, he had continued just a little further along the opposite bank before finding a route south-
wards through grim suptopia, so avoiding the reach where
lay the tiny eyot of his memories. Today it was Thursday,
and he found himself once again on the hilly side of the
water on a bright, clear morning, tramping along the bridleway that would, he knew, eventually run near the spot he
had been avoiding. But today he made no efforts at diversion, following the twitching of his nose with barely a
moment's hesitation. "If I walk past it, well then, past it I
shall walk," he said. "What harm can it do now, anyway?
There's that great 'field' in the way, too."

As ever, the track ahead of him was empty of fellow animals, though from the main road far off beyond the river
he could hear this startling motorbike-scream, that derang-
ing siren-warble, to remind him of flows elsewhere. He pat-
tered on, thinking of nothing absolutely-in-particular, but
with brief, isolated fragments of the scenes he had witnessed at the old mink's table still resurfacing to challenge
him. Each time this happened he would slow down almost
to the point of stopping, searching the banks alongside the
track for evidence that some flowers still grew *here*, at least.
More than once he repeated—less as instruction than as
hoped-for possibility— "I should do *something*.—I *should*.
... But what, Mole? What should you—could you—would
you—DO?"

Within thirty minutes of setting off he had reached the
length of bridleway he had first crossed at a right angle all

those weeks ago in order to drop down to the eyot. Here, unhesitatingly, he sat on a section of steep bank where one vigorous patch of marjoram and grass still resisted the encroachment of brambles. His view of the river was completely blocked by more bramble, walling-in the bridleway's opposite side, but this did not worry him: he did not want to be able to look down towards it.

The bank here happened to be made at just the right kind of angle for lying back on, and one part in particular was upholstered by long, soft grasses. The temptation was too much, and the Mole deckchaired himself upon it. The curve of the bank was a perfect fit, and after no more than three minutes in the hot sun his eyelids began to droop.

"… Even if the Nozone layer does pack in," said Mr McMinc, "we already got that covered—hey, Matt?" "… One last spin of the wheel!" cried Mr Wyvern-Toad, cackling gleefully. "Then to perdition!" "… We shall go on, just as we always have done," snarled Mr McMinc, "till the last pandamned tree on the *planet* has been felled."

The Mole covered his face with his handkerchief, and let out a shuddering sigh. "O dear, O dear, O dear," he breathed. He closed his eyes again. "I should find the Badger," he thought, and "… I should find the *Badger!*" he whispered. But he got no further with this line of thought. For at the very moment the words were forming on his lips he heard a new sound in the eddying overlay of traffic noise, far-off aircraft rumbling and isolated points of birdsong. Then—it was just as he completed the whispered words—this new sound also ceased. He lay quite still now, gripping at a clump of grass with his left paw, and listening with every eardrum in his body.

"—The pipes? …" he breathed, a moment later. And as he did so, once again he seemed to hear the very thing he was describing. But this time the notes floated on after he had spoken, for three, four seconds, intertwining themselves with the chortlings of a mistle-thrush that drifted up to him from somewhere far away along the riverbank. Very, very gently, the Mole removed his handkerchief from his face and sat up, staring into the bramble-bank that blocked his view to the water.

He waited like this for another three minutes without so much as the flick of a whisker, hearing neither the thrush nor the other, more elusive music. Then, out of the traffic-thrum and wind-whisperings, the thrush sang again; and for just a few seconds—woven into and around it like ivy twining its way around the intricacies of a wrought iron gateway—there came a sound as of pipes, blown quietly and at no great distance by some figure seated, where else than on a tiny sliver of willow-studded land, in the midst of the flowing stream?

The Mole got to his feet very slowly indeed, fearing that one abrupt movement on his part might be enough to silence the music, and gazed down over the ragged tops of brambles on which a few blooms were already opening. But he could see nothing of the eyot from here, and little enough of the water: all the riparian trees were fully open now. And long as he waited on there after that, he heard no more of the piping, or the mistle-thrush.

"*I must bring them to the island,*" he said finally. "—Mr Rette. Mr Wyvern-Toad! That is what I have to do, isn't it? *Isn't* it, Mole? If you can get them to go there—perhaps they will hear it too. Perhaps they will hear it, and—" He halted, struggling. But beneath any surface confusion, the idea was there clear enough. "—it might make them change. It might make them *change.*"

What that change would entail, or what might result from it, the Mole could not begin to say. But it did not matter: he had all he needed now by way of motivation. "It will make them change," he said out loud, with something close to confidence. "And I must—I *must* find the Badger!"

In the relatively short time it took the Mole to return to the Rette stronghold after lunch, the sky clouded over from the west. The clouds were heavy almost at once, irising-down the day's former early summer brilliance into something only slightly less gloomy than a mid-January day when snow is in the offing. Once he got the gates open, the Mole was surprised to find Mr Rette's *Blumenduft* parked there on the gravel, some bits of it still ticking as it cooled down. He went inside to the house to top up his thermos flask, expecting to find the driver inside. But the place was silent, unoccupied.

Whilst he waited for the kettle to boil, the Mole turned on the kitchen radio. "… can expect this weakened outer rim of the vast weather system surrounding Hurricane Clarabelle to work its way gradually up from the south during the next thirty-six hours or so," said a now familiar voice, "as a series of fronts. The first of these is quite weak and will probably produce only a sprinkling of rain here and there, but it is going to get much worse, I'm afraid, as the rest comes through tomorrow and into Saturday. By teatime tomorrow we can expect storm-force winds or stronger all across the southern counties, and up into the Midlands later, and of course we will be keeping you updated on that in later bulletins. So all together, I'm afraid, not a very seasonal—"

"O *dear!*" thought the Mole. "What a rotten nuisance!" He had not expected to meet Hurricane Clarabelle at all in this life, even less twice over.

But he was not to be deterred. He stuffed a waterproof into his rucksack alongside the thermos, opened the front door again, and set off briskly along the best route he knew towards the Badger's plantation-sett.

It was only after he entered the outer edge of the plantation itself, a good two hours later, that the Mole slowed
his pace to something closer to his everyday exploring-
amble. He had to go slowly here anyway, since until now he
had not been into this wood along anything resembling a
direct route, and so had to guess his way on in the direction of the hidden entrances. He was helped in his search
by the Clearway, which he could hear breathing through the
trees after traversing no more than a few hundred yards of
the track. He paused once, looking back with a little jerk
of apprehension. Surely he wasn't being followed here *again*?
His memories of this place—at least, until the point when
he had been admitted to the Badger's retreat—were not
good ones. Just as on his first visit, he began to walk a little faster.

But this time no pursued or pursuers materialised
behind him, and in minutes he came up against the barrier
of the Clearway itself. He looked down and along it and—
thinking he recognised an over-bridge—turned left along
the narrow gap between the fence and the rows of trees. He
was getting close now: he was sure of it. Another two to
three minutes and he had reached the point where he and
the Badger had stood briefly, watching the diuturnal flow,
and here he turned left again. It was here ... here, somewhere ... under one or other of these near-identical match-
stick trees. There would be brash pulled over it—he
expected that. Experimentally, he dragged a twist of broken
branchwood away from the base of a tree, but found nothing beneath except needles and twigs. He tried the next tree
along, to no better effect. He looked back towards the
Clearway fence, squinting, checking his orientation, musing. "Ah!" he said, and moved three trees up, in parallel to
the road. Here, with his foot, he roughly smeared aside an
arc of needles; and beneath them he saw the old stained
planking of one of the "coal-cellar" doors.

But what on earth was he to do now? Where was the doorbell? ("Silly question," he thought.) Should he knock three times and wait? Shout down through the wood? Tentatively, he tried knocking—not very loudly—looking about him as he did so. There was a hollow and desolate thudding echo. He peered a little more closely at the even layer of needles on the doors: they looked very much as if the trees had dropped them there. He tapped again, much more energetically, but nothing more than the echo came back to greet him.

"O dear," said the Mole. He did not need to be told, now, that there was no one there.

What could he do but retrace his steps? For one moment he considered leaving a note, but since he had nothing definite or useful to put in it he decided not to. He returned to the long mossy ride and trudged off unhappily. No more than thirty paces along it, he heard his own name spoken.

"Mole," the voice said again, all but inaudibly.

The Mole stopped, staring about him, to find nothing but trees.

"Over here."

One of the trees had indeed spoken to him. The Mole walked towards it with his mouth wide open. Beyond its luxuriant sprays of blue-green needles he could just make out a shape in colours marginally different to that of foliage, and then a face showed itself—an unsmiling, grimly determined face. It was the one-eyed hare.

"Come on," he said, and without further comment or greeting he led the Mole off—the one animal striding, the other running to keep up—into the pitchy gloom beneath the trees. The Hare slowed his pace a little here, and the two animals continued on for many minutes before emerging into a wide grassy clearing, beyond which they plunged once more into seemingly impenetrable coppice under a canopy of full-grown oaks and beeches. Beyond that they were in tree-belts where many of the trees were dead or dying, surrounded by regulation ploughland; then again into a small and isolated wood. At last the Hare bent to pull aside a piece of half-rotted, leaf-strewn green canvas, and three minutes later the Mole found himself standing in another of the many obscure subterranean bases of the Animale Restoration Front.

<hr />

The scene before him now—as he waited in the shadows at the Hare's request—was as odd as any other the Mole had seen in this world. The chamber was a large one, though not the largest in the sett. In it, with their backs to him, sat the Badger and the Otter, framing between them a small hedgehog in a bulging quilted jacket, with a battered fold-up table beyond. On this—and it was the very last thing the Mole might have expected to find here—stood a row of dimly glowing window-boxes, each linked up by a tangled plait of wires and small boxlike objects to a whirring and ancient-looking turbine-generator. This was being powered, for want of a better word, by two of the big young badgers, each of them seated at an anchored-down bicycle whose back wheel had been removed and linked up as a drive unit by way of what looked like a set of scaled down windmill gears. Both sons' faces wore an expression of dutiful boredom.

"You must see it, Otter!" the Badger was saying. "There has to be a way forward for us here. Don't you see that through this we are able to speak easily, instantly—for the very first time—with anyone out there who is sympathetic to the cause? *Anyone.* Not just ARF Wiltshire, or ARF Surrey. I guarantee you: where there are still burrowers surviving there will have been resistance. They will have done as we have done. If they are out there on the other side of the *world*, we can find them." He slapped a screen-box. "—Yes. Through this!"

"On-ly may-be fa-ther—" grunted son One, pedalling, "with a-no-ther po-wer in-put—?"

"Patience, Melos!" said the Badger. "—Patience!"

The Otter shook his head defiantly, and with an irritation that suggested this debate had already seen some airing. "This equipment is the spawn of Weaselworld!" he said. "I'm telling you, Badger, it will let through *nothing* but the weasel view of things. What else can it have been made for? If we use it, trust me, we shall become like them. And they will find their way back to us along these wires quicker than if we sent them an *At Home* card with a map in it!"

"But we *must learn*, Otter! I don't like this apparatus any more than you do. But I am not going to ignore a way forward when I see one." He placed a paw on the Hedgehog's shoulder. "Can you call up some more?"

"Sure thing," responded the small round animal, tapping. "Let me try ... Let's just follow this entry here— O.K.? ... *University of Gosport—Lowland Countryside Survey?* Looks good ..." He tapped, and tapped. "Oh, yeah. What do you want here? 'Numbers of lapwing, snipe, woodcock, lesser spotted woodpecker, willow tit, grasshopper warbler, tree pipit, redpoll, good grief, starling ... all declined by more than fifty per cent in past ... twenty-five years ...'"

"—You must see this, Otter. You must see it! This agrees, interlocks, with that earlier study from the Fenland. Roughly the same drop for five, six species—slightly different timespan. Independently of one another, they are saying the same thing.—Can you widen it? If that's the word?"

"Okey-dokey. Why don't we try ... Kew Gardens? They have—no, I have a better idea. We'll go to the Global Nature Club first. They go for the macro, so we hear. And

right away, here——see? You've *got* to be impressed by this!
Even as you're depressed. 'One quarter of world's topsoil
probably lost in past fifty years'? 'One third of world's forest cover gone over same period' ...?"

"One quarter of the world's *topsoil*?" echoed the Otter in
a whisper.

"Why should we be surprised?" said the Badger. His
tone was ironic, but he could not hold back a sigh.

"... 'One in ten of world's tree species headed for
extinction' ..." quoted the little hedgehog brightly. "Now
there——see?——bottom right?——that's taken from a study
funded by the Dutch *government*."

"Can't be too many weasels in power in Holland yet,
Otter," said the Badger. "——Which is good. Which is
good!"

"Extinctions ... extinctions ... You want extinctions, we
can do you extinctions ... Tropical forests, could be losing
species at the rate of——" The Hedgehog paused. "Three
every *hour*?" He sniffed, his jauntiness pricked like a soap
bubble. "Blimey."

The Badger inhaled very deeply, and exhaled very deeply,
breath and sigh bound together by the force of his emotion. He shook his head silently.

"We should build a Mausoleum Of Made-Extinct
Creatures," said a standing rabbit blackly. "Record every
one of them that goes. Carve their names. *Picture* them. A
great stone tablet. Leave it somewhere underground for
animals of the future to uncover. So that they can see the
vastness of the crime."

"Your optimism's good to hear, Rabbit," said the Otter.
"You expect there will still *be* animals, capable of reading,
in any future you care to name?"

"A point," replied the Rabbit, grinning a Golgotha-grin.

But the Badger did not smile. "They die because their
homes are destroyed.——You see? It does not matter where

it is on this earth, it will always be the same thing. It always has been the same thing. Here, the hedges are destroyed, the woodlands are put under conifers or grubbed up for plough-and-poison. There, the forest itself is set alight. Our homes are destroyed. Their homes are destroyed. It's the same. All that's different now is the speed at which it's happening."

The Otter leaned forward and put his nose between his paws, staring.

"—Do you see it now?" said the Badger. "It's not just that these studies are being made. This is the way the knowledge is coming through now. Here! On this—thing, yes. Filtering through. Day by day, day by day, through and into Weaselworld itself. How can they stop it? In this country; in every country. And we can tap directly into the flow. We can do it! Here, now, anywhere we want. We can link up with it. We may even be able to talk to the animals who are doing these studies. And we can be *heard*. It's as open to us as to any other animal. We can find friends, Otter. We can make them!"

The Otter continued to stare at the screen nearest to him. Then, barely turning to the Hedgehog, he said, "*Can they trace back to a—er—an* input, or whatever, with these things?"

"Now that I can't tell you. I can find out, though. When d'you need to know?"

The Otter continued to stare ahead, rubbing heavily along the line of his scar. Then, abruptly, he leapt from his chair, seeing the Mole and the Hare for the first time as he did so. "You know what my instinct is, Badger?" he said, in something between a shout and a sob. "My instinct is still to fight.—Yes, and I mean *fight*! Disable their machinery! Blow up their chemical stores! At least, then, we do one thing at a time, and know it's been done well."

The Badger paused, exhaling deeply, "... But my dear

friend, you must see that by changing ideas—*that* way we may have a chance of destroying something far bigger than any shedful of chemicals. Those things are just the means to an end. What if, now, we can begin to change the end itself?"

The quilt-muffled hedgehog had by now tapped away the last of the death-toll charts, replacing them on both screens with a bold-print message. It read simply, "HELLO, WORLD!"

"—But if it isn't the *Mole!*" cried the Badger, who had at last moved sufficiently to notice the new arrival. "Welcome back, Mole!—And who is this you have with you?"

The Mole turned to find another animal standing at the foot of the flight of steps behind him, his head and neck covered by a black cloth bag, his arms pinned back and in the grip of the third of the Badger sons. "He was following the Mole," said the son. (It was William.) "That's what it looked like. Tailing him all the way up to the Defoliation base. He didn't say anything, but I thought we'd better bring him in."

The bag was roughly plucked away to reveal nothing other than the stricken and staring face of Mr Gordon R. Rette. "... three species ..." he whispered, "... every *hour?* ..." His eyes wandered across the group in front of him. "Whu—wha—where am I? Who—"

"Were you following this mole?" demanded the Badger.

"I was.—In a way I was, I suppose. Yes. I came home, you see. I—ha, ha—I took the afternoon off. I—Mr Mole? Mr Mole. I wasn't well. I just, you know—I couldn't *do* it any more. Not this morning. I just couldn't. I came home. I was out there on the boat—no idea why, really—just wandered out there on to it. Sat there with my skipper's cap on. I saw you leave, with your rucksack. And I thought, *I'd* like to go for a walk like that. Just—go. Just open the gate—like that, you know, and—go. And before I knew it

I was out there myself, following in the direction you'd gone. To—" (He let out a light, distracted, slightly disturbing laugh) "see what it was like? To—walk. I only caught sight of you twice—miles off—but it was enough for me to follow the way you went. I'm sorry—I had no idea you—" He looked about him with large, confused eyes.

"That's it, then," said William. "A Weaselworld spy, caught in the act of spying by—well, er—" He grinned.

"—No—" said Mr Rette. "I'm not a *spy*." He laughed again, in a timbre a little closer to the everyday. "—Am I, Mole?"

"O, no, you aren't," responded the Mole firmly. "He isn't.—He isn't."

The Water Rat raised clenched but twisted fingers to his forehead. "Where does it all go to?" he asked of no one in particular. "The topsoil?"

"I wish we could tell you," responded the Badger. "Into the sea, presumably. You are—let me get this right—you are the Mole's, er, 'colleague', aren't you?"

"You could put it like that."

"Toad Transoceanic?"

"Yes."

The Badger nodded grimly.

"Er ... Fa—ther?" said Pedalling Son Number One, in a not un-aggrieved tone. "Can we *stop* now, Fa—ther?"

"Stop—what? Oh! Yes, Melos. At ease. Switch to backup."

"Thanks for telling us so soon, Father."

⚊⚋⚌⚍⚎

The Mole stared again through the great plate glass window of the Rettes' living room. The weather outside was bad enough by now to penetrate even so near absolute a sound-barrier as this: each time the shrubs and little trees danced in the garden, and the short grass of the lawn flickered and rippled crazily around them, their movements were accompanied by a muffled but uneasy shushing.

All the Mole could do now was wait, and hope it got no worse again. It was mid-afternoon on the day after his visit to the A.R.F. hideaway, and he was standing here now since—amazingly—the Water Rat had taken very little persuading before he agreed to go along with the plan he had put to him and the other animals present. The Mole knew he had not expressed himself well—putting things well wasn't one of his strengths. Had any of them *quite* believed him—even the Badger himself—when he had told them what he had heard (what he thought he had heard) at the eyot? And he was still smarting now, just a little, at the Otter's repeated barbs: "What difference is it ever going to make, Mole! Even if he *did* hear something there? And what'll you do then if he does, take the chairmals of every other giant corporation in the world down there one by one in a coracle for 'illumination'?"

But one thing had changed already, and that in itself was extraordinary. For when the Mole described the sounds he had heard, and told the gathering what he believed to be their source, one animal in particular had listened with deeply furrowed brow-fur and unblinking, hollow eyes. So that—when the Mole asked him if he would, at least, *try* to get the chairmal of Toad Transoceanic to join them on the island—Mr Rette had agreed, quietly, soberly, and without so much as a hint of sarcasm.

And that was where things stood. Hesitant, nervy and sometimes a little confused he may have been, but it had been the Rat himself who had eventually suggested a strategy. The Toad would never in a million years waste his time making a trip to a tiny river-island, he said, unless he believed it might be significantly to his advantage. But they did have one card they could perhaps play here, since the Toad had great faith in the Mole's ability to make things happen—as he so often did, the Rat had added, in a rather crabbed tone. So: if, for example, he were to be told that the Mole had found someone—a "person of importance"—whom it was essential he should meet at once—that he had in fact arranged a rendezvous to that end ... He would be there. He was certain it would be enough. And if nothing happened—well, then, it would not be impossible to explain away: unfortunately, the contact had not shown up. The "deal" would just have to wait a little longer.

But until he exited his wardrobe this morning, the Mole had forgotten about the weather. He had had to sit through a detailed report on "maverick" To-We MP Mrs Malvolia Gerbills' *Keep Bromley Indigenously-Furred* campaign to get the three-minutes-to-eight bulletin, which told him things were most likely to be at their worst across the south during the early afternoon. "Some structural damage was inevitable", and "drivers of high-sided vehicles" were being strongly advised not to. The Mole watched the shrubs bend, and flick back, and bend again: he couldn't imagine being out there now on one of the little ratlets' skateboards, let alone in a "high-sided vehicle".

He waited another hour like this, mostly on guard by the window, willing each bush-bending burst to be gentler than the last. Then, when he was least expecting it, he heard a door opening, and voices; and a moment later Messrs Rette and Wyvern-Toad were there in front of him exactly as he had hoped.

"Mr Mole, Mr Mole!" said the Toad, beaming. "This is all most intriguing! I hadn't taken you for a mal of intrigue, on top of all your other gifts. ... But of course, I could hardly fail to respond to your call! Are we, er—are we to know, who exactly this person is ... whom you ...?"

The Toad gestured with his hands as if he thought it might be the Mole's turn to speak; and it was only then the Mole himself realised that—since he was not, in fact, a mal of intrigue or anything resembling one—he had no reply of any kind prepared. "Um—ah—"

There was a brief pause, of an uncomfortable sub-type.

"—I think it might be better, W-T," said Mr Rette, looking out of the window himself now, "if we leave that detail until the meeting itself? I'm sure you'll understand immediately the time arrives."

"... Fine, Gordon. Fine!" said Mr Wyvern-Toad with just a trace of amusement. "After all, why should one object to the *sotto voce* approach? Good to see one's, er, newer colleagues applying it so creatively! I hope we have water-proofs?"

"On the boat," said Mr Rette. "Oilskins, plenty. I have umbrellas in the hall."

The umbrellas might better have been left in the hall. Within thirty paces two had turned inside out, and moments later the third was wrenched wholesale from the Mole's grasp and rose up like a round black kite to which no one had attached any string, to soar out of sight over the barricade of mourning-conifers. All three animals found themselves staggering in each new blast, and the wind and the rain together plastered their clothes hard to them, so that by the time they reached the boat there was hardly any point in getting the oilskins on, at least for the general purpose of keeping dry. But they did so anyway, whilst meantime the dragonsbreath stench of the water rose to their nostrils from the churning water. At least, today, it was tempered a little by the freshness of the rain in the air.

The Toad sniffed, and seemed about to speak, but said nothing. A few moments later, as Mr Rette was firing up the engine, he said, "Hasn't Mollusk sponsored a scheme

somewhere on this stretch of river, Gordon? I'm a bit
undercranked on that sector at the moment.—Some water
vole habitat thing, is it? A couple of hundred metres, somewhere upstream of here?"

"Afraid I'm a bit undercranked on that myself, W-T,"
answered Mr Rette, who was still breathing heavily after the
last few minutes' exertions. "I'll 'gress the dats for you"

"Oh.—No. No matter."

Even before the Rat had made any attempt to get the big
white boat out from its moorings it was riding the waters
much like a Cornish lifeboat out on a mission. "I have
never seen it like this!" said the Rat. "What has happened
to the river?"

The Toad scanned the altogether ghastly view of brown-
grey floodwaters surging seawards between banks that were
already barely visible, and must certainly have been over-
topped already wherever the watermeadows were at their
lowest. Even as he watched, one of the alders on the far
bank—its heavy-leafed upper branches tousling and twisting as if in the suction-current of some outsized vacuum
cleaner—fell towards the water, taking a section of the
bank with it into the flood.

"Will you be able to get this thing down there?" asked
the Toad in a much less confident voice than usual, both
hands gripping tightly at a fat chromiumed rail.

"Oh, don't worry about that, W-T!" shouted the Rat,
grimacing. "Master of the high seas, you know! One week
in every year, at least.—Getting back might be a problem,
though," he added, in a voice designed not to be heard.

"And I ... I do rather wonder, Mr Mole, if under these
conditions a *small island*—that is the venue, isn't it?—in the
middle of the—er—river—is the most sensible place to
effect a meeting?"

This thought precisely—this thought only—had been
dominating the Mole's mind from the moment he saw the

churn of the waters from close to, and so, once again, he
was rather stumped for anything to say.

But once again Mr Rette came to his rescue. "We can
only try!" he said. He spoke, the Mole thought, surprised,
with a certain relish, grinning as he backed the boat on full
shuddering power just a few yards into the current before
making the turn that would free it to rush away downstream with its engine barely working at all.

"Amazing!" shouted the Water Rat as, every few
moments, he wrestled with some new sideways force. "This
river has *waves* today!" The wind's biggest gusts were strong
enough now to lift the water from the tops of these crests,
blasting it across the line of the current in a raggedy, pelt-
ing mist.

It took them little more than seven minutes to reach
their first view of the eyot. And a tiny frail sliver of earth
it did seem to the Mole now, its line of black pollard willows stuck up, no less resiliently and stubbornly, the river
waters surging past them with all the force of a lava-flow.

"Is *that* it?" shouted the Rat.

"Yes!"

"... What?" said Mr Wyvern-Toad. "What did you say?
What is it?"

"Um—that," said the Mole. "There.—With the willows."

The Toad gaped, his jaw dropping as low beneath his
face as Nature allowed. "That tiny little—! We're going to
wait *there*, next to *that*?! In *this*?!—Mr Mole, I do hope this
meeting proves as rewarding as Gordon has hinted it would
be! And I *do* hope the individual in question hasn't decided
to take a raincheck!"

("Take a rain-check?" thought the Mole, who had, he
believed, been doing exactly that ever since he got up.)

"—It's angled slightly, isn't it?" shouted the Water Rat,
nodding ahead to the island.

The Mole followed his gaze, trying to remember. "—Yes," he said. "Yes! Go round to the other side—between it and the riverbank, that's it—it might break up the current enough for us to—"

None too soon, the Rat wrested his bucking and rolling craft over towards the left bank, throwing both engines into reverse as he did so. The boat rode on at what seemed at first like undiminished speed, with the trees on the riverbank positively flashing past. But as they drew closer to the eyot they found that the main force of the river was being channelled elsewhere, thundering on seaward at ten thousand tons-per-minute beyond the little island's right-hand flank. This drop in force was just enough to allow the motors to bite, and the Mole watched in relief as oaks and alders began to pass by more slowly, and then—as the Rat increased the power—more slowly still; and then, finally, not at all.

"Throw down the gangway!" shouted the captain, and the Mole, following the line of his pointing arm, leapt into duty as under-mariner, to the best of his abilities. Five minutes later, rocking and dancing on the race of brown waters, the big boat was moored to one of the inner willow-pollards—securely, too, for as long as the pollard itself could keep its roots down.

"—Well!" said Mr Wyvern-Toad, whose skin now was less amphibian green than the colour of the flipside of a whitebeam leaf. He did attempt a grin, but there was little in it of his usual workaday confidence. "We—ahh—wait here, then, Mr Mole, I take it? I *do* hope, not for very long."

"—No," said the Mole, adding unhesitatingly, "we'll have to get out."

"*Get out?!*"

"On to the island."

"But there is no sign of the animal yet!"

"He may not turn up," said the Mole, "if we don't get out." It was the best he could do.

"I prefer my islands larger.—Considerably larger!" said Mr Wyvern-Toad. "And in far kindlier climes than *this*." He kept his gaze on the Mole another few seconds, quizzing him with eyes at once puzzled and wary. "You've not let me down yet," he said, an observation that seemed to be enough in itself to decide him. Retying the knot on his sou-wester, the Toad made slowly for the gangway.

The three small animals had only just succeeded in dragging themselves into the lee of the largest available pollard when they heard a portentous creaking-groan from the field nearest to them. Another tree was coming down—it was a big oak, one of several in a belt running up from the river—and they were able to watch the last heroic stages of its fall before it hit the ploughland in an explosion of top-branches and a great rending of timber that twisted and sliced it jaggedly open along the rust-and-cream centre of its bole. All three animals looked instinctively for something to clutch at as this sight was thrust upon them.

"This river doesn't have to get any *higher*!" shouted the Rat in a high tone, against the gale, the fur of his exposed snout rain-blasted into much the same condition as some long-drowned Elizabethan's velvetings. "It's inches from the top of the bank here already!"

The Toad's open-jawed gaze—which had been fixed in horror on the fallen tree—moved slowly in the direction of the nearby pouring waters. He did not in fact *shout* "I don't LIKE this!" or "I want to GO HOME!" He had no need, since both propositions were very clearly inscribed across his features. "He has *five minutes*, Mr Mole!" he yelled tremulously, after a pause. "No deal is worth more than five minutes of this!"

For his own part, the Mole could do no more than turn to look out around the edge of the firm and unyielding willow-pollard, staring with one eye and then squinting with two into the spiralling blast of rain-mist and water. There must be a change—some sign of a change, or—he would not allow his heart to sink—but, well, *something* must happen!

But he could see nothing new. He pulled back, wiping his eyes as best he could with no handkerchief to hand, then twisted round to squint once more. He had hardly put his face to the wind before he withdrew again, urgently pricking up his ears. For in those few moments the gale had, if possible, grown stronger still and its howling was everywhere, everywhere about them. It was as if the atmosphere itself was being played by it like the strings of some limitless and insubstantial Aeolian harp. And into this infinity of sound had come another, more focused, *closer* set of sounds—a deep, thrumming musical "chord" that ran on in the howlings like a release of dye in a torrent of water.

The Mole listened on now, motionless and intent, as this music strenthened to distinctness, unambiguously present, faded away and returned; and it was then he realised what its source must be. For the strings of this harp were substantial enough—he had walked under them once himself—those quietly sizzling, arm-thick cables that ran on tapering giant skeletons to a certain point in the field to their north here, dived to the ground, then reappeared on the far side of the river.

"Three minutes!" shouted the Toad. "*Damn* this sou-wester! It's coming down my neck!"

"It's coming *over!*" bawled the Rat, his voice higher now by at least an augmented fourth. "It is! It's beginning to come over the top here!"

The Mole turned and peered, turned and peered, wiping each new jet-blast of water out of his eyes only to be half blinded again in an instant. Yet now, he thought, he could see a change, though it was a thing of the most difficult-to-get-hold-of kind. Beyond the wind-tunnel rain the sky was all cloud; but since he last got a proper look at it the patterning of the clouds themselves had changed. What had been simple ridges of grey, stretching from one side of the sky to the other, had become—at least, in the centre, above the valley itself—a quite extraordinary knotting-together of black-dark and paler short ridges, not running horizontally but tilted, many of them, at an angle of forty-five degrees to the horizon. It was as if the clouds had become tangled together here and were trying now—with forces quite beyond imagining—to wrench themselves apart even as a skyful of others were compressing up against them.

"O—o—o—o—o—o—o!" said the Mole, entirely to himself.

"*One* minute!" yelled the Toad in an exasperated voice.

"It's covering the first of the tree roots!" wailed the Rat, but even as he did so he staggered forward—luckily for him, into the lee of the sheltering pollard—pushed there by a sudden doubling, or trebling, in the force of the wind at his shoulder. The white boat was barely visible now beyond the horizontal bandings of rain, mist, and air, snatching and hauling at its mooring-ropes, and from both sides they could all hear further sounds of big trees groaning to the ground.

But this was not the only new sound they heard as all three did at last cling tight together in their terror. The music of the cables too had doubled, or trebled, in intensity, and from both sides of them now a deep-bass, many-noted howling thrum came to them, penetrating even the roarings of the gale and waters. And bound up with this, in a way quite beyond describing, there was—to the Mole's ears at least—another sound as well.

The Mole turned to face the quailing, clutching Toad and stared into his face for what he hoped to see there. "*Do you hear them?!*" he yelled, into the nearest available ear. The

Toad returned his gaze with eyes not at all unlike small cricket balls, incomprehension wresting rudely with blind funk for control of his features.

"—*Do* you?!" shouted the Mole again. "—*The pipes!* THE PIPES!"

The Toad continued to stare helplessly, his eyes fixed on the Mole as if athirst for any kind of explanation, even one that made no sense. Beyond him the Water Rat was staring too now, up and out into the patterns of gale-channelled rain and spume. He was breathing more deeply than the Mole had ever seen him breathe, and on his face, fear aside, there was something akin to exhilaration.

"Will you—" The Mole halted, stymied. What could he *ask*? How could he *ask* it? "Will you do things ... you know!—do things *differently* now?" he demanded at last, waving his one free arm to clarify the point.

"'Differently'?" repeated the Toad, staring first to his left and then to his right. He spoke in a voice so small it was all but lost in the sounds around him. "Oh ... yes, *yes*! Yes! I'll do *anything* 'differently' ... if only we can get away from here alive!"

"WA-A-A-ATER CO-O-O OMING!!" shrieked the Rat at highest available volume. He had turned again to look beyond the tree, only to be confronted by a sight more terrifying than any yet: a miniature tidal-wave, no less, of four to five feet in height, rushing down upon them and already less than a hundred yards away. "Hang on to the BRA-A-A-ANCHES!!"

All three animals scrabbled hectically at the pollard, clutching and clawing for a grip on any available part of it, even the short, slender branchlets which had grown out from its stumps since last it was cut. Luckily for them, the tree had a deep split in the centre of its bole, into which both Rat and Mole were able to insert an arm. But the Toad had nothing to hang on to except the other two and slipped down as the big wave struck, clinging only to the Rat's tail. He was more than half immersed by the water, and as he flailed around for a better grip his jacket burst open and a string of very large denomination banknotes and small, rectangular cards bearing words like *Gold* and *Platinum* began to wash out from the pockets and swirl off downstream like demented fishes. Against the force of this flood even a grasp of mortal terror might not have been enough to keep him in place, but the Rat, and then the Mole, were still somehow able to grab on to the neck of his waterproof as he wailed out, all but inaudibly, "Sa-a-a-ave me-e-e-e-e!! Don't let me-e-e-e-e go-o-o-o-o!!"

"I never let *anyone* go, W-T!" yelled the Rat, into the howling of the wind and the roaring of the water.

The long wave passed, and after that the water-level began to drop behind it, so that in a matter of three to four minutes the highest parts of the eyot were visible once more. The force of the gale was also dropping back a little too now, and soon it was no stronger—perhaps even a little less strong—than it had been when they set out. Supporting one another, and still clinging hard together, the three bedraggled animals stumbled and slid their way back towards the boat.

"... so," said the Otter, his face the very picture of scepticism triumphant, "you went out into the worst storm hereabouts since 1627. You sat on an island in a hurricane until it was under water. You nearly got drowned in a tidal wave (if you can *have* a tidal wave on a river). But that's all just fine because the Chief Executive Animal of Toad Transoceanic has seen the light, and is now a completely changed mal. *You hope.*"

"He did say he'd start doing things differently," replied

the Mole doggedly. "He *said* it. He *did*."

"On the island."

"Yes."

"In the hurricane."

" Yes!"

"During the tidal wave."

"... Yes."

"And what did he say, Mole, once he was back in the warm and the dry, and bathed, and scented, with a nice fresh suit on, and his third gin and tonic in his hand?"

"He asked me who it was I'd wanted him to meet there."

"—oh! Oh well! In *that* case! And what did you tell him?"

"I said—I said we had met him."

The Otter paused, though not for long. "And *he* said—?"

"He didn't *say* anything, much. He just—he stared at me. He did. He stared. He went pale again. He did say something like 'And what *is that* supposed to—?' Mean, I suppose. Not much more, though. He went very quiet after that. Wasn't his usual self at all."

"Well, he'll be down here tomorrow, then," said the Otter drily. "Crack of dawn. Head to tail in best penitent's sackcloth, offering himself on bended knee as an A.R.F. novice—"

"Otter, please!" said the Badger, who had been listening to this and the Mole's earlier account of events in the deepest of silences.

"'High Priest Of Weaselmind Recants'," persisted the scathing swimmer, and he was not the only one who was laughing now. "Ha, ha, ha! 'Abandons Transnational Helmsmalship To Take Up Post As Burrows Campaigner'! Ha, ha—oh, ha, ha, ha, ha, ha!"

"Ignore him, Mole!" said the Badger. "If the very event he's describing happened right here and now in front of his eyes, this otter would still say he didn't believe it."

The Otter stopped laughing, and rubbed the back of his neck with a heavy paw.

"I—um—" said the Mole.

"Go on, Mole," said the Badger encouragingly. "We are all of us impressed at the risk you took. And grateful. You must know that."

The Otter stared at the rough earth floor.

"O—well," said the Mole dismissively. "It's just—these bits of paper I've got here. Haven't the foggiest idea what use they'd be, but—I've been using the back of them for my diary. 'Least, I meant to. But there's all this—stuff on them about Mr McMinc's companies. Blowed if I can understand it."

The Mole produced the sheaf of paper from his rucksack and passed it to the Badger, who looked through it slowly, with ever widening eyes. "'CONFIDENTIAL'," he read, "'World Mystery Consortium Talks ... McMinc Core Strategization Program-Program ... McMinc: Global Franchize ... Long Term Amalgamabsorbtion Evolutive Supraview ... Attn. Mr McMinc/Inner Circle: *Total* Excluzional Access' ...!"

The Hare began to speak but the Badger silenced him, leafing on through the sheets of paper and now and then turning back to some with deepening concentration. "And it is all—*completely*—up to date!" he said. "To the beginning of last week! Mole—Mole! Have you any idea what you've brought us here?"

"Don't s'pose it's good news," replied the Mole.

"No," said the big animal, and then his face lit up in a momentary show of warmth and admiration. "But it's very good news—fantastically good news—that we've got hold of it. No, Mole, believe me! I won't exaggerate, but this is *something. Now* we will see how far we can reach out with—" He gestured to the row of screens. "Sorry, boys! We will sort out this power problem. First thing—everything else will have to wait now. In the meantime, though, it looks as though you may be getting a little more exercise."

Sons groaned at all points of the compass. "*Thanks, Mole!*" grunted Son Number Four.

"This will convince you, my friend," said the Badger. "If anything can. We will send *this* out into the world." He tossed the papers across to the Otter. "Every channel we can find. Then, let's see what happens."

The Otter began to read, saying nothing, and did not speak again for quite some time.

Later that morning, the Badger invited the Mole out for another little stroll across the woodland floor. The Mole had sat, increasingly sunken and dejected-looking, as the group of animals around him developed their plan to publish the McMinc strategy documents. It was not that he wasn't pleased to have (apparently) been of help to them. That was splendid—just splendid. But he was not *of* them, and as he listened on to their debate, and the way that they put things, he knew for certain—so that he couldn't hide it from himself—that he never would be.

"You want to go back," said the Badger, laying his big arm across the Mole's low shoulder. "Don't you?"

"I can't go back," replied the Mole, in the voice of a newly-born runt flea.

"Do you *want* to go, Mole?—Tell me. *Do* you?" insisted the Badger, almost growling at him.

"Yes O yes O yes!" cried the Mole. "But it's impossible!"

The A.R.F. leader did not reply at once. He inhaled deeply, then paused, turning to look at the Mole directly. "We can get you back," he said. "I think so, anyway. The entrance is there somewhere under the new ThriftaCenta— is that right?"

"—But it's completely *buried!*"

"Only concrete," said the Badger. "That's just another job of work, Mole. We can uncover it—we can, yes!—if you can lead us to the right spot. And you can do that, can't you?"

"Yes!"

"We have a—er—sympathiser, working there now, as it happens. He should be able to get us in there without too much trouble. Fine, then, Mole, so: when?" demanded the Badger in his no-nonsense way. "Tomorrow night? That too soon?"

"N ..." The Mole fell silent as, out of nowhere, a great tide of sadness rose up in him. But it passed. "... No," he said.

"You should stay with us tonight. We'll need you on the spot."

"O but, Mr Rette—and—"

"We'll get a message to him."

They walked on under the high canopy of the wood, but also in the dense shelter of a broad swathe of old, unmanaged hazel coppice. The Badger fell silent, thinking through the details of the incursion he would now soon be leading."

Then the Mole himself stopped. "—Badger?"

"—Yes?"

"There was one thing I wanted to tell you."

"Go on."

The Mole scratched his head. "Well—I—" He snorted, in frustration at himself. "It's just that I *did see* him.—I'm sure I did."

The Badger's mind had been more than half on other things, but there was something in the Mole's tone that made him pay attention.

"I *saw* him.—Not last night, no. But when I was away, cycling, in the East. Under a—under a little maple tree."

The Badger did not take his eyes off the Mole now, and

very slowly his expression softened. Gone was the animal of action and hard-won principle, and in his place there stood, perhaps, some earlier, younger incarnation: an animal capable of looking at the mysteries of Nature and observing them, at once searchingly and with a dreamer's eyes, without surprise that they should be there.

"Do you believe me?" asked the Mole.

"Of course."

"He was waiting."

The Badger breathed a hard, long sigh. "... *Waiting.*"

"It was just—how it felt."

The Badger walked a few paces away from the Mole through the hazels and took hold of a firm, shining stem. He pulled it to him, staring down at the detail—the million-formed complexity—in one of its leaves. "*Waiting!*" he repeated, looking about him now exactly as if he could make out in every leaf in sight, down to the tiniest, the same complexities spread all about him. He said no more, and neither did the Mole, but returned to the hidden entrance of his sett-h.q. with what did seem to his small companion a fresh vigour in his step.

The final hours of the Mole's chequered sojourn in Weaselworld were so filled with preparations that for the most part he was barely aware of them as time at all. With the help of a ground-plan of the Retco ThriftaCenta supplied to them by the A.R.F. sympathiser (another young hedgehog), the small band of animals worked out their plan of action. The 'hog in question was to remain in the store at closing time, hidden inside a 100-pack Retco 750g-for-the-price-of-500g Maizeflakes crate, emerging from it at two a.m. exactly to let in the excavators through a side door to the Employees' Rest Area and Changing

Rooms. There would be two night watchmals on duty, both of whom would have to be rendered temporarily unconscious: the Otter was placed in charge of the chloroform squad. Pickaxes would be used to cut into the appropriate small area of floor, and the Mole would be able to tell them where that was. Access to the Employees' Area side door was to be along the western cotoneaster-shrubberies, where the car park night-lights penetrated least.

Mr Rette had been telephoned at home, and a message of suitable ambiguity left on his answering machine. The Mole feared that neither he nor anyone else there had received it, and that in any case it might be just too ambiguous; and as the evening wore on he became more and more agitated. He could *not* leave again—and finally—like this without saying a proper goodbye!

By ten o'clock, seeing how unhappy he was, the Badger was seriously considering sending out another son direct to the Rette house, in addition to the son who was already waiting at the tollbridge-phonebox rendezvous. But he did not have to do it. Twenty minutes later, that same toll-bridge-phonebox-son arrived with the rat himself.

"Well, Mole!" he said, attempting perkiness with about as much success as a flood-drenched carpet taking a crack at flight. "You're—er—off for, ah, good, then, I hear?"

"Yes," said the Mole. For one disorientating moment he was filled with pity at the sight of the animal, whose high-flying mood of the other afternoon now seemed remote indeed.

"Which way are you—ah—headed, then?"

"Down the—down the hole I came up."

"Ah."

"After they've dug it open for me again."

"Ah. Yes, of course. I see. Ha ha. But ... er ... well ... *after* that?"

"I'm going home," said the Mole, suppressing the sigh he might have sighed if he had been able to believe his own words. "I'm going back home."

"I would have brought Justin," said the Rat. "I'm sure he'd have loved to see you off. But he'd—I am slightly amazed, to be honest. He left a note saying he'd *gone off* somewhere, on his *bike*. 'To recalibrate the index-twixtodes'. Whatever they may be."

"—O!" responded the Mole, his whiskers gaining a little in altitude as, indeed, had Mr Rette's. "O! How nice! —'Fraid I didn't readjust the saddle."

"I'm sure he can cope. Suppose he's getting old enough now to make decisions on his own."

"Yes."

"... I wanted to thank—" said both animals, as near simultaneously as if they'd been rehearsing for it.

"Oh, but, no. No!"

"No, no, but—no!"

"Not *me*.—You."

"No, you. *You*."

"But—"

"O—"

"But—it's true!" said the Rat, gaining a split second's advantage on the beginning of a sentence. "Things look ... different. If I can put it like that. Things do look different. I am going to change something. I can't say how, yet. I don't know, really. I'm not talking to anyone about this yet. It's so confidential it's not even confidential. But you know, I couldn't have begun to *think*—"

"O, no! But *I*—"

"—No, Mole. You're wrong there. You did something. You—I don't know. You altered the chemistry. I couldn't have *hoped*—" The Rat opened his hands in place of words, smiling a weary but, now, almost entirely undrenched smile.

"Well," said the Mole. "I'm very pleased, I'm sure. Very

pleased. And—you've been most, most—*most*—kind."

The Rat snorted. "After my fashion," he said.

"Time!" shouted the Hare, marching through the sett on the roundup.

"May I—Well, would you mind if I joined you, for the sendoff?" asked Mr Rette of the Badger, who had just come in to the chamber. The Otter, also present but standing behind the Rat, signalled not, but the Badger said simply, "We're a bit low on disguises, Rat. But you didn't look *too* bad in that black bag the other day."

Just over three hours later, on a signal from the Otter, a select band of eight well-disguised animals—four of them carrying pickaxes—made their first cautious entry into the silent, half-mile-long cavern-hall of the Retco Thrifta-Centa, less than 2 minutes by car from Junction 13A of the C4.

The Mole was in the lead—at least, in the sense that he was on the scent for the point where the tunnel entrance was buried. Seeing the great looming space of the building and the line of empty tills stretching away to an absurdity of tininess, he halted, stalled for a moment by impending terror. But the Badger, at his shoulder, whispered him on.

"—Do you have something?"

"… Yes."

"Why—er—why are we *here*, exactly?" said the Rat, looking about him with blank eyes.

"Don't wait, Mole," said the Badger firmly. "Do as your whiskers tell you."

The Mole did as his whiskers told him, not hesitating any further except where he had to. Walking very slowly at first, he turned down the two hundred or so yards of Frozen Chips and Pizzas, moving onward in a southerly

direction into the vanishing perspective of Frozen Cream
Cakes, Puddings and Ice Creams. Here he halted, puzzling,
before returning to the crossing aisle and then confidently
tracking on northwards. A special end-stall (unstocked)
labelled 'Pre-Peeled Oranges' went by, as did another
marked 'NEW! *Liquabag* Pre-Cracked Eggs'. For fifty feet,
the Mole went west, along Chilled Cheeses, where unfortunately he lost the scent again by the Woldeslyme. Nothing daunted, though, he marched on in the same direction,
the small band of axe-toting animals close behind him with
the Hare taking up the rearguard. He picked up the trail
again just as soon as he had got out into Luxury and Pre-
packed Breads (where the labels on the sliced brown bread
showed harvest waggons, full of corn), swerving around a
tiny carousel marked 'Organic Produce' into the fridge-lit
maw of Fruit and Veg. Here, puzzling, the Mole sniffed
long and hard by the Mothylene-treated tomatoes, took
three paces—then another five—and stopped dead in front
of the cryogenically-arrested pears.

"This it?" whispered the Badger.

"Yes," whispered the Mole.

" —Sure, now?"

The Mole sighed a long, shuddering sigh. "I'm sure," he
said.

"All right then," said the Badger, felt-tipping an X in a
circle on the floor. "We are going to go through this in
—ten minutes, at the outside. Get noisy, team!"

"Why—er—why are you doing *that*?" asked the Rat all
but inaudibly as the first blows fell. To the Mole's blank
amazement, the various layers of flooring—surface tiles,
insulation, lump-concrete, membrane—yielded to the
relentless force of the young badgers in particular like tof-
fee brittle to the impacts of a coal hammer. After little
more than eight minutes the Badger was able to call a halt
to the work, stepping forward to wrench away one last big

chunk of greystuff. Beneath this, the earth was clearly visible.

"You had better—survey it," said the Badger.

The Mole got into the hole and took a tentative scrabble. Then he began to dig more vigorously—in the general direction of the pears, but with the slightest of yaws toward the peewees and zykolafruit—penetrating down so far that only the bottoms of his feet were in sight. They remained like this, all but unmoving, for nearly thirty seconds and then, with an exultant fountaining of earth, the Mole resurfaced. "I've *got* it!" he shouted. "I can feel it! It's easy, its easy! I know just which way to go! *I know!*"

"All right then Mole," said the Badger, removing a small object from his pocket. "Do you *know* what this is?"

"Um ... Ah ... Have seen one, once ..."

"It's a *compass*. If anything did go wrong—"

"It won't—"

"If it *did*, the nearest way out is due west. You see? You understand? That way, On and out beyond that wall. Keep *this* on 'north'—here—and then go straight towards the 'W'.—Got that? It has a light in it. Press—here. And remember, you will have to go down deeper round the edge-foundations."

"Thank you, Badger. Thank you! And all of you. For everything. Most—Most kind."

"You'd come up beyond the Burgerburg. There are shrubberies every forty yards."

"Yes.—Well—"

Silently, one by one, and as best he could, the Mole embraced each of the animals present, for all the world like a warrior turning away from the field of battle.

"I shan't forget you," he said.

"Oh, I think you may, Mole," said the Badger. He shrugged, acceptingly, and smiled, though it was a sad smile. "That is what my mother taught me. If you go back.—When you go back. You may have no choice about forgetting us—everything here. It may be for the best."

The Mole looked back at him and at the Rat—who was by now speechlessly clutching and twisting at his rolled up head-mask—and all the rest of them. "O," he said. "—Well—come what may, I hope you—you know, all of you—win through, in the end."

"—You see, Mole, who knows?" said the Badger, leaning forward to him. "Maybe this thing here isn't a *time*-tunnel at all." ("Tu-tu-tu-*time* tunnel?" breathed the Rat.) "It would be well worth debating—"

"Badger!" hissed the Hare. "Let's get going!"

"... but, er, perhaps not under quite these circumstances. Who knows, though, Mole? Could it be something more like a *possibility*-tunnel? Could all of us here be caught up in what is, in reality, just one possibility out of many? Don't worry, Mole! We won't give up fighting to make it other than it is. Where is the world we need, I wonder? Somewhere due west from your hole, if you can find a tunnel to take you there? Somewhere south-by-southeast, on a fine spring morning? You choose!" He smiled again, and raised his heavy paw in salute.

"Goodbye—"

"Goodbye!" said the Mole, turning to the earth beneath him. And he felt such tenderness then for all those suffering creatures he was about to leave behind him—such tenderness, he could not bear to look at them again.

For the first three minutes the Mole found himself digging blind through the earth itself, and as his tears flowed so the soil began to stick to the growing patch of wet fur around his eyes. Even so, he bored his way on with absolute determination, responding to the pull he felt ahead of him now like a calling voice. He had no need of the Badger's compass, and gradually the soil began to feel less compacted, so that as he progressed he found he could abandon all such sophistications as the squoozle and the squiggle, and was able simply to scrabble and scrooge, or scratch and scrape. And as this happened, so the Mole became conscious of a new sensation in himself. It was as if with the loosening of the soil all that had so weighed on him and distracted him these many past weeks—weeks?—*was* it weeks?—had lost its grip on him and was lightening, dispersing, releasing him back to a new but also an old—O yes, yes, a very old!—simplicity.

Now, the soil—the sandy, gravelly soil—was loose enough for him to push through almost without digging. Now, it was giving way before him. And now—now, *now!*—he had cleared his way free into the tunnel itself, bending ahead of him there to the left—he could recognise the bend—in the direction of one place and one place only. Joyfully he scurried along it, shouting, "You're going home, Mole! You're going home!"

But the tunnel had always been unstable, and his small shout, and perhaps the pattering of his feet, were just enough to start the roof collapsing in behind him. He rushed on with the tunnel closing itself up in his footsteps, and in a matter of a few seconds more he had tumbled out on to the floor of his kitchen, with a mess of soil and bits of gravel rattling out of the caved-in passageway behind him.

The Mole clambered to his feet and stepped around the cupboard, positively marvelling at everything he saw in front of him. There it was—O! there it all was—his very own kitchen: the old dresser, the simply stocked shelves, the door in the passage beyond down to his tiny beer-cellar, the three old beech chairs and the table with his biscuit box, teapot and cosy just waiting there on top. (The Mole felt very emotional at the sight of his teapot and cosy.) And in

the little parlour beyond—as he walked into it now—
everything was exactly as it should be: the two sleeping-
bunks in the wall, the old armchairs on castors, and
there—waiting only for a match to be put to it—the wood
fire he had laid in the grate just last night.

Ten minutes later the fire was blazing merrily, the Mole
had filled his hot water bottle and put it into the bed, and
the kettle was on the boil again for tea. But he felt so tired
now! Every muscle in his body was groaning. *What* a day he
had had, with all that whitewashing, but at least now he—

"O no, O *blow!*" he muttered, turning to the cupboard
which he had quite forgotten to haul back into place. "You
can't leave it like *that*, Mole! O, and *what* is all this mess here,
now?" He stood, fists on hips, staring at the pile of earth
and gravel which had, it seemed, collapsed out of the wall
while his back was turned.

Exhausted as he was, the Mole's love of tidiness still had
the upper hand. It took him ten minutes more to take the
earth outside and sweep up after it, and then tug the big
old wall-cupboard back to where it always stood.

As he lay in his bunk not very much later, happily
clutching his hot water bottle and gazing, already very
heavy-lidded, into the dying blaze of the fire, the Mole did
breathe something to himself—one of those senseless
things an animal says sometimes when poised at the very
edge of sleep. "I ... have been on a journey," he whispered.
"A journey ... a long, long, journey ..."

Next morning he was dragged up from the deepest and
most blissful depths of sleep by the clonking of his bell
and a far-off, insistent rapping. Still in his pyjamas, and
yawning one long yawn on top of the next, the Mole stumbled blearily upward in the direction of his front door.

This, with an element of fumbling, he at last pulled open on the beaming and expectant face of his dear old friend the Water Rat, resplendently strawed and striped as he was today in boater and blazer.

"Why, *Moly!*" cried the Rat. "Whatever are you *doing*? Don't you know it's already half past *eight*?"

"I was asleep," mumbled the Mole.

"I can see that! And we are going to have to get you un-asleep, old fellow, and quick about it! *Look* at this day! *Look* at that sky! *Look* at the trees there, dancing in the breeze! Any animal who is not on the River today—*and* by quarter past nine at the latest—is a sad, sad beast indeed!"

"Must have been all the whitewashin'—"

"O, not another *word* about the blessed whitewashing! Can't you hear the River calling, Moly? Aren't your palms already itching for the oars?—Now then. Step lively!"

Delighted as he was to see his friend, the Mole remained a touch on the quiet side over his hurried breakfast. It was just as if he was trying to remember something—not that it mattered in the slightest, really—but the beginning of a thought, or picture, or *something*, seemed forever at the corner of his mind, yet obstinately refused to come out and be looked at.

"I feel as if I've been dreaming absolutely all night long," he said, yawning again. "Though I can't remember a single bit of it. Not a thing! Although—"

"Do finish that cracker, Moly, there's a good fellow!"

"I feel as though I've been in—" The Mole paused. He *would* get hold of it. "I feel as though I've been in far, far places …"

The Water Rat turned, and looked at him. For one moment his face lost its urging expression. "… Mole, you've not been at the pickled gherkins again, have you?" he demanded. "O, here! Let *me* pour the tea!"

The picture was still there, though, lurking in the very

corner of a corner. It was as if he remembered—something awful—O, *awful!*—yet with good things in it, too. But the harder he puzzled at it, the more it seemed to shrink, and dwindle, and grow less insistent, so that by the time he was downing the last of his tea, and half way to the door, the Mole was quite incapable of believing that the thing he'd *thought* he'd remembered—or anything faintly resembling it—could ever have existed on the face of this earth.

Later on—after he had passed the sculls back to the Water Rat and gingerly swapped places with him, and sat back into the cushiony seat at the stern of the boat—the Mole said suddenly, "O, Ratty, it's *so* good to be here! Really, you know, it's almost too much!—The River—the sunlight—the willows there—the fields and hedges all going by—"

Grinning broadly, the Rat looked back at him. "Now *there* speaks an animal with whitewash on his fur!"

"—O, Ratty! Ratty!" said the Mole out of nowhere. "Do say you will never change!"

The Water Rat looked back at him and it was as if, now, for the merest fraction of a second, the shadow of the tail of the smallest cloud in the sky had passed across his face. "Change?" he said. "Change! Whatever can you mean? Moly, my dear Moly, *why* should *I* ever change? Why should *I* ever want to do anything except what I do already?"

"Blessed if I know, Ratty. Blessed if I know why I said it, now—blessed if I do!"

"Of course you are! And I'm not at all surprised. Messing about in boats, my dear fellow! I've said it before, and I shall very probably say it again, and no apologising either. There is nothing, Moly—absolutely *nothing*—half so much worth doing in this life as messing about in boats."

"Just that ..." he said, though the small craft had travelled several lengths downstream before he did so. It was a warm morning, with only the gentlest of breezes. The sun was emerging from behind a single bank of cloud and the blue of the sky was there in the River, across one expanse and then the next. Water lights were playing and dancing around the Rat's whiskers, and a look of dreamy contentment had settled on his face. "Just that, Moly," he repeated quietly. "Simply messing—you know ... Yes ... Simply messing about in ..."

**UBI SAEVA INDIGNATIO ULTERIUS
COR LACERARE NEQUIT**

ENDNOTE

With the exception of a few imaginary details and link passages, the descriptions of landscapes, both rural and urban, in this novel are based on direct observation. But anyone looking for such locations on the ground in the order in which they are described would be quickly frustrated, since the England of Weaselworld resembles nothing so much as a patchwork quilt whose source elements have been cut up, reshaped and transposed in shameless pursuit of narrative convenience. This said, the general trajectory of the Mole's journey east could be traced without too much difficulty.

It may also be worth noting that the inspiration for the setting for the Mole's first emergence into Weaselworld does not lie in the Thames Valley, as might be expected. However, it can be found very near to it, and is in a river valley.

G.L.J.